About the Auth..

Liz Heron grew up in Scotland and studied at Glasgow University. After living in Paris, Madrid and Venice, she embarked on a freelance writing life in London, contributing to a range of publications. Alongside literary translation, her own books include *Truth, Dare or Promise*, a compilation of essays on childhood, and *Streets of Desire*, an anthology of women's 20th-century writing on the world's great cities. Her short-story collection, *A Red River*, was published in 1996.

She writes a blog, mainly on film, as well as art, books and politics.

www.lizheron.wordpress.com

THE HOURGLASS

LIZ HERON

Unbound Digital

This edition first published in 2018

Unbound

6th Floor Mutual House, 70 Conduit Street, London W1S 2GF

www.unbound.com

© Liz Heron, 2018

This book is a work of fiction and, except in the case of historical fact, any resemblance to actual persons, living or dead, is purely coincidental.

ISBN (eBook): 978-1-912618-47-7
ISBN (Paperback): 978-1-912618-46-0

Printed and bound in Great Britain by Clays Ltd, Elcograf S.p.A.

For Ursula, Tansy and Céleste

E per gli amici di Venezia

Dear Reader,

The book you are holding came about in a rather different way to most others. It was funded directly by readers through a new website: Unbound.

Unbound is the creation of three writers. We started the company because we believed there had to be a better deal for both writers and readers. On the Unbound website, authors share the ideas for the books they want to write directly with readers. If enough of you support the book by pledging for it in advance, we produce a beautifully bound special subscribers' edition and distribute a regular edition and e-book wherever books are sold, in shops and online.

This new way of publishing is actually a very old idea (Samuel Johnson funded his dictionary this way). We're just using the internet to build each writer a network of patrons. Here, at the back of this book, you'll find the names of all the people who made it happen.

Publishing in this way means readers are no longer just passive consumers of the books they buy, and authors are free to write the books they really want. They get a much fairer return too – half the profits their books generate, rather than a tiny percentage of the cover price.

If you're not yet a subscriber, we hope that you'll want to join our publishing revolution and have your name listed in one of our books in the future. To get you started, here is a £5 discount on your first pledge. Just visit unbound.com, make your pledge and type HOURGLASS18 in the promo code box when you check out.

Thank you for your support,

Dan, Justin and John
Founders, Unbound

Super Patrons

Chris Arch
Lucy Bland
Robert Brett
Lesley Caldwell
Sandra Cavallo
Hanna Chalmers
Clare Coope
Robert Cox
Kevin Davey
Gillian Dyer
Denis Echard
Susan Egert
Penny Elder
Judith Elkan
Anna Fodorova
Judy Forshaw
Giorgio Giandomenici
Harriett Gilbert
Joanna Goldsworthy
VC Green
Sally Greenhill
Hermione Harris
Pauline Henderson
Tansy Huws
Ursula Huws
Malcolm Imrie
Esther Kinsky
Caroline Knowles
Bobbie Lamming
Sheila Lecoeur
Robert Lumley
Katherine Marles

Colleen McCann
Jennie McDonnell
Mandy Merck
Christopher Methley
Maggie Murray
Mica Nava
Bruno Noble
Sue O'Sullivan
Irene Payne
Ruth Petrie
Lisa Vine and John Pipal
Eddie Playfair
Adrian Rifkin
Joanna Rosenthall
Sheila Rowbotham
Ann Rumley
Joanna Ryan
Bill Schwarz
Amanda Sebestyen
Lynne Segal
Naomi Segal
Lucio Sponza
Ifor Stoddart
Robert Tollemache
Susan Trangmar
Martin Upham
Julia Vellacott
Joyce Vetterlein
Ginette Vincendeau
Hilary Wainwright
Valerie Walkerdine
Stan C Waterman
David Yelding

For the modern woman, ageing is no longer just a stage reached on a linear continuum. As present time accelerates, the past expands to accommodate the breadth and variety of her experience and the sense of infinite potential her female ancestors could not have had. Against the brevity of future time, those years might well be centuries.

Elfriede Mueller, *Millennium Island*

Acknowledgements

My thanks to everyone whose support through crowdfunding has made publication of *The Hourglass* possible. As for the writing of it, I'm indebted to my friends Malcolm Imrie, Ruthie Petrie, Janet Rée and Adrian Rifkin, who read and commented on the manuscript at various stages. Conversations with a good many other friends also sustained me, as did the generous grant I received from the Royal Literary Fund some years ago on the strength of my last book – awarded for me to keep on writing. At last I have something to show for this valued encouragement.

NIGHT

Dusk settles on rooftops and drapes the flaring chimney stacks. Below, the city empties out its crowds and relaxes into twilit life, its corners and alleys replenished with mystery, their stone-cast secrets all the more alluring.

Ombre start to flow in earnest, fist-sized tumblers downed in every *osteria*, one quickly after another. An *ombra* is a glass of wine: a word that recalls the noonday shade where wine was sold in centuries gone by. Mostly it's men who drink and talk in such places, their voices rumbling into laughter or argument.

A woman in a long grey coat, blonde, middle-aged, walks the length of the market at San Leonardo. Light bulbs strung above the stalls make mounds of pears and fennel gleam; they accentuate the spikiness of artichokes. Food seen like this entices, prompting thoughts of candlelit feasts. She stops and buys red peppers, a bundle of salad leaves thrust into a brown paper bag; she chooses them for colour, not from appetite.

Where San Leonardo broadens out, the woman turns into a *calle* by the facade of a former theatre. The *calle* narrows just before a bridge and here she goes through a high double entrance into a vaulted hall, gloomy and smelling of watery decay. She climbs the stairs, unlocks her door; inside, in the dark, she pauses, taking breath, head lifted, like a fugitive finally slowed by refuge. Darkness remains until she reaches a room at the corridor's end. Once the *sala*, grand and many-win-dowed, of this old palazzo with its Flemish-sounding name, the room is now split in two, the larger space packed with antiquarian bric-a-brac for furnishings, the other with its overspill, crated and strewn about. Either she is leaving or she has just arrived.

At the touch of a switch, light skitters across the bare scagliola floor; its intricate pattern of mosaic flowers makes it lovelier than the mar-ble it mimics and not so chill to walk on. She kicks off her shoes, high heels in soft blue suede. They fall toe to toe, as if exhausted.

Sitting on the sofa, she shivers in the silence of these rooms. Music will warm them.

She selects a CD and goes into the kitchen to pour herself a whisky.

People pass by on the *fondamenta*, a canal's breadth away, and hear the strains of Mozart through the open window. An old recording, its tempo fast, the trio of singers still clear, the insistence on women's faithlessness unmistakable behind the music's effervescence.

> *È la fede delle femmine*
> *Come l'araba fenice…*

A constant woman? As mythical as the phoenix!

Part One

Cures

There is as much difference between us and ourselves as between
us and others.
Michel de Montaigne

1

Descent began with a catastrophic lurch. Aiming not to notice, he turned his attention to the book in his hand, the only Henry James he'd ever come close to finishing, a short one, set, of course, in Venice: '... She unfolded the white paper and made a motion for me to take from her a small oval portrait...' They were circling now, above the sporadic tilting glow of the city's lights. These dissolved and through the darkness two parallel rows of winking blue runway studs loomed closer. Too close, perhaps, so fast. But the plane must have hit its designated spot on target, for the landing was serene, the bounce of wheels almost elegant, until the final rush to standstill ended in a bump.

Courtesies kept stampede in check, the comforting admission of an ordeal shared.

At the bus stop he found himself beside the couple he'd sat next to. They were lucky, she said: the last bus to Venice was due in two minutes. Had he a ticket? Paul shook his head and her companion took one from his wallet. Smiling, he waved away the proffered note.

They crossed the moonless lagoon over a low-lying bridge. A neon Campari sign reared out of the dark and they dipped into a square cluttered with buses. The couple showed him where to catch the boat to his hotel and turned in the opposite direction, the wheels of their suitcases noisily grinding. With the hubbub of arrival dispersed, he suddenly craved sleep.

On deck, in motion, the watery tang of the air on his face, his tiredness left him.

He'd been here before, at too young an age for recall: not long before his mother died. Gliding past the moss-edged palaces with their stuttering reflections in the Grand Canal, he had a sense of experience submerged. A wishful remembering, or the imprint of an endlessly pictured Venice?

San Stae. The boat juddered against the swaying platform, beyond it a forecourt where three-branched lamps lit steps rising from the water. Stone figures in dramatic silhouette crowned a tall white church. He allowed himself a sigh of satisfaction.

His well-plotted map led him through a shuttered maze: a long straight alley, a turning, a bridge, another, the length of an embankment and the twist of a final alley – what here was called a *calle*. At last, one more bridge and he found the place, a crooked little square, its darkness diluted only by the thin glow of the hotel sign. The night resonance of footsteps faded to nothing.

The whole atmosphere so suggested an empty theatre set that he was startled when a voice crackled through the entry phone and the door clicked free of its lock.

Behind the desk a bleary-eyed old man pointed his key towards the steep staircase.

– First floor.

Before getting into bed, Paul opened the window. It was set below an overhanging balcony. Outside, in a garden sheltered by a sturdy dense-leafed tree, everything rustled – with what might have been the murmur of a breeze or else the pattering of rain. Whatever it was, and he couldn't reach past the overhang to test the moisture of the air, it made the garden active and vibrant, a presence separate from the inert stones that surrounded it, and joined instead to the deep night sky above.

He slept soundly, but when he woke he knew he had dreamed of what this trip was meant to leave behind.

After breakfast, he made the call.

– Mrs Forrest, *per favore.*

A female voice replied in English.

– She's not here, but she's back this afternoon. Can I give her a message?

– Just tell her Paul Geddes rang, please. I'll try again, this evening. (The silence made him pause.) If that's all right.

– I'll let her know.

Entering the Querini Stampalia, his mind tingled at the thought of what he might find in the library, but when he saw that the building had a picture gallery, a sudden inclination took him there first. Research would have its excitements soon enough and his singer's secrets would still be waiting for discovery.

The Geography Lesson was a small canvas he might have missed had Longhi's genre pictures not already drawn his interest: scenes of bourgeois life as the Republic moved towards its fall. This one offered something more than illustration.

A woman seated at a small round table forms the centre of the painting. Her right hand rests atop a globe and holds a pair of compasses; the left points to its surface. Four figures surround her: a corpulent red-faced man sitting, a younger one standing, and, waiting in the background with a tray and a coffee pot, two female servants. All of them look at the central figure with her globe of the world and her atlas lying open at the hem of her dress, a pale ocean of blue silk out from which peeps the toe of an even paler shoe. She's all paleness: white skin and rose-blonde head. Except for that coquettishly distracting toe, she could represent the luminosity of knowledge. She shines, the painting's light source – no other is visible. Not with an easy radiance as she might were beauty her reason for being there, but with a teacher's straining will.

Are the men attentive listeners or merely struck by a woman's presumption to teach them? They look doubtful. Perhaps that's the point. Doubt: a necessary prelude to enlightenment. In the background, a raised swag of curtain discloses shelves of books leaning and sliding in the disarray of use, the untidy haste of a reader's hand, the lady being that reader.

Longhi's ideal instrument had yet to be invented, Paul decided. He was the photo-documentarist of his day, without a camera. Would a photograph have revealed more about the nameless lady with the globe?

He had idled long enough. Time to get to work.

In the connecting rooms that circled back to the delivery desk, the old floorboards creaked. The domestic shape of the palazzo remained intact from when the last of the Querini line bequeathed his books and the building to the city, so that poor scholars might come and

read after a working day. The gloom didn't bother Paul; it was char-
acterful in a library with a city's 1,000-year history written into ink-
rusted documents and accumulated tomes. Only one area had been
modernised, with computer terminals among the runs of reference
books in different languages.

On-screen browsing, then a hunt through the paper catalogues,
yielded plenty of relevant detail, theatrical mostly, yet, against expec-
tations, he found no evidence that Esme Maguire had played a part in
the musical life of Venice.

What he'd found here might be useful later on. Anyway, there were
other libraries in prospect, and one sure source: Mrs Forrest. He had
no idea where; the address gave no clue, just a long number and the
name of the district. This city wasn't made of streets, but meanders.

Outside the Querini Stampalia the quality of the light amazed him,
as it had that morning, only now it blazed. Suddenly Venice felt like a
reward, a fresh sunlit start. Esme Maguire was long dead and couldn't
harm him, or make him feel guilty.

He loved opera, with a passion all the stronger for having erupted
only two winters before, a *coup de foudre* that lifted music and song to
a realm of new and subtle experience. Encountering not her voice but
her half-told story in a magazine article, he saw Maguire as a woman
hemmed in by history, perhaps even part of it. That piqued his interest.

On a café terrace selected at random, he ordered a cappuccino and
took in the blur of life on the square, aware of its brightness, nothing
more. A football grazed his shoe before a child rushed in to kick it past
another boy who lunged at him too late, their movements rousing
him from reverie. He watched them play. When he got up to leave
a flower seller barred his way, a slight young man, a dark Asian face.
No, grazie. He shook his head to make the refusal definitive, the roses
still thrust forward. It was the third time that one of these youths had
approached him. About to turn away, he relented. Why shouldn't he
buy a rose from someone who so obviously needed to sell it?

In exchange for the note he placed in the young man's hand, to
his surprise he received not one but a bunch of yellow roses tied with
purple ribbon.

2

Back in his room, smoothing out the magazine's rumpled pages, he scrutinised the photographs again: Esme Maguire in profile as Senta, her face hidden by the starched wings of a headdress, and as *Faust*'s Marguerite, praying. In their grainy shadows she remained indistinct, and now, after his morning's failed pursuit, he even had the ridiculous impression she was hiding.

By their dates, both pictures placed her at least in her mid-forties. Nothing unusual in that; great singers go on being young girls on stage until they retire. Melba sang Mimi at 65, and Maguire's near contemporary, Adelina Patti, kept going in her sixties, cashing in on the early recording boom.

He really had little to go on. A handful of roles, an emergence from provincial obscurity on the cusp of middle age. Bringing Maguire to life would be easier if she'd left some recordings.

Yet her muteness in a dawning age of recorded sound was part of the attraction. Maguire's absence from the catalogues cast her into an earlier world than that of the scratchy vocal ghosts in the Neophone archive, enhancing her appeal. Why hadn't she recorded?

She tantalised.

Wagner and Verdi must have known her, yet there's no word from either. He had found a reference to a Parisian-Irish beauty with a 'belated future' in a Meyerbeer letter. And a link to an exile from the Paris Commune, the geographer Élisée Reclus: a recent study of the Commune's aftermath footnoted a letter from a Madame Maguire mentioning a portrait of him. The only published piece to raise her from footnote status was this article in *Discovering Opera*. It had transformed his flicker of interest into the beginnings of ardour. The enigmatic Esme revived his spirits; he'd fallen a little in love with her.

Six o'clock. Nearby bells pealed. Taking the hint, he poured a large measure from the bottle of Grouse he'd brought as a precaution and raised his glass to the face in the dressing-table mirror. All well, despite its pallor.

The phone interrupted this self-appraisal.

– Mr Geddes? It's Eva Forrest. I thought I'd try the hotel you mentioned in your letter. I'm surprised they had a room at short notice. You've been lucky…

He got no further than a friendly 'Ah!' of recognition. The voice sailed past it, silky… a touch glacial.

– Does nine this evening suit you?

– Yes, where…

– When you get off the boat, just walk straight ahead – that's the general idea, except for a few zigs and zags: right first, then left. The name on the doorbell is Lensky, not Forrest. Joe Lensky was my last husband…

He had a vision of a multiply-married socialite in furs. The accent might well have been Hungarian. Eva Forrest's English was a long way from Zsa Zsa Gabor's, but the comparison amused him.

As soon as he pressed the doorbell, the street door opened and he stepped into a high entrance hall. Deep inside rose a stone staircase worn from centuries of footfall. A statue of a lion with a pitted face stood guard at its foot. He had no idea which floor he was headed for, but on the second landing, just before the stair light went out, he saw a door was ajar. In the dark now, he knocked loudly, calling out: Hello. *Buona sera.*

– Come in, Mr Geddes.

He moved towards a figure beckoning at the end of a high-ceilinged corridor streaked with light from a few dim wall lamps. In the glimmer of a doorway, he saw Eva Forrest's face. She reached out and he felt her hand brush his arm as she drew him into the room. The shadows, her fleeting touch, made the gesture momentarily intimate. The sudden glare of the room's interior dispelled that sensation. And the rush of her words.

– Do make yourself comfortable. I recommend the blue sofa. It sags less. This is the only room fit for company. The flat was tenanted after Joe died, then it languished. I came back before Christmas, after six years, and I thought I'd stay on. You can see I haven't got far with sprucing it up.

In the face of this loquacity, he said nothing. Mrs Forrest would have chattered on, he surmised, needing neither prompt nor response, had he not remembered the flowers: the yellow roses, retrieved from the tumbler he had propped them in and retied with the purple ribbon.

– I'm sorry they're not wrapped; they're only from a street seller.
– How kind of you. I'll put them in water straightaway.

This with a warmth that unsettled him.

She left the room. Quickly she returned with the roses in a globe of purplish glass that matched the ribbon. Motioning him to sit down, she returned to her commentary. He continued to hover.

– I've cleared a couple of rooms to have them done up and I've crammed stuff in here. Joe was a collector. Of course, there are things of mine too. So many boxes.

She gestured towards an open door, where he glimpsed tea chests and cardboard crates.

The room floundered in a muddle of precious things and antiques in need of repair. A chaise longue in tattered plum brocade promised luxury only after reupholstering, a pair of scuffed screech-yellow armchairs were piled with fabric samples and assorted papers. Sundry objects converged on the fireplace. On the mantelpiece, under a large mirror, a row of clocks gleamed in their ormolu and tortoiseshell casings. Paintings, photographs and fragments of tapestry jostled for space. He searched for some neutral response to this mess of extravagance.

– That's unusual.

He stooped to peer at a clock crowned with a Tyrolean-style roof. Mother-of-pearl and emerald chips flashed among the gold. It reminded him of the gingerbread house in *Hansel and Gretel*; he thought it vulgar.

– Yes! It *is* fanciful, isn't it? Belonged to Wagner. Do sit down.
– Wagner?

He gave the clock a disbelieving look before taking his allotted place on the blue sofa.

– Maybe you know he died in Venice, not far from here, in the palazzo that's now the casino. You can arrange to visit his apartments;

they're a kind of shrine, I suppose. He was a great one for fancy wall-paper – a far cry from the roulette wheels and one-armed bandits downstairs.

– I have to admit, I've only seen one Wagner opera: *The Flying Dutchman*.

– Yes… the ship's captain condemned to sail the seas for all eternity; a living death, unless he can find the love of a faithful woman.

She smiled for effect, theatrically.

– And die in earnest.

He nodded, his own smile ironic.

– You might like a drink, Mr Geddes. Whisky, I imagine.

Thus far he'd avoided her bustling gaze. Now he fixed her with an amiable stare.

– That would be very nice. How can you tell I'm a whisky drinker?

– Well, for one thing, you're a Scot, aren't you? And then I…

She faltered.

– I think I'll have one too.

She left the room again.

He wasn't sure he liked her. A rich woman of a certain age with time on her hands, well versed in things of the world, things that cost a lot, that went with the grey-blonde chignon, the gold bracelets, the mink probably awaiting winter resurrection in one of those light-green wardrobes lining the corridor. But she was no fool, and it shamed him to think she'd smelled the whisky on his breath. All the same, she'd made it obvious.

She returned with a tray.

– Please help yourself to ice.

– Thank you, it's fine neat.

Silence. The gingerbread clock had a loud tick.

He sat cradling his glass, delaying his prepared words. But she didn't speak and her mild blue eyes became expectant.

– Mrs Forrest, I'm very grateful to you… in the first place for responding to my advertisement for information in *Discovering Opera*, and for agreeing to see me. You wrote that it might be possible for me to look at Esme Maguire's papers. I hope not to take up too much of your time.

– I'll be happy to help.

Nevertheless, her tone made him think she might want proof of his worthiness. He took his first sip of whisky. A malt.

– I may have said, I don't have a musical biography in mind. Music's not my field, though I do love opera. Its power to convey extremes of emotion... and there's a historical richness to it, playing out the conflicts and ideas of its time. What interests me most from the historical point of view is the 19th century – opera enacting the fight for national independence. There's something that intrigues me too, and you may have a view... why are all those heroines motherless? Why the significance of fathers and daughters, with mothers not just absent but unmentioned?

– It's true. At least in Verdi... I hadn't really thought about it.

He supposed she'd go on; she gestured in his direction and he resumed.

– Esme Maguire didn't have a straightforward career, maybe because of personal things, who knows. It could be she lived better for being less of an artist; perhaps she chose marriage, motherhood... I have no idea whether her voice was a great one; I have some idea of the range she had, and the vocal power, apparently praised by critics. She didn't last, so she might have lacked whatever it takes to make a great artist...

Thinking aloud, not measuring how coherent his words might sound, he paused to check Eva Forrest's response and was struck by her expression. For the first time her face was unguarded, her eyes lively with feeling. It had certainly been a beautiful face. The recognition jolted him, since it showed him the face was still beautiful, shaped by intelligence, and surely by a deeper experience than his spoiledwidow fantasy had allowed.

He waited, seeing the eyes veiled again. She spoke lightly.

– We might ask the same questions about many artists who didn't fulfil their potential, don't you agree? History is full of them. So many obstacles to achievement.

– It's still worth considering one who might yield some interesting answers.

With a curt nod of agreement, she got up.

– Please wait a moment, Mr Geddes. I have all sorts of things here: letters, notebooks, even, I think, rough drafts for libretti. Nearly everything's in French, the rest in Italian or German. My husband had read them – he bought most of them at auction, and there's stuff he may have inherited. Music history was his great passion. I'll look them out. But there's something I can give you now. I put my hands on it just before you got here. I've been curious about her too.

She disappeared through the doorway where the tea chests lurked. He heard a heavy drawer slide open and a rustling of papers. She came back holding a crumpled yellow folio.

– I've only glanced at this, but I assume it's about her. Please let me have it back tomorrow. We can make a photocopy if you think it's useful. Let's say around one, and we'll have a bite at my local trattoria.

For all this declared willingness he suspected something steely in her, some calculation. Yet when she handed him the sheet of paper, he felt an immediate surge of gratitude that provoked an anachronistic impulse to kiss her hand. Surprised at himself, he stifled it. He felt drunk, after only two swallows of whisky. There was still some in the glass. His hostess hadn't touched her drink at all.

3

The curtain goes up.

I stand in a circle of light. The sound locked fast in my throat escapes, liberated by darkness, by the hush of an audience now faithful to their part as listeners, forgetting one another and themselves for my sake. And by my own exulting joy. The notes climb free of my body into the vault of the stage, their vibrations joining the orchestra's ebb and flow, filling the crowded space, travelling far from my doubts, my terrors.

They sing me into life.

I become Amelia or Delilah, Senta or Jenůfa, or Marguerite, just as I have been Euridice and Elvira, and a host of others. Until that moment I am a ghost stepped out of her living body's clothes, leaving a trail of gowns and mantles, discarded gloves and veils and shoes, a wardrobe that is the passing of time.

I stand in a circle of light and I am renewed. In this play of roles, of changing names and costumes, I am at last invariable. What for others I perform, I myself inhabit. I am sheltered by the light, by the back-drop and the flats, the sure abode of illusion. Being on stage revives me, and the touch of an Almaviva, a Don Giovanni or an Orpheus reassures me I am flesh and blood.

In my many different heroines I am one. They are my heart, my centre and my harmony. In them and on stage I've come home. Thus I am my truest self.

4

Eva, she had said as he was leaving: no more Mrs Forrest. A good sign. So was the warm, untroubled air, pierced only by birdsong. And the small, sunlit square she had chosen for their meeting. Enclosed in a decor of Byzantine curves and bas-reliefs, Renaissance pilasters and windows with pointed Gothic arches, it mixed styles and periods in such congenial proportions they felt like those of a lived-in room: a room you could enter at one end by stealth, through the outstretched arms of two narrow alleys. A bridge at the other offered the square's only visible opening. He viewed its comings and goings from his café table.

– Hello, Paul.

He started. She had arrived from around the shady corner behind him. They shook hands and he ordered her a drink. Tocai, she said.

Opposite him, squinting in the sun's glare, she burrowed in her handbag for dark glasses. When she put them on and looked straight at him she was grave, trying out her newly hidden face, he thought. Then she flashed a smile. This friendliness matched her more relaxed and younger style; she wore jeans and her hair combed out loose. From behind the shaded lenses, she too was assessing. It didn't bother him. She asked if he'd had trouble finding the way.

– I thought I was lost, then here I was. It's beautiful.

– Always a pleasure to show visitors my favourite places. Venice has endless discoveries in store for you. Did you say you've been before?

– But too young to remember.

Wanting to change the subject, he reached for his bag and took out the stiff envelope containing the folio.

– This paper of hers. It seems she really was devoted to her art. 'My truest self.'

– Yes, though it's just a first impression. Who knows?

– First impressions count. We're often right about them.

– We should trust our instincts?

– I've always thought so.

– So that applies to meeting people, for the first time?

17

The remark struck him as meaningful and he nodded, saying nothing.

He turned the talk towards a neutral subject: architecture, the building behind them, with its high loggia, and who might have lived there in the past. She gave insouciant answers, humouring him, he thought. A hostile murmur in his head warned him against over-personal exchanges. If there were a price to be paid for access to Maguire's papers, he would prefer it to be monetary. Eva Forrest was attractive, albeit not his type: a few years older than himself and much richer. Clashing with his excitement, unease had impinged on his sleep the night before. Now it assumed a form he could recognise.

– Maybe we should go and eat. You mentioned a place nearby…

At once he noticed the wine still in her glass.

– Forgive me. I didn't mean to hurry you.

– We have time. I've booked a table.

The restaurant was crowded, not with tourists but the noise and banter of people who called the waiters by name and were addressed likewise in return. Eva was evidently one of these regulars, but despite her reservation and the owner's warm handclasp, apologies were called for. Some confusion over dates: tomorrow instead of today. No table.

– They can set one up outside, in the shade. Would you mind? It's not too chilly.

Paul had no objection. He admired the view, an irreproachably charming ensemble of bridges and canals, and congratulated Eva on her choice.

– It's a family trattoria.

They ate grilled fish. He relaxed and let the present take over. He was being churlish, his suspicions unfair. Wine and well-being loosened his tongue; he talked about London, and where he came from. She said she'd been to Scotland, Edinburgh, never to the West. And there were Scottish writers she admired: Stevenson, Scott for his novels, Burns for his songs, Smollett and Susan Ferrier.

– Ferrier? I don't know her.

– She wrote novels in the 19th century. I've read only one of them. *Marriage.*

– I see. So you're not up to date with the literary generations?

He was laughing and she joined in.

– You too are fond of the past. You seek it out with your biographies. Why is that?

Not wishing to mislead, he told her that his 'biographies', the credentials he had offered in the first place, amounted to no more than a few slender monographs – one on a Scots-Italian lieutenant who had fought with Garibaldi, and a longer account of a Paris print-worker's household in the revolutionary year of 1848. These were researched and written in time left over from teaching social history, and published for an academic audience.

– Were they well received?

– Only within their specialised world. The forgotten interest me more than the great and good. It's a way of understanding social patterns and how they've shifted.

This sounded worthy and dry, he saw at once, schemes and patterns being the opposite of what he meant, which was what it might be like to be alive a century or more ago.

– That past may be remote, the 1840s say, but it isn't separate from us. We shouldn't deny the limits of experience at any given time; otherwise, we deny the value of what took people beyond those limits: action, imagination, solidarity, utopianism. I'm curious too about how our ancestors were both like us and unlike us. It would be wonderful to interview those people; all we have is what they've written down.

– You have strong feelings about these things.

He caught a note of surprise and said nothing, aware of being cautious. He reflected on where this project diverged from what he'd done before. Letters sent from the front to a mother or wife, letters pleading with a creditor or arguing with a bureaucrat – these were the closest he'd come to the secrets of a man's soul.

Eva broke the silence.

– It's true that the world keeps changing. The past can only exist for us in smithereens; even in our own span of life we forget so much. Yet some things stay the same: how love feels, being a parent, being young or growing old – the cycle of life, in other words. What do you think about that?

– Societies have made vastly differing rules about choices in love. Medical advances affect health and bodily suffering. People live longer than a century ago, and usually look younger. And we all know human experience is varied, and rarely uncomplicated.

– That's probably why I prefer novels to history books. They suggest how like and unlike us other people are, now as well as in the past.

– Perhaps you're wise. In that case, you should be up to date with your reading.

She smiled at his mock sternness.

They had coffee and Paul dealt with the bill.

She looked at her watch.

– I have to go. Perhaps we can meet again soon. Once you've read this, I hope.

She took a blue folder from her bag and placed it on the table.

– Thank you, Eva.

He spoke so softly that, without meaning to, he made her name sound like a caress. Drawing back, he saw in her eyes a small glimmer of anxiety that contradicted the answering smile.

5

– Will the signorina eat a candied plum?

It was his aunt who offered me the sweet. A blonde, buxom woman with a kind smile. She spoke idly.

– Have you met my dear nephew?

My unbitten plum in one hand, I followed her across that pale hard floor with its mosaic of jade-stemmed lilies entwined around the edges, to where he sat, his gaze intent on the sea green of the canal. I felt eyes upon me and was glad of my finery, the figured silk where long-tailed birds fluttered as I moved, the half-cape of sage green velvet.

We were there because of me; I'd sung in Padua the week before, at the house of a silk merchant my mother had dealings with. More invitations had come our way through the merchant's family in Venice. Our hosts had sent a gondola to bring us to this fine palazzo, even though my mother wouldn't let me sing that day because the autumn dampness of the city made me cough too much.

I watched him from the moment we arrived. He had a proud, self-possessed way of walking, impervious to people; at another's approach his face became alert, then I'd see it slowly altering from warmth to warning, or the other way around. When he chose his seat by the window, turning his back on the room, I lost my hope of us meeting.

His aunt said, that voice of hers both gentle and peremptory – Lorenzo, my lamb – and he turned, his look bruised with insult at this childish endearment, then acquiescent for affection's sake. She introduced us. On his face I saw happy recognition, as if he'd been waiting all his life for a girl called Elena, Elena Merlo in particular, and he must have seen the same on mine, the joy of finding the very Lorenzo I'd been seeking without knowing it.

– Signorina.

Speech might have been that family's currency, what made their fortune. One single word and Lorenzo's voice would never leave me. The tender inflections that everyone heard, the low dark timbre that people always stopped for, became a caress for me alone.

He stood, offering no more than bright courtesy. I inclined my head as I had been taught; he took my hand and bowed. That first look between us denied formality. Ease dissolved it, the sudden rightness of being together.

I was smitten too by that place, my good fortune at being thought interesting there, a prodigy. It was late afternoon, the light burnishing reflections in that drawing room, the ladies' gowns clothing them in the twilight brilliance of fireflies. Somewhere a viol was being played, and happiness seemed to scent the air I breathed.

Our mirrored eyes needed to conceal the intensity they found.

It was new to me, something my 14-year-old mind could hardly grasp, a passion of the senses muffled by my innocence.

Lorenzo was 15. His family had settled here a century before, merchants from Antwerp. He was the youngest of five children and the only son. Rumour would always put his paternity in doubt, insisting that his beautiful mother had a lover. Whispers. This city thrived on them, buoyed by gossip and water.

His aunt told him I was a stranger, in want of youthful company.

– You are to entertain this signorina, tell her something of the palazzo we are in, the lineage and nobility of our hosts.

She left us and he performed this duty. Dutiful likewise, I listened. I heard no dull recital of histories and grandeur, only the eloquence of feeling.

Then we stood together by that window, looking out, not at each other, but almost touching, thrilled by nearness, made speechless by it for a while.

– How long will you stay in Venice?

I could hardly answer, my tongue tangled with the fear of never seeing him again.

– We leave tomorrow.

So much in Venice was soft with water's motion, but the merchants and their loud complaining voices had wearied my mother. Her business was done.

He swung round, shock on his face.

– We'll come back.

I spoke with no notion whether this was true.

– Then we'll meet again… we must. Do you promise?

I promised. Never had I felt so solemn, so bound. To steady myself, with the hand next to his (in the other I still held the plum) I gripped the frame of the window. He lifted my fingers into his and pressed his palm on mine.

– I'll remember your hands. And your blue eyes.

His own eyes were hazel-brown. I looked into them and let out a sound between laughter and a sigh. Again I struggled to speak.

– I sing; that is, people often ask me to sing for them, I mean, they ask my mother, if she'll allow me.

While anxious not to appear vain, I needed to say this important thing about myself.

– And you'll sing for me one day.

That was when his aunt appeared beside us, to take him home.

We looked at one another for as long as we could before the claims of others made us separate. The powerless young, at the beck and call of parents' plans.

Next morning the lagoon's surface thickened under heavy clouds. I had slept little from wrestling with my longing, inchoate, a secret even to myself.

We were due to leave when the storm broke. The boatman would not take us, so in the furious wind, our wet cloaks whipped around us, amid the din of shouts and rattling shutters, we returned along the *fondamenta* and waited. I would have waited forever, loath to part from Venice, from him.

My reprieve was short-lived; at four we sailed out.

Scarcely had we slid through the shadow of the bridge of spires and I saw him again. Watching our gondola, and making a quick little bow when he saw he was seen. This fleeting privilege of the unexpected added one more memory. Strange to think that others remember things of us that we shall never know, glimpses to which we are blind. What if I had not chanced to see Lorenzo seeing me? Were there times when I never did?

I looked back. He was gone and the stone masks on the bridge of spires mocked me.

We returned a year later and stayed for a month, it must have been October. He was betrothed.

Foreigners thronged the Piazza and packed the city, more of them than I remembered from before. I overheard talk of this, of the new bordellos, the multitude of gaming houses. I saw Lorenzo's face in crowds, and knew that these encounters were not accidental. Masks and crowds gave us opportunities, even though I went nowhere unaccompanied, always with my mother or a duenna. You can lose your mother in a crowd, and a duenna even faster, with a ready excuse of getting lost by the time you find your way home.

Lorenzo contrived our first meeting alone with the help of coin and a servant. At Rialto, in a small room at the back of a storehouse behind the money changers' stalls. In that world we could be invisible; amid the buying and selling and heaving of goods, the frantic daily business of our surroundings, no one had time or thought to notice our comings and goings, the two of us masked.

Kisses, on every inch of face and lips. The bliss of being held by him. And our hands exploring this closeness, moved by a physical conviction of being not two bodies but a whole, with a single beating heart. We lay on the dusty floor, his cloak spread beneath us, wanting more of skin to touch and more than touch. Eyes adoring, fingers straying inside collars, stroking seams and circling buttons, plucking at velvet and felted wool, restless yet aware of the risk we dared not run.

– I love you.

– I love you.

The symmetry of these truly meant declarations was undone by his reminder.

– I cannot marry you, Elena my love. Two years from now I'll have a wife who'll bring great wealth and partnership in trade. My father is bound to this marriage by contract. I have no choice.

We met there twice, then once at a closer place, almost under my mother's nose, so that we could be together every day, he said.

– Stay, find a way, he urged, when one scant week remained of my stay in Venice.

His pleas confused me with false hope.

That reckless rendezvous was when she saw us, from across the Rio dei Pensieri, turning the corner by the dyer's shop after parting, him first, me following, flushed and dishevelled.

My dear mother, Madonna Merlo, had been vexed with me from the day she rubbed my sticky fingers clean and threw away the candied plum I clutched unthinking as I returned to sit with her, that new-found ecstasy brimming in my eyes.

– I told myself it was the bliss of music I saw written on your face. I've believed your little lies since, loving you too much to trust my suspicions.

She demanded my promise that I'd never see him again. I screamed.
– No! No!

I ran from the room but she caught me and blocked my path to the door.

– You're a fool. He won't marry you. Do you want to ruin your life?

She wept, seeing my stubbornness. I wept too, from being found out, from hurting her. From the fury of being thwarted, I screamed again, that I would go to him, make him marry me, for he must because he loved me. Well knowing the futility of it.

My cheeks burned less from her gentle slap than from humiliation.

The truth was that my mother and I had no ties of blood, yet the seed of gratitude planted in my heart had taken root as love. My conscience pricked and I surrendered.

– Elena, my dear, there is time enough for you to find your heart's desire.

Within an hour she dispatched me to Mira on the Brenta river, to the house of an old friend, a lady who would keep me under lock and key until we set out for Genoa. The Brenta boat, the *burchiello*, left from a nearby canal.

I did not see Lorenzo for many years. By then my life had changed, much more than anyone, even I, could know.

6

In front of him lay the sheaf of papers, tied with thin green ribbon. The handwriting was minuscule, crammed into the centre of the page, very different from the careless, ample script of the first single folio.

He pulled gently at the ribbon; it loosened and he set it to one side, his finger running its curled length. These small gestures were ritualistic, an attempt at detachment, controlling the thrill of contact with the past, while also heightening it.

Before reading, before reaching for the magnifying glass, he glanced through the pages. Among them he found traces of a distant body. A pale eyelash. Granular flecks, pinkish like face powder. The edge-print of an inky thumb. A smudge that might have held the moisture of a tear or the dampness of a sweating hand, a drop of water splashed from a glass or a passing gondola.

His pleasure was deepened by these intrusions of the physical. They intimated life and breath, an existence in the senses.

In the act of this imagining, he aimed to banish thoughts of quite another body, a living one. It was Eva he found himself thinking of, wanting to dwell on the memory of her presence only hours before, wanting to revise the memory of their first encounter last night, which by now seemed long ago. These hankerings were unwelcome.

7

Our house in Genoa had a loggia, perfect for the mild air of the Gulf in winter, which we always spent there. We'd returned from Venice in November and my mother meant to stay for the sake of my delicate constitution. But mercantile necessities intervened, so at Christmas we found ourselves in Prague. Bitter cold, and colder still in Buda, our next stop. A heavy fog smothered the Danube and drifted over the city; it made me cough and shiver despite my fur cloak. I pitied the poor who went hungry and ragged in those damp streets.

– We'll go south. You need sun and warmth, my girl. Naples is the place for that, and I have an introduction to someone there who might be worth dealing with.

– I'd like Naples, I'm sure.

I said this with little enthusiasm, though she didn't notice. My mother was torn between concern for my health and the fragility of business interests run by a widow in a world of men she could not rely on. For myself, I'd rather have gone home to Genoa, our loggia and my lessons: our usual quiet winter fare. But I sensed some urgency in these travels.

Alas, all plans went awry at Udine when fever caught up with me. Anxious now, my mother took us to Venice, thinking of a doctor she knew.

We arrived on the eve of my 16th birthday. Though we had sent the maid ahead, our customary lodgings were taken, and Doctor Molin was away.

That night was a delirium of black water and streaming torches that set the *fondamenta* ablaze and spiralled into liquid fire below it. I had a coughing fit as they carried me from the boat; too weak to raise my handkerchief, I felt the flux of blood on my chin. Voices hurt me. My breath half strangled, I wanted silence. Then came oblivion, a loss of consciousness that my mother feared meant death.

Seven days it lasted, she said. My return to the light was slow, gradual, amazed.

Dimness at first. Figures came and went through it, bringing sound: footsteps, words that hung half-uttered in the air or fell with soft insistence. Halting perceptions that left me unanchored from my body, without pain or feeling of life. This must have been my brain's dreamlike invention, for my eyes would not open.

I could give no sign to the world.

A hand held mine, its touch fleshless, my own hand as if separate from me, refusing to obey my wish for its response. Even my sense of hand, the word, was clouded. Hand, *mano*. I struggled to find some picture there, to give form to the hand in my mind, to loosen its inertia, to reach and combine with the one that held it. This striving for a sensation through an image had a different outcome.

– Hand.

My lips and tongue formed the word. My eyes stayed closed, my fingers leaden, but speech ushered me back from the realm of the lost. Exhausted by this effort, I slept again.

When I woke, I could see. A trembling arrow point of gold loomed close. It became a candle flame that revealed my mother's face, sculpted on one side by the light that showed me another's: male, bearded, stooping to see me over her shoulder. A stranger's face, yet in it too I saw the joy her smile proclaimed, and a wilder joy, uncontained, hectic-eyed. Then it waned into eager uncertainty. Whose was this face that troubled me as I fought against the haze of lowered consciousness?

The man receded into the dark of the room, then came back, holding a small blue bottle, stoppering it tightly and giving it to my mother. He whispered and I heard.

– Every day, ten drops, until she has strength.

Over-exercised, my senses succumbed. I slept fitfully, perhaps for hours. Again I heard a voice: this time its melody, its shape, before the words.

– Elena, Elena… are you well? Can you hear me?

– Yes, mother.

Deep sleep claimed me at once, until I woke to a wonderful aroma that announced a meat broth. Aided by my mother, I supped this first food with convalescent relish. No sooner had I swallowed the last mouthful than I lapsed into another healing slumber.

Awakening revealed the world to me complete.

A clear February noon poured southern light across my pillow. Next to my bed, a table bore the remnants of a simple meal: a bowl with a shining spoon in it, a heel of bread, a glass stained purple. Sun glowed on the wood of a chest and through the window I saw the naked blue of the sky.

In no time I was beside it, greedy for a sight of life beyond my sick room. I looked down over red-tiled rooftops.

Hundreds of oars ploughed the wide canal. Black gondolas, skiffs and bright-painted *sandoli* laden with merchandise crowded past. Either side of this busy street of water were *fondamenta* thick with passers-by and vendors. I could hear the close echoes of purposeful steps and the muscular babble of speech. These Venetians bellowed, as they have always done, the boatmen loudest of all, querulous or plangent, as if holding back a sob. Walkers hurried in the habit of the quick Venetian pace; they dallied, contradicting haste to stop and pass the time of day. Talk flowed unhindered by time, and in that almost Levantine city of loud-mouthed buying and selling and eternal conversation my alert ears gathered sound: voices raised and lowered, the calls of birds and cats, the splash of water and its traffic, all distinct, in a natural amplification against air and stone. High above, I possessed its sea tang, its stenches and its fragrances. Intoxicated by my rebirth, I was home.

With each day of health regained I breathed more deeply and saw with sharper eyes. And when I heard music, I heard what I had never heard before. The spaces around it. What it answers.

My heightened faculties ebbed and flowed. Sometimes I sweltered in their heat, assaulted by sensation. I also discovered an ordinary stillness that pulled me from the surface of the world and deep into myself. I needed this route to self-possession.

How my new state had come about, and what its consequences would be, I did not learn for many years. Illnesses fade, discarded by the recall of mind and body. But I remembered everything, while knowing that some piece of memory was missing. One day I asked my mother if I had really seen a bearded man by my sickbed. My doctor, she said, to whom I owed my recovery, called to Verona as I started to get well. She sent him word of my extraordinary progress.

Over the years I was troubled by a dream whose cloudy insistence sent me towards that memory.

8

On the phone she was pressed for time, issuing brusque directions to meet her near the University, close by the notary's office where she had business to attend to.

He scanned the packed terrace of Caffè Rosso without seeing her, until the languid wave of something held aloft caught his attention. Squeezing past boisterous student tables, he observed how sleek she was. The chignon again, a grey wool jacket with dark red silk underneath. She made him think of Grace Kelly, then of Chris – not a resemblance but a shared talent for self-transformation. Chris was well versed in shape-shifting, artificial ageing, pouring herself into whatever mould the play required. That must have made deception easier.

Eva's smile was cool, her greeting impersonal.

– I like this area. So full of life.

Tall trees against the bluish light, the chatter of starlings atop a low brick tower, the cries of children at play. It had charm, but he'd expected somewhere quieter for their meeting. He found her aloofness as baffling as the papers.

– I read what you gave me.

– What did you think?

Paul frowned.

– Are you sure they're Maguire's? I see no connection. This is someone writing about the 17th century. It reads like fiction.

He made an effort to sound surprised rather than irritated.

– I did wonder, but they're filed as hers. She wrote all kinds of things, perhaps even fiction. Anyway, there's more. I've done photocopies. It might make sense in the long run.

He took the large envelope and thanked her, prepared for another disappointment. A delaying tactic, to withhold the real papers? Could she have a buyer in mind?

He caught a waiter's eye.

– Another drink, Eva?

She shook her head. He ordered a beer for himself.

– I have to make a phone call. Excuse me.

He watched her weave between the tables and reach the open square. Earlier, he had thought of inviting her for dinner but he guessed she already had plans. And no designs on him, it seemed. His relief conflicted with the need for her to be interested in helping him.

She had looked through him, her eyes dark and opaque, not the blue he'd remembered. Their vacancy of emotion had prompted a dislike that now quickened. A capricious nature: prickly, superficial. He couldn't abide women who blew hot and cold.

– Are you okay, Paul? You're not unwell?

He opened his eyes and gaped at her blankly. Mild concern showed in her eyes.

– What's wrong?

Her voice was gentle. He straightened up, stifling a yawn.

– Sorry. I'm shattered. I've walked around a lot, went to a couple of libraries, and the Correr Museum. I skipped lunch, I should get something to eat before turning in. Thanks…

She stopped him.

– Come and have dinner with me. It'll be no bother; I've ordered a roast chicken from the *rosticceria* near home. Though we'll have to hurry or they'll be closed.

– No, I've imposed on you enough.

– It's too late to argue.

Her manner became playful. She wagged a silencing finger, then set off across the square, making it hard to do anything but follow.

It must have been the phone call, he concluded; someone had cried off sharing the chicken.

Over dinner he talked about Chris, spooling out an edited version of the break-up.

– Fourteen years? You should have married her, Paul. You could have had a baby.

He helped himself to an artichoke. Her remarks struck him as presumptuous.

They provoked a small surge of memory. An accidental pregnancy, the miscarriage solving their doubts. On this they had agreed. Yet the estrangement started then. Three years ago. He chewed on the artichoke, avoiding Eva's gaze.

Salads from the fridge crowded the kitchen table, roasted peppers that had come with the chicken, an almost empty bottle of Prosecco, another waiting to be opened. The meal's freshness and abundance confirmed that she'd planned for a guest whose replacement he was.

– Marriage had no importance. For our generation it was different.
– Different?

He realised his gaffe. He saw her now as being not much older than himself, and age wasn't really what he meant.

– I'm sorry. I didn't mean to…
– How old do you think I am?

The question was good-humoured.

– The same as me, I imagine… maybe younger.

She laughed.

– I like men who lie to me about my age.

This made him smile.

– It's not that. What I meant was background: culture, not age, a refusal of marriage as an institution. So I've never been married, and you have. More than once, from what you've said.

– Yes, several times… So that makes me seem older?

– In a way. In ways of the world. The unmarried… there's a rite of passage we declined. Many of us saw marriage as a sham. You know, the legacy of the Sixties, a decade much derided, but important. It seems very far away now that we've crossed into a new millennium. I find it hard to believe this is 2000 – it seems almost fictional.

– Time is a strange thing…

This, murmured… then, with half-comic emphasis:

– I thought *highly* of the Sixties.

Lifting her glass, she went on.

– I have an American friend – you might even meet her; she comes to Venice a lot – you could compare reminiscences. So here's to the Sixties. May their spirit thrive!

They clinked glasses.

– And babies? Christine could have had one without you being married.

– She's had one with her new husband. She'd put it off because of her acting career. He's a successful director and that's helped, so everything has worked out well for her.

Her scrutiny made him feel probed for the true feelings behind these words. He waited, suddenly uncomfortable.

– Not for you?

– Well, she's the one who left... after starting an affair. I don't feel good about that. I mean, I didn't; I'm fine now.

He shrugged, faltering. Eva shot him a quizzical look.

– Really?

– Yes. Time sets the heart to rights – in most cases. Along with a trip to Venice.

She smiled agreement, sympathy in her eyes.

– You still haven't said how old you think I am.

– You wouldn't be aiming to embarrass me?

She raised her eyebrows.

– I'll tell you one thing: I've lived long enough to feel I've had many different lives.

Leaning back in his chair, his smile broad and sardonic, he gave her a blatantly assessing look.

– It does sound as if your life has been eventful.

Her features betrayed an inward start. It pleased him. He liked her better now.

She pointed at the envelope.

– Read this.

– I will, right away.

He was joking, feigning instant subservience to her command. She took him seriously.

– No. Read it at your hotel. Forget her for now. Eat. Drink.

This time he obeyed in earnest, tipsy, but alert enough to grasp how much Eva Forrest expected to be in charge.

9

The mother who bore me had been a lady's maid and sewed for the shopkeepers' wives. My father looked after horses at the inn.

A raw wind blew down from the steep corridors of snow to the north of our town, and a shiver of winter has stayed in my bones from those days and nights so near the mountains. I was the third girl, with a brother a year younger. My mother died giving birth to yet another sister. None of this lives in me with certainty, just the chill of that childhood.

Madonna Merlo was the wealthy widow of a Genoese merchant. She had travelled widely in the wake of her husband's death, settling accounts, collecting monies owed and seeing the world he had kept her from. As a woman of great energies, she found a taste for striking bargains on cloth and glass and leather. Her children had both died in infancy. While these old sorrows travelled with her, so did her new-discovered appetite for life, and a generosity for which the city of her birth is unreputed. Genoese, people sneer, when encountering stinginess.

Chance brought her to our town, and gave her news of our misfortune. She wasn't looking for a child to love but, chance again, she heard me sing and lost her heart. After questions on my likes and dislikes and what little learning I had, she persuaded my father to part with me for my own sake and his.

– She is special. I can make her gift flower, I can give her a life of comfort, and ease your burden for the loss of her.

I had no say in the matter, for all my tears. I never knew how much his choice was governed by gold, but the family was the richer for my going.

– You were a child who would be wondered at. To become your mother was a privilege.

She had in mind my vocal gifts.

In time these words strengthened me, lessening the pain of being abandoned by my mother in death, sold by my father. From the start Donna Merlo accepted my grief and consoled me with her heartfelt

37

promises of happiness. At first I called her aunt, but I so much wished for a mother that she did indeed become one. We both had blue eyes and light hair.

How different my life would have been had she not taken me on her travels.

Her riches were finite. The boatman took us west, towards Santa Chiara and beyond, leaving the palaces of Canal Grande to those with fatter purses. Venice was costly in those years, its Levant trade in ruins, its prices high from shipping goods in wartime, but my mother was aiming to sell, not buy. She took an apartment in that unfashionable part of the city where orchards and kitchen gardens spread between those alleys of water, which everywhere else were lined with stone.

Next to our house, wax was made for candles and spread in the sun to whiten and dry. On the other side was a soap factory, and across the canal a dyer's shop – the city abounded in those, for colours were among its closely guarded secrets. Amid these industrious surroundings ostentation had no place, yet while the building we lived in was plain on the outside, it made up for its want of decoration with interiors of gracious, light-struck proportions, and a perfumed garden at the back. Our high windows overlooked the Rio dei Pensieri, and it is in this well-named river of thoughts that I have often searched for clues to my strange fate.

10

After the roast-chicken dinner, some distance was called for. He needed a day without seeing her; he had to ration his time.

Until six he trawled through library catalogues, ordering sundry books and documents, finding no trace of Esme Maguire. According to *Discovering Opera*, Maguire saw out the 19th century in Venice, but it seemed she'd done no singing, at least not on the stage. He scoured two conscientious histories of the Fenice, to no avail. No opera playbills or programmes mentioned her name. He even perused the records of subscribers to see if she figured as a regular member of the audience.

For the first time, he wondered whether the whole enterprise might be futile. He'd found nothing that made sense – except for that first folio. My truest self. The rest lacked credibility, and the shared initials of Maguire and the fictitious Elena Merlo roused suspicions. Be patient, Eva had said, shrugging off the doubts he voiced. When he asked if he might search the papers himself, she'd been horrified.

What if there really were another interested party?

He had four more days.

Weary as he was, he preferred to walk to his hotel rather than join the crowds waiting for the vaporetto. Getting to Rialto was quicker on foot: a straight line rather than the boat's zigzag progress. Only ten minutes. Once over the bridge he felt on home ground; it was quieter, subsiding into a place where people actually lived.

A woman emerged from a shop and for a moment he thought she was Eva. She had her back to him, hurrying ahead; the same height, hair colour, something in her walk. But the clothes weren't right: close-fitting black trousers and a blue denim jacket.

He watched until she was lost in the bend of the alley. In the nearest bar he ordered a whisky.

When he passed the shop it proved to be a stationer's with a jumble of stuff in the window, some of it dusty. Not Eva's style; she was fastidious.

Another bar waylaid him close to his hotel. He had a glass of wine and a snack.

She kept breaking into his thoughts. It had been ill-mannered not to ring today. He risked her annoyance.

Between the door and the reception desk he glimpsed a woman sitting in the small lounge. As he picked up his key, a hand touched his arm and he heard aloud the voice that had murmured in his head all the way from San Marco.

– Hello, Paul.

She handed him a bulky envelope.

– I've been out all day and I thought you might have rung. No need to keep you waiting for the next instalment.

Startled, registering blue denim, black trousers, he didn't take in what she said.

– Eva? What are you doing here?

A shadow crossed her face.

– I'm sorry, it's unexpected. You've come here specially.

Her poise returned as he grew flustered.

– I had some errands in the neighbourhood.

The poise was easier to respond to.

– That's really kind of you. Listen, I was heading out for a pizza. Would you join me?

Pizza had just popped into his head. Fittingly spontaneous, a casual sort of meal rather than a 'dinner' invitation that might be misinterpreted.

She pursed her mouth, then brightened.

– Why not!

He drank two glasses of water before touching any wine.

– What if I'd been out till late?

– I don't know. I didn't want to leave the papers, in case they got mislaid.

She took a deep breath.

– The truth is… I wanted to see you.

– Why?

His voice controlled a spasm of alarm.

LIZ HERON

– I'm giving you these papers to read and… you're the first person to see them since Joe died.

He nodded.

– So… I want to get to know you better.

This was said with such disarming sweetness that he failed to remind himself how much he'd already given way to Eva's curiosity, despite his wish to be detached. As he held back the compound of fear and desire that she provoked in him, caution came too late for him to stop her next words.

– I'd like to take you on a little boat trip. What about tomorrow?

41

11

Our gondola set us down at the water gate of a fine high palace on the Grand Canal, its facade of Istrian stone, not deceptive stuccoed brick. Either side of this portal were the words *Non Nobis* – Not Unto Us. I wondered at them. Every stone in this city has its story; over time the stories are remade, the stones unchanged.

For 14 years I'd been away. For 10 I was married, now widowed.

My mother chose a husband for me wisely, a good man. She had long been patient with my refusals and was finally firm. At 18, she said, my past was lengthening and without a fortune my future remained insecure. Though she had managed her business with prudence, she had not known how to weather wars and speculation, the embargoes of trade and the vagaries of fashion, so her capital had dwindled and we lived more frugally than before. We had our home in Marseille, after moving from Genoa in a rush of selling up and packing, threatened by bankruptcy or some other evil. I never knew which.

At 42, Jean-Albert was a little older than his rival, Monsieur Lenoir, an engineer who had worked on Vauban's fortifications at Valenciennes and Luxembourg.

– He really seems younger than Lenoir, mother, and not so dull.

I sighed. With my modest dowry I had scant hopes of being a young man's bride.

– Yes, Elena. Lenoir is a bore, and I would not wish a dreary husband on you. Jean-Albert has an open mind and a young man's energy.

His looks did not entirely displease me. He had read and travelled, he collected curiosities. His family's money came from soap, more of which was made in Marseille than in Venice. He had studied law. Much of his time was spent educating me. A model bourgeois husband. Kind-hearted too.

When he died, I had other things to thank him for. Still young, I was an independent woman, a widow of sufficient means. I knew

Latin and Greek and had known a man's love. I had returned it. Without passion. My husband had been kind, never forcing his ardour on
me, valuing my daughterly fondness. No children came, leaving me
without regret. I lacked the urge for mothering.

Non Nobis. I stepped inside that palazzo and sneezed.

I went on sneezing, uncontrollably. More and more heads turned.
My first Venetian entrance after years of exile and instead of being a
triumph it was causing me embarrassment.

I fled outside. A chair was brought. In the fresh air I recovered.

– My dear, what's the matter?

Rolande, my sister-in-law, the youngest of my husband's three siblings, bent close and looked into my reddening eyes. I dabbed at them
with a handkerchief.

– Dust.

We had arrived two days before, both of us in widow's weeds that
enjoyed the benefit of a French dressmaker's cut, and as soon as we
entered the Cannaregio Canal, I felt the air stir around me. I could
hear words whispered between a couple on the *fondamenta*, the tread
of a cat above as we sailed beneath the new three-arched bridge. I
could taste the city's sweet-salt tang in my mouth. Venice heightened
my senses.

But the dust inside the Palazzo Calergi had almost choked me.

When I regained my composure, we returned to the *salone* to
be introduced: Madame Bourdon (myself) and Madame Robert. We
attracted interest, whether for our novelty or our French looks – in
this new Venice, whose empire had shrunk, elegance succeeded. Or
else some pictured the bills of exchange we carried in our purses – the
very word Marseille spoke money. I listened and smiled, by instinct
saying little. Rolande chattered with a seemingly guileless charm.

My eyes darted about in hope of recognition. They met with disappointment. A remote enough hope, since I had no way of knowing
whether Lorenzo were alive or dead. But Venice had revived those
memories of girlhood.

– Madame is looking for someone?

The man at my elbow was old, around 60 I thought, his gaze neither lustful nor greedy, merely inquisitive. Yet he made me nervous.

– No, I am curious about my fellow guests. It's natural, don't you agree?

This provoked a fleeting frown, then a smile that displayed a mouthful of good teeth, extraordinary for someone so old.

– Quite, Madame. Let me introduce myself so you can dispense with curiosity on my own account and make use of whatever assistance I can provide regarding your questions about others.

Davide Perulli was of the lower nobility and without a title of his own. When younger, he had been a man of science and even practised as a physician, although his family disapproved. We talked, or rather he did, which reassured me, for it altered my impression of prying eyes, and soon he had told me about his life, about Venice and its recent alterations. He appeared to know everyone.

It was on the tip of my tongue to name Lorenzo when he enquired if this was my first visit to the city. Instantly, he answered for me.

– No, Madame, I see you have been here before. You are at home.

Commonplace as these words were, they put me on my guard. I mistrusted his apparent openness – maybe a trap designed to lure me into confidences. He wanted something from me.

– Sir, you are right, but I was very young.

– How young, Madame?

– A girl. Perhaps 14 or 15.

– Might we have met?

He held my eyes.

– I hardly know.

– I believe we did. Something about you is familiar.

I blushed, from a sense of being found out. Yet all I had to hide was the guilt of my desire to see Lorenzo. Guilt I'd betrayed, from Perulli's next words.

– There *is* someone you seek here, if I am not mistaken.

I looked away and caught Rolande's eye.

– I must join my sister, Signor Perulli. Perhaps we'll meet again.

– I'm sure of it.

He bowed.

– Your sister, you say. And how is your mother? Still in good health, I trust.

Back turned, I ignored the question.

In the atrium I felt safe enough to stop.

– Why such haste? Who was that gentleman?

Rolande was eager for some mystery to unfold, but accepted my shrugs.

– He pretended to know me. I can't say I liked him.

This piqued her curiosity.

Outside, we took a gondola from San Marcuola. When we reached the *bacino* my heart lifted at the sight of so many ships' sails and the sparkle of the open water. For the rest of that day I basked in the glorious light of Venice and the optimism it inspires.

I got it into my head that Perulli brought on the sneezes. It struck me as strange that he often crossed my path.

A lady I came to know described him as a shady character whom some thought it best to avoid.

– He's a magus, they say.

Perulli had combined his medicine with alchemical magic, with spells and doubtful potions that made some patients sicker and gave others wild, delirious dreams. The rumours fuelled by these maladies had forced him to give up doctoring.

I laughed, though disturbed at hearing of his power to harm.

– What nonsense.

Superstitious notions did not attract me, nor had they entered my education, guided by my mother's common sense and Jean-Albert's scepticism. Many, however, believed in witchcraft. The Spanish emperor's impotence was blamed on hexing by a witch, and this feeble invalid's want of an heir was causing talk of war the length and breadth of Europe. War looming again, just when Doge Valier, with the other powers in the Holy League, had signed a treaty ending struggle with the Turks. They now ruled much of Venice's old empire in Greece but had fled at last from the lands of Bosnia and Serbia, returning them to Christendom.

That night a dream woke me with a shudder. A dream all too familiar. It lingered as I lay awake, Rolande sleeping in the bed close to mine, an oar slapping the water outside – this and her breath the only sounds. The dream haunted by a memory, where a bearded man held out a cup to me. Drink this, he said, and I did. That man became Perulli.

Next morning, Rolande, alert as ever, quizzed my dark-circled eyes.

– Is your trouble a sweet one, or not?

It was a year since my husband, her brother, had died, and she believed that young and childless as I was, I should waste no time in marrying again. Her three daughters already had husbands.

– Who is there to give me sweet trouble?

– You are the one to know.

At a gathering she had heard me raise Lorenzo's name, and heard the answer. He was alive and in Venice. He and his wife, that wealthy girl I had envied, had two sons. I believed I would see him sooner or later, but doubted it would make me happy.

– Madame Bourdon, welcome, how do you do? Your mother fares well, I trust. My father held her in high regard.

I had sent my mother's letter of introduction to a young English merchant and banker, the son of a man she had known when her business still prospered. His name was Joseph Smith. He was wealthy and rumour had it that he supplied the British army.

Before meeting his other guests, I gave him a brief account of our fortunes.

In his L-shaped *salone* overlooking the Grand Canal, artists, poets, booksellers and pamphleteers mingled with Flemish and English merchants.

– Merchants can be well read too. He whispered this, a touch of mischief in his voice.

Smith was a man of very many parts, a Midas whose ease with making money was matched by alert tastes and the polymathic knowledge required in one who collects costly treasures: rare books and precious gems as well as the fine drawings and paintings he bought from artists who interested him. Giuseppe, as he was known in Venice, settled me

beside one of these, a woman I judged of my own age, with an immediately candid and searching gaze that I felt obliged to return. Hers
struck me as a rather stony face, unforgiving in its scrutiny of mine.
I began to feel out of my depth: a woman artist, a species I had never
met before. Rosalba Carriera.

But the face creased into a generous smile and with it I noticed a
softening dimple in Rosalba's chin. This alteration encouraged me to
speak.

– We're the only women here.

– There's one you haven't noticed.

She gestured towards a young woman in satin standing alone by
the balcony door.

– Giuseppe's wife, Caterina. She's English too, and a singer. Before
she married, that is, in London.

I wanted to know which roles she might have sung, but Rosalba
shrugged, so I asked instead about her own work. She painted miniatures on ivory, and had begun to do portraits in pastels. I remembered
seeing one of these, of a white-wigged Venetian beauty, and how it
shimmered with different shades of whiteness.

Giuseppe, she said, was a valuable patron to have. A connoisseur,
a clever man who managed, somehow, to live several lives simulta-
neously: trading, banking, dealing in art, and welcoming guests, for
he liked to surround himself with dazzling talk and those it pleased to
hear it.

– Too many talents for just one life. I wonder, does he ever sleep?

She laughed at her own question, then proposed to walk about
the room with me and tell me who was who, which she did. Only
one name was familiar, that of Ricci, a painter. She left me with Mrs
Smith, striking and slender, polite enough, but resistant to my curiosity, only saying she was not English but Scottish, had sung at Drury
Lane and would sing no more. In the face of this woman's unhappy
hauteur, I did not speak of my own childhood gifts as a singer.

With Rolande I was a frequent visitor to Smith's palazzo and in
these gatherings I discovered a new brightness of language and possibility – until the evening Lorenzo entered the room, eclipsing all of
this dawning light; Lorenzo, no longer a boy, but a young man in

his prime. The cool self I had acquired was lost to my memory of the fiery girl he had known. I became her again.

He kissed my hand, held it in his. Rolande made sure to leave us alone. By the evening's end we felt that time had never separated us.

– Do you sing still?

– Only at home.

I told him of my early longings to make a life in music, and how, out of fear for my virtue and my marriage prospects, my mother had discouraged these as I grew older.

– You should not waste a gift that makes you who you are. I admired the girl with that voice. I loved her.

Joy flooded through me. The light in his eyes showed that this feeling was more than a memory. We fixed a rendezvous.

Next morning a message came to postpone it.

Finally I saw him, in secret, at the house of his closest friend, in its secluded high-walled garden.

We sat, intoxicated, relishing the sight of one another, before we fell into a new conversation, narrating our lives, our travels, and what we had learned in the course of the years. Our happiness was no carnal rapture; we didn't touch, yet no boundary remained between us. A missing part of me had been restored.

I marvelled at our closeness under the skin. Each pierced the core and the heart of the other.

– Trade is my world; it takes me to Amsterdam and Bruges, and even once to Greece. I was always meant to do as my father had done but I sometimes hanker after other kinds of life.

– Be glad of your life. I envy your freedom as a man.

– I too am constrained. My choices were made for me.

He shook his head, giving me a look of helpless sorrow. I couldn't answer this muteness; I wanted him to show more courage.

It was early in the autumn. A dish of fruit stood on the table between us and in silence we sucked on those small dark grapes whose coarse skin encloses the fragrant flavour of strawberries.

This vein of conversation led us both to silence. He'd look at me, then look away, his turmoil visible.

– It's dangerous for us to be here. My wife is a jealous woman. If they knew of our meeting, her brothers would ruin me and rob me of my sons. My beloved boys are already influenced by their uncles. Those men have boundless wealth and a vicious sense of family honour.

This outburst astonished me. All that joined the two of us was feeling, not flesh, and we had met just once after many years of separation. I was angry that he should make me the cause of such fright.

– Your fears amaze me. I have always seen you as proud and strong.

– You have no children.

Was this what it meant to have a child? To forfeit the best of oneself?

At our parting he held me close, crushing my body against his, yet without any kiss. In this embrace I felt him push me away, the words unsaid: I long for you but you cannot have me.

He left, telling me to wait, in case we should be seen together. I quivered with rage and thwarted desire. Tears hung in my eyes. Again I was the girl he'd abandoned, only with an adult woman's powerful longings. I dug my nails into my palms and wept.

On the table some grapes remained, and beside them the thick and bitter skins we'd discarded from our mouths as we ate the sweet, soft pulp. I took them all, his and mine, to mingle them together on my tongue. I sucked at them, then spat them on the ground. It would have shocked him to see.

Advised by a servant, I left the garden through a courtyard where the cook kept a herbarium. From there ran a short *calle* that brought me to the hubbub of the *ruga*. I glimpsed a tall figure, masked but unmistakable, disappear among the crowd. Perulli's dark green coattails. Even here, for all our caution, he had found me, and it struck me as uncanny. Why did this man keep me in his sights? It made me afraid.

Rolande saw my reddened eyes, and waited for me to speak. In vain. That night I lay awake in an ecstasy of uncertainty, my blood racing. Was I to leave or stay, perversely hope or resign myself to a future without Lorenzo? And what of Perulli, his motives for stalking me?

Finally I told my sister everything. She could see that I suffered, but had no understanding of such passion.

– What is this love that hurts you? Love is serene, love is content-ment, it does not destroy, it nourishes.

– Love is fever, love is longing, love is oneness. And need.

– You need him? For what?

– As a swift needs the air, as the spider needs corners.

Rolande concluded that some madness gripped me.

The day after this thorny conversation I was walking on the Riva, seeking respite in the sun-dazzle of the lagoon and the movement of ships bound for the open sea, when I found myself face-to-face with the man I considered my enemy: Davide Perulli.

I felt weak at the sight of him, paralysed by a humiliating fear. Perulli fixed me with his compelling eyes.

I knew I had to speak or terror would swallow me up. It took great effort to stop my voice from trembling.

– Signor Perulli, what do you want from me? Why do you follow me?

He shook his head in vehement denial. I asked again, my tone more insistent.

– What have I done?

This time, he cringed and stepped back.

– I am to blame. Forgive me.

To my amazement, with a gesture of despair he covered his face with his hands and sobbed. My fear dissolved into puzzlement and an unexpected pity.

Passers-by gaped, at him, and at me, the apparent cause of his dis-tress. At a loss to help him, I ended the encounter.

– Signor Perulli, go home. Do not trouble yourself over me. I am well.

The strength in my voice surprised me, its command pronounced as a kindly meant request. Perulli heeded it and walked away.

I saw Lorenzo one more time. As things turned out, I could not wait for his promised message. A week after our meeting in the gar-den, word arrived from Marseille that my mother had fallen gravely

ill. Always robust, she had been in the best of health before our departure; leaving her had given me no qualms.

For Lorenzo's sake, I could not risk approaching him. With little
time in hand, I dispensed with caution and went to Giuseppe Smith.

– I have need of discretion, Giuseppe, and you're the only man in
Venice who can help me. I beg you to hear me out.

He rewarded my audacity with a kindness I had never suspected of
the English. Asking no questions, he sent for Lorenzo to come on a
matter of urgent business, and put a room at my disposal.

Frantic with impatience, I watched the clock on the mantelshelf.
Rolande was taking care of bills at our lodgings. We were due to leave
within the hour.

It was a plain English clock in a case of inlaid wood. I stared at the
face, willing it to slow down.

The servant returned. Lorenzo was on his way. The clock's ticking
sounded softer and less hostile.

From the window I caught sight of him in the *calle* below. He
looked up and I read surprised love in his eyes, his whole face tender
and quickening, revealing the boy I first knew, not a man weighed
down by worries and mistakes.

I saw a change, though. His hair had been darker at our last meeting. Now it was quite grey.

Time slowed again as I listened for his tread on the stairs, and a
small eternity passed before the door opened and Smith showed him
in, leaving us alone.

His embrace was cold and fleeting, the reek of rejection issued from
his lips. There is no magic about sudden terror on the breath: fear
sours the juices in the stomach. The mouth that brushed my cheek
betrayed it.

I stood back. His eyes withdrew from mine. I spoke of my departure and heard only wounding politeness that wished me a safe journey and my mother a speedy recovery. He bowed and left. A mere
five minutes had passed since his arrival. With nothing more to wait
for, I was bereft. A claw reached into my heart and tore at it, the pain
enraging me.

Rolande saw me now not as mad but ill and did her best to give me solace. With the miles we put behind us my disappointment receded, and the closer we got to Marseille the more my thoughts dwelled on my mother. Whatever else might hurt me, losing her would be the sharpest grief of all. I pushed dread out of my mind; she shall live, I said, sure that my will could make it so.

My mother lived long enough to take leave of me. She was lucid at first, and gave me sensible counsel about taking care of money and health, about finding a new husband and choosing him well. Dusk gathered and the room filled with shadows as her strength dwindled.

– I don't want to leave you.

Her voice was heartbreakingly small.

Stemmed tears drenched the hand I took in mine. In the darkness now, I no longer saw her face. A maid brought a candle and I sent her away.

Before her consciousness faded, I asked about Davide Perulli. The name brought no recognition. I described him.

– Yes. The doctor who saved your life.

I heard the gladness in that weakened voice, but the words startled me, although I'd half known the reason for the dream Perulli evoked. Why so furtive, and for what did he blame himself?

After my mother's death, nothing mattered. Perulli's behaviour shrank into trivial recollection. I fretted, riven by guilt, convinced that with me beside her she would not have succumbed to her sudden, fatal illness.

Without my mother's gifts to me, who would I have been? I was no one's daughter now. I needed to learn new and lonely things, knowing that I too must die one day.

How sorely I took her death. Perhaps I was also mourning Lorenzo, though he had left my waking thoughts, clinging only to my dreams.

Two years passed. With each new season, I regained some meagre joy in living. But life's taste altered to thirst-quenching water, not heady wine. The future lay flat before me: a vista of duties and small pleasures to be shared with Rolande, my nieces and their families. Nothing pressed or threatened, nothing was promised.

The unexpected happened. The deaths I looked back on and the war being fought elsewhere in Europe played their part. I know my urge for life to be vivid; I am fond of change and drama, I wrest them out of any dullness. But this had its own reflection in fate's mirror. I fell in love.

My mother would not have approved.

I had been loved by Jean-Albert. I loved Lorenzo as I loved my heartbeat, and for all his cowardice he too loved me, a passion in my very being that had grown as part of me since childhood. François was my first love choice as an adult woman.

He was a tall, lean man whose languid eyes would clamour when something fired his passions. He loved to dance, had a sweet tooth and chose soldiering for want of any other chance to make his way. Although he was no scholar, there was one book he always carried with him: an old volume of Montaigne. It was his *vade mecum*; he said it showed him what men have in common in the workings of the body and the mind, and taught him too about the comedy of folly and the variousness of human nature. Yet he deemed it not always wise and sometimes laughably foolish, and this disagreement made him argue with Montaigne, which he did aloud, reading to me and commenting in between, altering the timbre and tone of his voice. He was so lively, eloquent and entertaining that he would have made a fine actor.

How reckless to lose my heart to an army man, a cavalry officer serving under the Duc de Villars.

I was swept into the war with him, even though I had never seen glory in the art of killing at some king's behest.

We married.

12

The French roads were best. Once we reached the Spanish Nether-
lands there were only dirt tracks and stony ground. I broke my shoulder when a front wheel spun off its axle and I fell through the carriage
door. Bruises, gashes, falls in ditches – I shrugged them off, always on
the move, heedless of discomfort.

All of Europe was embroiled in this mess of conflicts between Hab-
sburgs and Bourbons that lasted 13 years. Alliances shifted, plans were
waylaid. Sometimes I caught up with François' regiment, or else I'd
travel ahead to where victory was expected. When I took rooms in
Vienna to await François' arrival my French wardrobe had me taken
for a spy, but my Italian papers saved me. In vain, though. No conquering Frenchmen entered the city, for the march on Vienna was
cancelled and Villars, his nose out of joint, returned to France to fight
a local war. My husband went with him. I followed, always begging
for news of his regiment, sparing no expense to reach it whenever
muddle and carnage forced us apart. Our reunions were worth all that.
La belle Hélène, he would call me, each time we met after separations,
making my name French, taking my hand and drawing me close.

If I sound frivolous, let me be forgiven. I never saw the phantasms
of the battlefield; nor did I even glimpse the rising smoke, the con-
flagrations. Once, twice perhaps, I heard the boom of artillery a long
way off. I chose to forget my fear, my nausea and disgust at what my
husband told me of the horror wrought on human flesh by swords
and cannon: of bodies split in half, guts spilled, heads blown off, skulls
crushed and splintered.

Instead, I remember what I wore at officers' dinners and balls.
I remember the champagne I drank, the compliments I received,
the pain of parting, the relief of reunion, the blind confusion of
rumour and my persistent need for wifely optimism. Such intensity
was unknown to me, our partnership of love and danger made me
newly alive.

So much might have been different, had Villars not been persuaded to relent and rally France against the English. For the treaty-makers and cartographers, and for me.

My husband was killed near the war's end. Crueller still, he had survived the slaughter at Malplaquet. In the letter he wrote to me from there, he looked forward to retirement on a handsome pension. He died absurdly, in Villars' easy taking of Landau.

After his death, I thought of how he might have become sundry other things than a soldier, had opportunity allowed, and mourned all the more the stilling of his quicksilver being. That book of his was sent to me along with his few other possessions, and I too have kept it with me, consulting its torn and spattered pages and forever hearing François speak its words.

The news only reached me a week later, but on the day he died I wept. I always knew he lived through the shedding of blood, that at all of those battles widows and orphans were made – a foul gamble in which others staked that blood. And because of our bond I knew when his time had come. In this uncanny knowledge of loss I was no seer, just humanly bound by love and instinct. Like everyone else, I could not foretell the future. However long my past might become.

In war's chaotic aftermath it took me months to reach Marseille. Though drawn towards home by a yearning for family comfort, I lacked the strength to travel far. Perhaps distance saved me; it forced me on each day towards yet another goal; it compelled my will against inertia and despair.

Desire held me from the moment I set eyes on François, and love had followed on its heels. In the first week of our marriage we rode to Baux; from the heights of the citadel we looked down on the countryside of Provence in the rugged throes of spring. A hawk hovered beneath us, the light was golden, the earth frantic with renewal. On that day, I felt I would never be happier. This memory returned with overpowering force and in my grief became voluptuous. It was there, on those heights, in that resplendent afternoon that I urged his spirit to dwell, far from the murderous scene of the German battlefield where his body would have lain. But how I missed his body, his warm, surrounding presence, his arms and mouth, the breath of him all over me. And because I was used to his absence in life, it was a while before I grasped that this new absence would never end.

La belle Hélène. I would whisper that love name, alone and sleepless in the dark, knowing I would never hear those words again from his lips, yet persuading myself to hear his voice in them, to make him live in me. In time I learned that the dead we loved do live in us, enlarging our spirit as we accept their gifts to us in life.

The year was 1714 and the last of the treaties was being signed. On my 44th birthday I reached Marseille and collapsed in Rolande's arms.

Only as I convalesced from my descent into mourning and illness did I notice she looked old. Her face had fallen into deep furrows and lost its tautness of expression. She was 11 years my senior and had a granddaughter soon to be a bride.

Two letters waited, both from Venice. The one from Lorenzo bore the date of François' death, and this moved me. Its tenderness struck me as inspired by shame for how he had treated me, and perhaps by some intuition of my sufferings. He wished me happiness.

Perulli's letter was the work of a man plagued by some inner daemon.

… I am old and don't expect to live much longer. I am tired and can hardly believe I once strove for life eternal. I was convinced I had found it at last, an elixir so potent it would halt all the havoc of ageing by an action of regeneration. I feared, however, that I might have failed to perfect it, and I lacked the courage to put it to the test myself. In the past, my experiments had sometimes cost others dear, leaving their minds prey to drastic imbalance of humours. They were willing, conscious of the risk they took, you were not, but you were dying… When I saw your recovery begin, I knew I had succeeded, but fled from seeing the consequences. So much could still go awry. Your mother wrote with news of your progress and I saw that my potion had done its great work. Alas, its effects on me were slight and short-lived, only strengthening my muscles, bones and teeth. Perhaps your youth was the elixir's necessary solvent; unlike me, you had not begun to age.

And then I saw you, no longer a girl, but fully grown to your womanly prime, your health and well-being enhanced by the strength-giving properties of my elixir. It will regenerate your body for many years to come: for three centuries, according to my first calculations, perhaps longer. Or its potency may diminish, so that you will age, but very slowly. It is my duty to warn you that your life will not be natural.

Nothing, however, will protect you from unnatural causes; you could die at any time from injury or poison or fire. But I do not wish you to suffer such a fate.

Have I cursed you? This is my dread. Time has made me see the error of opposing nature, and my guilt oppresses me. Neither you nor your mother had knowledge of my scheme. Without it you would have died, and I beg you to remember this when judging me. It may not be too late. You left Venice suddenly, before I could summon the courage to tell you these things. I believe I have devised an antidote. There is still time…

I wrote to Lorenzo with news of my bereavement. He sent his heartfelt condolences. Perulli's letter shocked me at first, but I gave it no importance. In the mirror I saw a grieving widow, exhausted by her journey, made pale by tears, her face gaunt from lack of sleep. No promise of eternal life looked back at me. I penned a note to set the man's troubled mind at rest. His failure to answer told me that either his courage had deserted him again or that he was dead. He had cured me and was merely raving in his dotage, or his 'experiments' had deranged his own mind.

War and mourning had deprived me of any senses grounded in normal life, those struggles without drama that are waged from day to day. It took a quieter adversity to sober me.

Our circumstances had worsened. The war had made some richer, most poorer. Taxes were high, bad harvests had put up prices. Rolande and I lived on the shrinking income of our family invest-ments and my pension from François. With time, it too lost value. King Louis had died and the Regent who now ruled promised us no better than we'd had. One morning, studying our accounts and see-ing no solution to our debts, I voiced a plan.

– I have always depended on others. I have never earned money of my own.

– My dear, you are no longer young, and there is little a woman of your standing can do to earn a living.

– I can teach music. I once had a voice considered exceptional, and had lessons as a girl. I shall need lessons now; I still have things I can sell to pay for them. It's true that I'm no longer young, yet I don't feel old. Not too old to begin something new. Is that what you meant?

Rolande peered at me through her thick eyeglasses.

– Come closer.

I kneeled in front of her. She placed a hand on my head and caressed it.

– I've noticed how well you look lately. You appear much younger than your years. It's extraordinary.

I too had noticed how youthful I looked compared with those around me. Yet don't we all delude ourselves about what the mirror tells us?

– It may be that my grief had aged me and now I feel restored. I have never had children, and the cares they bring add wrinkles, as you know.

She sighed. She considered me unfortunate for being childless, a high price to pay for a smooth brow. Later, I thought of Rolande's remark and felt I owed her words more credence than my own surmises had allowed.

– Do what you think best, my dear.

So I sold my jewellery, everything except a gold and sapphire ring François had given me – conqueror's booty, I suspected at the time. I could not part with it. He said the gem's blueness was right for my eyes.

13

Remember me...

Maestro Guzzi held his breath, wide-eyed, at each *Remember me*.

I had found a teacher, an Italian from Pavia, a stern and reserved man (the Pavesi are like that). But all the same, at my sixth lesson his jaw dropped when I sang my way through Dido's Lament. *When I am laid in earth.* I had meant to surprise him and had practised hard.

Maestro Guzzi surprised me, too, by adopting my talent and putting himself at its service. My progress continued to astonish him and, confident of my success, he arranged performances among the city's music lovers, then further afield. I was welcomed in aristocratic households and rewarded with generous patronage. I received invitations to the Savoy Court at Turin, and later to Milan, thriving on this favour and attention. As my voice grew in beauty and strength, it awakened fresh energies. My heightened senses, which surged and ebbed with change, were at a pitch of sensitivity, sharpening my instincts for the moods and intentions of others – a valuable resource when dealing with the powerful. My optimism matched this vitality. I was renewed by discovery of my longed-for self: the singer, the artist I was always meant to be. The future stretched ahead, charged with unknown life and possibility. Thus do the young perceive the world.

This rejuvenation would puzzle me only when I came home from travels to Vienna, to Paris, Buda, Parma and Bologna. Each time I found Rolande much older than before, and she would greet me with startled, rheumy eyes, as if I were a stranger.

Was I going mad, prey to a delusion that I could cheat time by my own resilient impulse to renewal, avoid growing old by creating a new bright self? A phoenix. I remembered Perulli's letter and had a moment's anguished thought that this disregarded clue to my fate had gone astray. But it was unlike me to throw away correspondence, and even that strange, importunate old man had connected me to Venice, the beloved city of my first passion.

The letter lay at the bottom of a chest, among old clothes, together with the last one from Lorenzo. Now Perulli's words transfixed me... *for three centuries... perhaps even longer.* I resisted his wild story. Whatever his medicine had done, it could surely not be this. I had no scrap of faith in magic – but others did. The letter could harm me; after dark, I threw it in the fire. A furious bruising anger possessed me as I watched it burn, a feeling that confused me until I found its seed in my fear that I had been condemned, the form of my life redesigned as monstrous, alien to the world. I spent a night wracked by terror, at a loss to understand. Knowing I could never speak of this made me feel all the lonelier. In my bones, I knew it best to stay away from Perulli; he was surely dead and would have left no trace of what he had done to me. If he had, return to Venice might be hazardous; I saw myself at the Inquisition's mercy.

Dissolving each into the other, my memory and my dream of this man haunted me still. I thought of that blue glass bottle in his hand and began a futile search for it among my mother's things, wanting its solidity as some kind of proof.

Rolande's death shocked me. My sister; we had shared three decades of family life. She was my companion and my prop, and she had never swerved from the paths marked out for her: wife, mother, widow, grandmother, a consolation to other women in their trials – myself, her eldest daughter, also widowed, and the neighbour whose children died in infancy. Death came to her by way of others' troubles, and it took her unawares. We cannot face death until it faces us.

She was in her prime when I first met her: strong, large-boned, her brown eyes candid and clear. That was how I wished to remember her, rather than as her dying shrivelled self. Age not only shrinks the body, it robs it of colour; hair, eyes, lashes, eyebrows fade, just as flesh's contours blur. She died a ghost of herself.

I had too many griefs to nurse by now to let this one strike me down. And no one left to lean on. I felt it unwise to linger in Marseille. With a first marriage, then a second, Elena Merlo had acquired new names; now she would have to take another, be reinvented for safety's sake.

In the mirror I saw a woman reaching her prime. The thought of a living eternity ahead overwhelmed me with sadness. Yet a different feeling impelled me to defy that empty future. It was elation, dawning power. I could own to being thirty-two and be believed: the age I was when I fell in love with François.

My natural life had ended.

14

They boarded the *motoscafo* at the stop beside the Guglie Bridge – the *guglie*, she told him, were the stone spires that capped the parapet. Crouching low in the water, their boat cruised up the Cannaregio Canal and entered the Northern Lagoon.

The sky billowed into vastness. He felt a child's excitement at an outing.

– I've no idea where we are on the map.

– St Mark's is the grand entrance, now we're at Venice's back door.

She sketched a topography of the fish-shaped city's shabby northern edge. Bell towers poked above the rooftops and, with a stream of questions, Paul searched for them on his fraying tourist map.

When she furnished dates and anecdotes he smiled his pleasure at her ready knowledge, touching her arm without thinking as he pointed at buildings or across the open stretch of water. He admired the baroque angels that reared up sideways on the skyline, their forms fluid, deliberately unaligned, striving, it seemed, to cast off their stone anchorage on the Jesuit church and swim to heaven through the watery air.

Beneath the angels, at Fondamente Nuove, they changed to the connection for Torcello, a more solid vessel, heavy with passengers. It swung out through marked channels deep enough to be safe amid the shallows. Paul sat opposite Eva, not close enough for conversation. Two teenage girls, sports bags on their shoulders, stood between them, rocking with the motion of increasing speed, revelling in it. He thought of the latest Maguire instalment, a story too absurd to be tantalising: a magus in a green tailcoat, an elixir of eternal life, the War of the Spanish Succession. Eva claimed not to have read it.

Getting to know him better, she'd said, wasn't about prying into his life, but feeling at ease. And how was he to know *her*: a chameleon, thoughtful and frivolous, imperious and kind, a modern independent woman, a vain parader of female spoils. Today, at ease, she flashed no jewels from rich husbands, no pearls.

When the crowds got off their eyes met: a moment's intensity, perhaps a threshold. What would the day bring? Should he let things take their course, or might it be unwise?

He knew better than to trust attraction. The sensible truth remained: Eva was a professional contact. What if sex were the only way to see the real Maguire papers – if they existed at all? He found the idea distasteful, not of sex itself, but an exchange of that nature. Then he disliked himself for these thoughts.

At Torcello the air was cooler, the sky a frail blue mist. They walked along a canal bank. Greenery replaced the stones of Venice.

– Wasn't your last husband English?

– Joe? No, his parents were Poles, but his mother remarried after she was widowed and the stepfather adopted him. That made him a Forrest as well as a Lensky. Having more than one identity can be a help… in business, I mean.

– I see. And your name before that?

– Murnau.

– German?

– Yes. A German husband.

– And what was your name before that? I mean your maiden name.

There was a short intake of breath before her eyebrows shot up.

– I'm sorry, I wasn't meaning to pry.

– Of course.

At the end of the path she stopped to shake some gravel from her sandal. She took it off and without thinking he reached down and caught her unshod foot, holding it for perhaps longer than was necessary, looking up at her as she looked down at him, both smiling, then relaxing into laughter. Not the laughter of embarrassment, but complicity.

The cathedral stood beyond a grassy forecourt where a stall sold lace and postcards. Lace from the neighbouring island of Burano, Eva told him, or more likely the sweatshops of China. She asked would he like a guided tour, and he said he'd been counting on it. In the manner of a proud schoolgirl with everything committed to memory, she plotted Torcello's 1,500-year history: refugees fleeing the Huns had come here from the mainland, settled and prospered as farmers and traders, built the first church, then rebuilt it as a cathedral. Here was a building finished in 1008, with solid vestiges from its earlier incarnations.

– I'm impressed. Thank you for that illuminating history lesson… So why was the island abandoned?

– Mud. Decay. The waters silted up. Transport and trade became difficult. Venice was growing powerful and overtaking Torcello.

– But Venice began here, didn't it?

– And this is the oldest church in the lagoon, to my mind the most beautiful.

Inside, in the gloom, the gold glow of the mosaics, the aquatic green of the marble all created a numinous underwater mood, as if the church had been drowned and risen from the bottom of the sea, its past life washed away, except the stones with human memories sealed inside them. Even the shutters on the windows were made of stone. The island itself struck him as sharing this opacity, an atmosphere of desertion never made good.

– Venice suits you, Paul.

– Why do you say that?

– Its melancholy becomes you. And melancholy's the other side of you, I think?

He eyed her in quizzical silence.

– Your curiosity, and that enthusiasm you have, youthful really. It's almost irresistible. Yet underneath there's the older, wiser you, sadder than the you on the surface, but the combination makes you interesting.

The silence persisted, his gaze now blank.

She stepped back in a flutter of uncertainty.

– I've offended you. It's my turn to apologise. Of course, I hardly know you.

He was slow to answer.

– No… I'm flattered, actually. In a way we're all strangers to ourselves. Aren't we?

The cloud lifted from her face.

He touched her arm, half-remembering he had done this on the boat deck.

– Wait for me, will you. I want some mementos of this place.

He was relieved to turn away, glad to walk back and see her standing there. She frowned at the sky.

– It's going to rain.

– A pity. So I can't persuade you to climb the *campanile* with me? There's 'an incomparable view of the lagoon from the top'.

He showed her the back of the postcard.

– How can I say no? Even if we get a little wet up there.

A young woman took their tickets, warning that the bells would ring on the hour. They're *very* loud, she emphasised, echoing their laughter as they walked on. Plenty of time, said Eva, it was twenty to. They made the ascent quickly, meeting people on their way down the winding stairs, and found themselves alone at the top, in the chill moist air where a thickening mist obliterated everything but the nearest small islands. As they re-entered the belfry the great bells lurched into their automated cycle, their oscillations speeding up with louder and louder clangings. Eva covered her ears. The noise became unbearable.

– Shall we go back down?

Paul had to mime the words. Eva mimed back.

– LET'S STAY.

Steps led to a wooden partition that gave some protection from the impact. They stood back from the barrier. The uproar of the bells deafened Paul's thoughts. He was enveloped in sensation, the vibrations shivering through him, not wholly unpleasant. A slight movement of his head made him aware of Eva's stillness, her eyes closed, lips parted in concentration. She turned and looked straight at him, her gaze alive and open, bluer than he'd seen it before.

They stayed like that, exchanging grim smiles, mutely mirthful, everything silenced by the tumult that detained them. Neither of them wanted to leave until it stopped.

At ground level, their ears still buzzed. When the threatened rain began to fall, they sought shelter and coffee in the bar halfway down the path to the landing stage. Paul had a dash of brandy in his macchiato.

– Was there any particular reason you brought me to Torcello?

– It's where Venice began, as you said. Some English writer called it Venice's grandmother. And it's what one does with visitors.

He looked at her sharply, but she was teasing.

– Which writer was that?

– The name escapes me.

They stayed in Torcello for dinner.

The light was waning when they boarded the Clodia. From the upper deck they surveyed the flatness of the lagoon, its channels marked out with the triangular forms of wooden stakes rising out of the water. Logs of oak, dark and weathered.

– They make me think of a ballroom on the sea, because they look as if they're dancing… waltzing.

Paul looked again. The poles leaned at different angles, seeming two in an embrace, or three huddled together whispering. The rippling of the water made them appear to move. It grew dark and their apices glowed with painted fluorescence. Seabirds alighted there, clustering at the tips, their wingbeats flickerings of eerie whiteness. Gradually, the water widened into an empty blackness lit with these beacons as far as the eye could see.

Night water, a chill wind driving behind them. He thought of the fear sea can incur. Here they were safe, trusting in the boat that carried them, the nearness of land and a city. He had an urge to dance with Eva. Venice was full of unused ballrooms.

By the time they got to her flat, the city was asleep.

15

Eva had left the green shutters open the night before. Outside, a boat's engine stalled, someone shouted in a loud *basso profondo* where the consonants all disappeared and he could make out no single word. Other voices answered with the same bellowing, almost drunken plangency. None of this woke her.

He watched as she slept. Years of insomnia had let him study the faces of women without their waking guard.

She lay on her back, her hair trailing damply across the blue-bordered pillowcase. Her lips were parted just enough for her teeth to show, the rise and fall of breath sending a quiver across her shoulders. He noted that her cheekbones were well modelled, the jawline firm, her throat taut. Then came the distinct jut of the collarbone and the rise of the breasts. All her contours were clear.

Gravity is kind to supine sleepers, though. It smoothed Eva's wrinkles, held back the forward fall of skin. She lay straight like a marble effigy, as if rehearsing the arrangement of her body for one of those tombs where the esteemed dead dwell forever in so many side chapels of Venice. They were always clothed, whereas she… Gently, he drew the sheet away to see. Across her stomach and thighs – rounded but nowhere flabby – he inspected moles, veins, the pale blonde hairs that clad the mound between her legs.

Thinking of a sleeper's vulnerability, seen but unseeing, the senses absent, the watcher as possessor or protector, he could feel powerful in this detachment, without fragility.

He shook off these omnipotent notions and felt the loneliness of being awake, Eva still wrapped in slumber, impervious to his very existence.

Unless her dreams paid him some attention, he thought as he got up and headed for the bathroom. He peed, observing the faded paintwork, the frieze of crazed art nouveau tiles, their painted tendrils lengthening to cover the expanse around the claw-footed bathtub. There were new glass shelves above the washbasin, crowded with expensive-looking jars and half-squeezed tubes of cosmetics, face creams, potions: the whole paraphernalia that women seemed to need.

Coffee was on his mind. He grabbed a large towel in lieu of a dressing gown and set off barefoot down the corridor. But nothing would make the gas light. Defeated, he turned back. At least the shower unit wasn't *fin–de–siècle*.

When he emerged from the shower Eva was there, fully awake and smiling, in a fluffy blue bathrobe, a cup of coffee already in her hand. He leaned to kiss her cheek. Repaying this coolness, she lifted the china cup to her lips and drank before making any response.

– Good morning, Paul. There's coffee in the pot. Did you sleep well?

After his calm contemplation of her unguarded nakedness, the desire he now felt at the sound of her voice was unexpected.

After sex, you lie there and expose some wound or other. If the sex has been good, has moved you, the pain or the memory is lulled and the telling more a gift than a bid for sympathy. See: I want you to know me, what I've suffered, what formed me, even gave me the strength that attracted you to me. See what I've overcome, and your telling is neutral, as if about someone else. You lie there in the lover's arms, or maybe you and she lie back, occasionally touching, both on the couch, confessional.

Lying next to her, lazily smiling, he almost spoke these thoughts, stopping just in time before he ruined this new intimacy a part of him was determined to set at a distance.

While the sun angled its way into the room, he told Eva about his mother, his words judicious.

– She died when I was six, the year after that family trip to Venice. It was a dream of hers, and the family chipped in to make it real because she wouldn't live much longer. All I remember is that she held and soothed me. She comforted and encompassed me; that's what I have of her and I suppose it's what matters.

When did these memories begin? The question disturbs him, for he worries that he's inventing, that they aren't true memories at all. He has no recall of her separateness, retains nothing of her beyond that primitive connection of body and voice, maybe just his imaginings of a mother. He spoke in a tone suggesting little more than idle curiosity.

– Your family must have told you things. Your father…

– Yes, but what my dad remembered was too mixed up with what he felt; sometimes stuff spilled out when he was… when he'd had too much to drink. It was my aunt Clem – her sister – who brought my mother to life for me, lifted her out of those faded old photographs.

– So what was she like?

He sat up, leaning on his pillow, animated now, looking her directly in the eye, observing the face of this woman he had just spent the night with, relishing her beauty, inwardly interrogating her responses.

– You know, I think she was a vamp. Clem always talked about the young men who'd been after Grace before she married my father. Well, I'm told she was generous and good-hearted, that she laughed a lot but had a quick temper – that went with her hair: red, two or three shades darker than mine.

– Are you like her?

– Well, there's the ever-youthful vitality that you spotted. It's a family trait… Or so I'm told.

– I see.

– And, seriously I mean, I'm told I look like her. We've the same eyes, they say; I can't see the resemblance, though it's hard to tell from the photos. I'm not like her in other ways… I wish I were; it would make her less of a stranger. She's been dead for so long and I only have the sum of her virtues and charms – nobody speaks ill, not to a dead woman's son.

His airiness wilted. Eva touched his cheek. He smiled; an ironic smile meant to conceal his awkwardness but barely succeeding. With this he slid out of bed.

– It's time I got going. I've some reading to catch up on and one or two libraries to labour in. As you know, I'm on the trail of another woman.

He pulled his clothes on quickly. It didn't seem the moment to enquire about the coveted papers.

– Take an umbrella from the hall stand. I think it's starting to rain.

– Thanks. I'll bring it back tonight, I mean if that's all right with you. Perhaps we can have dinner.

He bent to kiss her. She was thoughtful.

– Yes. That would be nice. But I'm thinking about whether you want to stay longer than you'd planned. It sounds as if you should, if you're serious about this project.

He blinked good-naturedly. What was she suggesting? His coolness belied a pandemonium of thoughts. There'd been safety in imminent departure.

– Serious? Well, of course I am; I've a flight booked, though, and the hotel room wouldn't be free.

– I know. The hotels are always full. And I won't invite you to stay here.

Laughter. She paused.

– I can, however, offer you a place to stay: a friend's flat that's empty. You'd only need to change your flight.

She was out of bed by now, padding off in her embroidered slippers. Still, he said nothing.

– Think about it, she called out.

From halfway down the corridor he heard her singing, loudly and with gusto.

Marlbrough s'en va t'en guerre
Marlbrough s'en va t'en guerre…

16

Ascension Day, 1750. Hot, bright and blowy. It was why the girls from the Pietà were there, orphans every one, foundlings at least. I still saw them as Vivaldi's children, even though he was nine years dead, but his strict musical regime had probably been softened, for here they were boisterous with the freedom of a holiday, the younger ones in a chaos of competing noise, until a whistle blast brought them to heel. More subdued, the older girls gazed about, at us and especially at the Turks in their rainbow-hued turbans. We passers-by stopped to stare back at them when a trio began playing mandolins and another group took turns at an aria of Porpora's, each aiming to outdo the others. An instructress, solemn-faced, shooed them into a garden with high walls and told them not to show off. We could still hear the music, with the sounds of more uproarious rivalry now that strangers' eyes were locked out.

Strollers crowded the Zattere, ablaze with the colours of swollen sails and ladies' daytime finery – and my French companion's well-cut mustard-yellow coat, streaming with lace at the wrists and the throat. I feasted my eyes on everything and told him that I truly prized my sight after our visit to Rosalba Carriera. She was an old woman now, half-blind and demented with the grief of it. I could still remember her when young, faintly.

There we had sat, in her house at San Vio, I beside that Frenchman in the height of fashion, two elderly Milanese brothers, a pious Spanish lady and her daughter, both of them veiled. We huddled in the shuttered gloom with the servants whispering and Rosalba on a throne-like chair of green brocade.

All the while she muttered, sometimes lapsing into a silent rage that consumed her quite entirely. If anyone said her name she would look about, stiffly throw out her arm and grimace as if apologising for an absence. We waited for her moments of lucidity and when these came, everyone in the room would hold their breath and listen, bodies seized with attention. When she finished, the two Spanish ladies would release a sigh. After which, we would talk among ourselves, an uneasy cluster of company.

In between our bursts of talk and her fitful replies, all you could hear was the splash of the water outside in the light, and a boatman's bellowing cry.

Monsieur Gaillard took me for a compatriot as soon as he heard my name. He followed me out when I left Rosalba's house and proposed we walk together. We made polite and mildly flirtatious conversation. By now I had practice at saying nothing with a pleasant turn of phrase. We rejoined the vulgar crowd, beneath the blaring sun, delighting in the sight of the red and indigo felucca sails. But my thoughts flitted back to that darkened room.

What memories pursue her of the light? Paris and Watteau, Vienna, princes, kings? In the end she had fame and the glory artists seek, after years of servility to patrons, reams of obsequious misspelled letters. The years since first meeting her had taught me much about art's alliance with ambition.

When young and in her prime she conjured a world of pale children and ivory doves, an Arcadia of ribboned pinks and blues and every shade of white on white. Hats and buttons, wigs and bows pronounced their lovely self-importance, secure in the delicate life bestowed on them by the incandescent outlines of the pastels in her hand. Yet they framed a deeper, secondary eloquence, a speech of the eyes. I had seen her portrait of Le Blond's son, a young boy with powdered hair and the weary expression of a man.

Another, her portrait of Madame Bordoni, had made me curious, although I never saw it, only heard it described. Its existence alone tantalised me. Faustina Bordoni, a youthful prodigy, as I had been; later, a rivalrous woman. Now married to Hasse and singing only his music, still singing at 50.

What had Rosalba seen in the singer's eyes? Might she answer the questions I've come to reckon with? She sat there, her wisdom dimmed yet obscurely persisting.

Alas, that gesture of looking about, unseeing, for her absent self, distressed me so much I could not speak, could not prompt her to remembered insight. The very thought of her age and mine held me speechless: she was born when I myself was already five years old.

That child was Elena, and now I had a different self, a necessary renaming. I still trembled at the prospect of discovery. Whatever unnatural qualities inhered in my body, it would not be immune to fire or stoning, or any cruelties inflicted on a witch. It was not indestructible, nor could it resist locked doors or iron bars, should someone decide I was fit for the madhouse. Avoiding such dangers forced me to become another.

Between the lives of Elena Merlo and her present self, there had been a blindness, a groping in pitch dark as the familiar components of my world dissolved. In time, I became accustomed.

When I was introduced, as Elise Muto, the singer, Rosalba stared at me and repeated the word. Singer. *I* sang once, she said, abruptly, turning her face away.

I knew this. Those with one outstanding gift often possess others. She had also played the violin.

At the last, Rosalba had delivered her own truth. In the interval of regained vision granted her by surgery, she made a portrait of herself. I wept when I saw it; it took me there to see her at San Vio. This self-portrait showed a spectre, vital and furious, haunting all her earlier visions of sweet lightness, giving them a glimmering anterior knowledge of time's warning: *col tempo*. There were laurels in her sparse grey hair, her face was bitter, naked. Despairing eyes looked out of it.

One, I could see clearly, was blue, the other seeming brown.

Was this discrepancy her rendering of the light, an effect of the cataracts, or an aspect of her gift? Is what the eye sees affected by its colour, by the nature of the lens's transparency, the different degrees of absorption and dispersion? Had one of her eyes, the brown one, aged more, losing that infant blue we all have at the start?

Before the flesh-and-blood Rosalba I could not tell, for her eyes were now milky and opaque.

Monsieur Gaillard had come for the Ascension fair and the new opera season. Rosalba's fame in France had led him to her house with the introduction of the French ambassador. I plied him with questions, for though trivial chatter came easily, I was loath to spend my time on it with those who could do better.

– Is it true that age blunts perception?

– What colour were La Carriera's eyes?

Too much time had passed for me to remember.

– Have you read Monsieur Diderot's *Letter on the Blind*? I found it in the bookshop at San Bartolomeo. It has much to say of how the senses shape our ideas and morality. They have put him in prison for it; did you know?

– And do you know about the Doge's telescope? How far it can see and which stars?

He shrugged away my questions and said he had thought me a pretty woman rather than a clever one. I laughed.

– Have I ceased to be pretty now that you think me clever?

– No, Madame. But your cleverness is what strikes me.

– In Venice you'll find many clever women, if you seek them out. But it's easy to avoid them too.

We parted at the Carità, where Gaillard waited for a gondola. I continued on foot, for I liked to walk in this season, before the day-time hours became too hot. Best of all, walking alone, enjoying the sounds and sights around me, the light on stone and water, the bird-song and the scent of hidden gardens. Just before San Barnaba there is a fountain with jasmine overhanging it. I had passed it at night, reeling in its perfume; by day it was more subtle, one note vying with many.

The intoxication of my senses had lessened since my youth, when their excess made me dizzy. My senses still served me well but my mind ached for what would expand its knowledge of the world beyond their reach.

In this world so different from the one that the closed, often win-dowless rooms of my girlhood could have led me to imagine, there remained less *terra incognita*. The earth and the heavens were being mapped, and the longer I lived, the more I travelled, the more I understood that horizons were limitless. I found myself delighting in abstraction, and relished the play of ideas in the fictions of the *philosophes*. Even the travellers' tales I read contained a universe of signs whose decipherment rewarded me with discovery. I did not know whether I was clever, but I was very curious.

I had returned to Venice to sing. At the San Luca Theatre, the one to which my mother had taken me, only then it had a different name, as did many things and places: the San Salvatore, where we had seen an opera by Castrovillari, whom no one remembers any more.

A woman singing at court or in the salons of the aristocracy incurred less risk to reputation than a singer on the public stage. Respectability decreed that I get myself a husband. I therefore contrived a marriage that would offer convenience without demands I did not care to meet. In Vicenza, through an intermediary, I met a man who, for complicated reasons of inheritance, needed a wife just as I needed to be one. His name was Giovanni Muto, a theatre architect, and he was as discreet as his name, now mine, suggests. We drew up an agreement that neither would impede the other's liberty. We led our lives apart, our households separate though within the same building. If we met by chance we would share a friendly kiss. Those who knew his taste was not for women would have seen nothing odd in our arrangement. From what he told me it was not uncommon.

So, thanks to the miracle of finding the right man, I was free to come and go as I pleased, free to repel the unwanted attentions of any suitor, free to live as I chose. Free to be faithful to the one I loved.

In the airy brightness of day, I cherished these freedoms. Sadness lurked behind the night's closed door, and I warded it off by reminding myself of the breath of life that still gusted through me, and the good ripe years I had known before I fell into this unshared future.

I went on, across San Barnaba, over the bridge on the opposite side from the church, and walked towards Santa Margarita. The *campo* was busy with vendors and I stopped to make a purchase from the man selling ink and rat poison. It was the former I required; my household was always well supplied with the latter, and with two cats besides. As well it might be. I counted six rats scurrying in my path between Campo Santa Margarita and the Rio dei Pensieri, where I and my husband lived, in the house I found for us, after a wait rewarded, the very one where I had lodged with my mother.

This house, not palatial, but spacious enough for bourgeois living, was of a peculiar though not unique design that particularly suited us, containing two apartments each with its own entrance from the *fondamenta*. Our floors alternated by means of long brackets of stairs that zigzagged between, each bypassing the one directly below. Thus, we had separation, and offered the servants fewer opportunities for spying and gossip. I could sometimes hear muffled steps and movements overhead, and take pleasure in knowing nothing of them. I could be alone with my books, my pen and paper, and my thoughts.

Not today, however. The moment I arrived my maid, Bettina, presented me with a list of things to be looked at or answered.

– Signora Elisa, the *parrucchiere* wants to know...

– Signora Elisa, you have two invitations to dine...

– Signora Elisa, the maestro sent word... a messenger came from Padua... your dresses have arrived...

It was the start of the season and I would sing that night. While performance was my element and it never worried me, the staging of an opera hinged not only on the singers' voices and the playing of the orchestra but on countless details and preparations: on costuming, powder, paint and glue, on candles, ropes and well-oiled pulleys, on feet well shod and tempers sweetened. I fixed a time with the coiffeur; accepted the grander invitation and declined the other while preferring neither; I answered the maestro that I would be at the theatre after a short rest; told the messenger I would reply the following day, thus delaying my decision about a small villa I thought I might buy on the Brenta... then I was able to try on my dresses.

These were simple, one in Bordeaux silk, the other pale blue, both trimmed alike with the cuffs and a narrow sash in fine lace, but with no panniers, no brocading or any other decoration. I wore too much heavy ornament on stage to want my own clothes to be lavish. In these times, artifice governed the opera as never before, in song and spectacle alike. I wished my life to be simple, even austere by the standards of Venice, where folly was festivity and masks permitted it. But I lived well without them; I had excitements and pleasures enough.

After five weeks of furtive enquiries, I established that Lorenzo was alive. I revised my first impulse to seek him out, foreseeing the shock of finding myself face-to-face with a very old man. Tormented to the point of despair by the gulf of years between us, I resolved not to see him unless fate should engineer it, and settled for the knowledge of his nearness. I still scanned crowded rooms and looked over my shoulder, but solitude at home spared me these compulsions.

At the house of an artist I had seen a Lendhof family portrait, painted, I was told, some 50 years before, soon after my last meeting with the painting's central figure. It marked the ennoblement purchased with 80,000 ducats out of his rich wife's coffers.

Her disappointed eyes consoled me.

So did singing. Song is not so easily forgotten as cities. Music resides in the fibres of the body as well as in the mind. It overrides time and can cure some of its ills. Without a note wrong, I remembered songs I had sung in my childhood. And yet that rough mountain dialect – my only language before Donna Merlo educated my tongue – seemed to have been spoken by a child who was not me. It was the child I became that I sought in the river of thoughts, the one who met Lorenzo, her life not yet saved by the magus Perulli. The child who might have had threescore years ahead, and not the threat of three hundred.

I chose the Bordeaux silk, as more suitable for entering and leaving the theatre, and set out in my gondola, prepared for an evening of triumph.

Joseph Smith was now the English consul. In his salon at Santa Sofia there was less talk of trade than 50 years before, and no talk of war whatsoever. His renown had grown along with the vast collections accreted around him – pictures, gems, glass and books, manuscripts, musical instruments and scores. He had aged with benevolent ease. In his seventies, he exerted a crafty, blue-eyed charm, while all the interest and variety of those he drew to his house kept a vibrancy in his person. It is said that the long-lived in general have blue eyes. I myself do not contradict this.

Mr Smith's keen look did not make me fear recognition.

– You once helped an aunt of mine, Elena Merlo, by bringing about a delicate assignation.

My former name meant nothing, but I gave him some clues and

he nodded, smiling with that polite, mysterious diffidence the English use to close all doors, softly, leaving those shut out in uncertainty of judgement.

From then on I was welcomed at his house.

I wondered still about Rosalba's eyes. Mr Smith had been a friend of her youth, so I asked him.

– What colour were they? It's hard to tell from her self-portraits.

– I'm afraid I have no recollection.

This failure of memory ignited a smile of compensation. He awarded me a genial introduction to Signor Longhi, enquiring whether he might have some notion of the answer to my question.

Longhi did not.

I was ignorant of his work, or I would have silenced my regret that it was now too late for me to sit for La Carriera.

– I much admire her portraits of Madame Bordoni.

– Indeed, I know them.

His smile was restrained.

Rosalba could have shown me myself, I was sure of it.

Painted and befeathered on stage, I was a creature entirely of artifice, a tragic queen abandoned, a daughter sacrificed, a vengeful slave. The glittering cloak of masquerade gave me rebirth, the orchestra inflamed me, the audience I beglamoured raised me to glorious, full-throated being. Singing, I had many selves, and I was true to all of them; but without these roles, without my voice, could I offer the world (or the mirror) any trueness deep in me? This doubt was no trifling vanity; what worth did I have as a woman caught in the stream of the years, my life forever drowning behind me?

– It is my belief that La Carriera's best portraits of ladies make them ageless, eternally young. Like La Bordoni, who still sings.

His smile now was more indulgent. He encouraged me to talk and I talked a great deal, avowing many things while concealing awkward truths. In the account of my travels I was careful to give a revised chronology, as women do when anxious to appear younger. I confessed my desire for sea voyages, for meetings with the scholarly ladies of Padua and Bologna, for a view of the night sky through a telescope such as the Doge had, for a dozen kinds of knowledge. He laughed and said I did not resemble a singer, for singers were rarely so talkative or curious. I took no offence, since as far as I could see Signor Longhi was good-natured.

It was unusual for me to chatter so much. I put it down to my excitement at this new Venice, at these new times. The midpoint of a century has a spaciousness about it when one is young enough to count on seeing its end. There is no abrupt change ahead into a fresh-dated future, no anxiety about losing the era to which one belongs. I had never felt so young in many years, and I became aware that my burning delight in present time and place made me not only curious but gregarious, for I wished to share my new enthusiasms, my naive well-read wonder.

I could be a vivid social being, then slip off through the night to be united with my deep, shadowy reflections in the river of thoughts. Thus my otherness was no longer due just to the passage of the years, but lay within me all the time. This experience of coexisting selves was new. The mask of silk or velvet I lifted to my face would always smooth the way between them. Could there be a better city for life doubled and divided?

Could there be a better time for me to uncover the truth of my strange nature? The secrets of the universe were being unlocked, its laws revised, light shed on darkness. We had Galileo and Newton to thank for all this in the first place. Now Doge Grimani was a Fellow of the Royal Society.

The laws of the universe. Hadn't I broken them, an irreducible exception to the rule? A freak of nature? Or living proof that magic still could work in the age of reason?

My curiosity took me often to the shop of Signor Pasquali at San Bartolomeo. At *La Felicità delle Lettere* I found more books by Diderot. I found Voltaire. And when he came to know of my thirst for learning, Mr Smith presented me with a dictionary of arts and sciences.

– It is Mr Ephraim Chambers' Cyclopaedia, translated from the English and published in Venice itself.

Many books were, for Venice enjoyed great freedom from censorship.

– How kind! What a perfect gift.

The Cyclopaedia had a great vogue in the city.

I sat reading in my garden in the summer's early morning sun, and as winter dusk fell into my drawing room I read by candlelight. On clear days I walked to the lagoon to see the snow-capped mountains that beckoned to my childhood. I thought of all the knowledge I held inside my head, the sights and scenes that no one else could picture from the past, and wondered if I could teach what I had learned. In the end, I failed to see how my several lives could be made useful by such meagre powers as mine. Were I a Chambers or a Diderot I could have transformed the world's vision of itself. All I could do was struggle with these thoughts. And live.

The blue dress bunched about me in a stiff rustle of skirts. Longhi arranged it this way and that, so as to gather shadow and reflections, letting it drop among the folds of the gold-yellow cloth that covered the table I sat by, and making it spread onto the tabletop so that the globe, a rather muddy-looking article, was embraced by the redeeming hues of sun and sky.

– Where are my knees to go?

My perplexity was genuine, for in all of his careful adjusting and positioning he seemed to have forgotten the limbs beneath the acreage of silk, and in all his courteous instructions that I move or turn a little to the right or to the left, he had neglected how I should sit, so I found myself cramped and twisted before he had even begun.

– My apologies, Elisa. It was not my intention for you to be uncomfortable.

Finally, having allowed me to fix on the posture around which my dress could be readily arrayed, Longhi was satisfied.

He had asked only that I should wear something pale, something light and unadorned, which he knew besides was how I liked to dress. I had put on the blue gown and had Bettina bring another for the sake of choice: a Venetian green with a thin cream stripe.

– The blue is perfect, Elisa.

I was to be the picture's focus. The other figures and the back-ground would be added later. This was not my portrait. I acted as substitute for the sitter in a scene he had devised and been forced to abandon, for the lady had died of a fever and her family had cancelled their commission. Longhi still wished to pursue the idea of it, being never at risk of wanting for a buyer.

He had not proposed that I sit as his model. That would have been impertinent. But he had told me of his notion for the scene, the unfor-tunate dead girl being one of those clever Paduan ladies I so admired, a doctor of the University, and he had wished to depict her as a source of knowledge, a globe in her hands and an atlas at her feet.

He dangled the bait.

– What a pity that you could not sit for me. You who have wished to sail to the very eyelashes of the world.

I had told him of the Portuguese travellers' accounts, and used this phrase of theirs.

– Why, Longhi? Does something prohibit me?

– No, but…

I stared at him hard.

– Elisa, this would not be you, the great Elisa Muto, or Elise.

He shrugged, seeing me frown.

The Italianising of my name was something I allowed to those around me every day, my intimates, my servants, but not in the the-atre. I could see, though, that Elisa Muto had a better ring to it.

– It would, I mean, not be a portrait, but a geography lesson.

I thought quickly and was pleased with his meaning.

– Longhi, I forgive it if you have judged me vain, but I have no distaste for anonymity.

– In that case, perhaps we could have you showing us exactly where to find the world's *sourcils*, Madame.

– Lashes, not brows, Longhi.

At times I was uncertain whether Longhi was having a joke at my expense.

When my role as a sitter had ended, the painting was far from finished. I had to wait until the whole canvas was filled before he would show me anything.

The stance of the figures struck me as artificial. Their gestures and poses were lifelike: the mild curiosity of the seated gentleman, the hunched concentration of the other, lorgnette raised and fixed on me, the servants hanging back. Yet the freezing of these movements and expressions was not quite convincing. It was as if everything had been drawn from the outlines in a camera obscura, which works well for views – of buildings, rivers and canals, quaysides, parks or landscaped gardens, but surely not interiors with human figures, though I knew that Longhi had painted directly from life. This effect was to do with the length of time encompassed in a scene: its flow and the stilling of the moment. Usually, it was longer, encapsulating time's duration, rather than arresting it.

I could hear the sound of the clock being stopped. A sudden click.

An illusion spoiled by my memory of how my arms had ached, the left particularly, from being held unsupported in that gesture of pointing at the globe; my wrist, I could see now, was the painting's exact centre. And this made me feel that of all the figures I was the most artificial. I was altogether unlike the rest. So pale as to be almost ethereal, while they were solid and high-coloured; so absent from them while I held their whole attention.

I was a figure from a different painting.

What I – she – reminded me of was one of Rosalba's pastel ladies. I hesitated before saying this to Longhi. He was watching and this expectancy moved me to speak.

His response was a smile with lowered eyes.

– Wasn't that what you wanted, Elisa, a portrait by La Carriera?

– I hardly thought that you would paint it, Longhi.

I injected some humour into my voice to cover my embarrassment.

– But wasn't it you, Elisa, who wore that dress, who powdered your skin and your hair to that shade of paleness. You came here with the ghost of that wish still in you.

I looked at my likeness and was startled by it now, by how Longhi had given me a detail not at all in keeping with Rosalba. The autumn had been chilly and I had suffered from the cold as I sat there. My fingers were unpowdered and Longhi had not spared their unrefined redness.

– You're probably right. In any case, as you said, it isn't me.

I inclined my head formally, conceding that the painting was the painter's.

Later, when I looked again at Rosalba's pretty ladies and gentlemen, they impressed me again as very fine, but I saw them as prisoners of their weightlessness.

I had contentment and the occasional challenge. By this I mean a rival, either on the stage or in the bedroom. As time passed, I surrendered my fidelity and occasionally took lovers. Despite these fleeting passions of the senses, I stayed constant to my one abiding love. I sang mostly arias by Jommelli, Galuppi and those a little more taxing, by Hasse, La Bordoni's husband. Now that a rhythm guided my days and my nights, Venice carrying me on its tides, I wanted life to rise and fall by my own urge. I had found my place to be, but I was restless.

It gnawed at me. Knowing Lorenzo was alive and in the city. Not knowing how much longer he would live. He would be close to 90. My frailer part wanted to see him again before I saw his grave.

One day I was in the Mercerie when, further on, I glimpsed a man I thought was him. A certainty gripped me and the jolt of it made me stumble. Without the press of people, I would have fallen. When I looked again he was gone and I convinced myself I had been mistaken. Strangers can remind us uncannily of those we have lost, a denial of death that might persist for years.

Nonetheless, still shaken, I inspected the shops I passed in search of this stooping man, a thin cloak of black silk thrown across his shoulder. Suddenly I saw him, two young servants at his side, in a dim interior where jewels and glass objects were displayed. I entered.

He stood with his back to me. On the counter in front of him glinted a snuff box of aventurine. I once had a cat whose eyes had flashed that same gold-bronze, and now this object, small and oval like an eye, held my mesmerised gaze. What if he should turn and be Lorenzo?

Without seeing his face, I knew him when he spoke. His voice was weak, that of an old man, but I recognised the rich, low timbre I had listened for across the years. Tears started in my eyes.

He asked for his purchase to be wrapped in a velvet cloth, and handed it to a servant, whom he addressed as Beppe, ordering him to take it to Signor the Marquis Poleni with his compliments. This name was familiar to me; not long before, I had met the marquis at Santa Sofia, a distinguished man, a scholar scientist.

When he left, still without my seeing his face, he turned his head a fraction, as if instinctively from being watched, and I shrank into the shop's recess. How could I have confronted him?

I recovered myself and left the shop. My quarry had disappeared but in the distance I saw the servant, Beppe, walking briskly towards Rialto. This gave me an idea. I knew I would lose him if I tried to hurry through the crowd, so when I noticed a young beggar girl sitting on the bridge I promised her some coins if she would run and tell him to wait for me at San Bartolomeo.

– One now, and two more when I reach him.

She dashed off and I proceeded at a decorous pace.

When I saw them, the girl was tugging at Beppe's sleeve in her desperation to detain him; he, wanting to be on his way and free of her dirty fingers, nonetheless looked about for my promised arrival.

– Wait, Beppe, I must speak to you.

First I had to keep my bargain with the girl, whose anxious face would not have left me any peace. She was pleased with her reward but instead of returning to her pitch she lingered, watching us.

– I know your name, Beppe, because I heard your master say it. Your master is one of the Lendhof family, if I am not mistaken.

– Yes, Signora. He is the Count.

– The Count Lorenzo.

I spoke with a slow nod, as if correcting him rather than eliciting confirmation.

– Yes, Signora, the Count Lorenzo.

– My grandmother knew him well in her youth.

And I told him my grandmother's name, the name by which Lorenzo knew me.

Beppe looked uneasy about my confidences. I decided on a plan.

– Will you tell your master I have spoken to you? Tell him who I am, the granddaughter of a lady he once knew.

And again I told him the name, this time asking him to repeat it.

– Elena Merlo, Signora.

He looked relieved, as if he had suspected me of some trick and I had proved my honesty by asking nothing more than that he remember my grandmother's name. I gave him a coin.

– Will you come and tell me what he says?

He nodded and I told him where to find me.

No sooner had he set off than the girl appeared at my side.

– Signora, can I be at your service? Have you more errands for me?

My first impulse was to chase her away; I told her no, but her dark eyes wouldn't leave me. Nor could I now ignore her wretched condition: undernourished, filthy, ragged and perhaps diseased.

Her name was Angela. I enquired where her parents were. She said they were dead but she had an aunt.

– Does your aunt treat you well?

– Sometimes she does, Signora… not when she is angry.

– And is she often angry?

Angela met my eyes in silence, weighing up the question, uncertain which answer I would prefer to hear.

– Are you French, Signora?

I accepted the evasion. I had no right to question her.

– Yes, I am.

In Italy I was always French, and in France an Italian.

– I am Madame Muto. You see, my name is Italian, because of my husband.

She looked straight at me, boldly this time, taking in my appearance; she summoned a quick smile.

– Goodbye, Signora.

– Goodbye, Angela.

That night I lay awake, my mind swayed by the conflict of emotions. Joy at my fleeting sight of Lorenzo, longing for a meeting while doubting the wisdom of it. Was it not better to remember him as he was than be dismayed by the wreck of him in old age? Would he look at me and see Elena Merlo in a face that must belong to her granddaughter? If he did not, it meant he had forgotten me and I could not bear that. Or would I be repulsed? I thought of my smooth hands clasping the withered skin of his. He was older than Rosalba Carriera; I shuddered. He was sliding towards death, while I was fully alive. Then I remembered my love for him and those other secret senses that joined us, and the body ceased to matter. Yet for him my presence would have no reality. How could I endure the absence of love's flame, scarcely the ashes of feeling between us? Finally, the thought that life remained in him became uppermost and urgent. I must approach him, and soon. He could die this very night, without my having seen his face again, or he mine.

I grappled with my fears, weeping, smiling, talking to Lorenzo as if he could hear and understand me. The Lorenzo I had known. I resolved to see him, no matter what. My turmoil probing ways and means, I recalled everything I had seen and heard from the moment I glimpsed Lorenzo to my conversation with the servant, Beppe. In the midst of this fervid recollection, the name of the Marquis Poleni made me realise I might open a door through this acquaintance. It was a slight one, but I knew he had a liking for the French, so I could take the liberty of writing him a note to invite him to the opera.

This small decision enabled me to sleep at last.

After only an hour I woke again. Now, caught in the ravel of my wakeful thoughts was the face of the child Angela, as if she formed part of my encounter with the old man Lorenzo had become. I considered why I had never had children of my own. Perhaps nature withheld from me the ordinary immortality of parenthood that was granted to others, for the very reason that my own mortality did not resemble theirs.

The truth was that I had never longed for a child and had done a great deal to avoid having one. Delay played a greater part in this purpose than refusal. No one since François had inspired enough love for me to wish that desire be made flesh of my body. With Lorenzo, how different my life would have been.

Some lives are complete: everything arrives in good time, and lasts until its natural ending: parents' death in old age, siblings side by side into adulthood, children as a consequence of carnal love, a pledge to the future. Others, like mine, contain premature partings and hopes denied survival, the foundering of all that would have made them whole. So, Angela in her wretchedness assumed the form of the absent child, the spirit of the daughter who had not come into being.

She must have been 10, at most 11. The aunt she spoke of I pictured as a prostitute or drunkard, perhaps both; I feared it would not be long before she put Angela to work.

I received the Marquis Poleni in my dressing room on the evening I was due to sing the title role in Jommelli's *Ifigenia in Aulide*. Though our meeting had to be brief, its outcome pleased me.

– I have heard you sing before, Madame. My compliments on your splendid voice. I look forward to hearing it tonight.

Once these courtesies had established a cordial atmosphere, I brought up the subject of Lorenzo, accounting for my connection in the version I had given to the servant, Beppe, from whom I so far had no word.

– I intend to pay a call on Count Lorenzo tomorrow. Would you do me the honour of accompanying me?

My heart jumped. Everything seemed suddenly simple and I wondered why I had kept myself waiting so long.

Such exaltation drove my voice that it was deemed to have reached fresh heights. In each moment of Ifigenia's struggle with fate, her sacrifice at her father's hands, her transformation by the goddess, I plunged headlong into the crucible of sound and feeling, so that these were intense and enmeshed. Ifigenia was a virginal girl, and the qualities of her singing demanded that illusion. With these demands I felt at one, and I triumphed.

Late in the afternoon of the following day the marquis sent his gondola for me and on the way – a much shorter distance than I ever had imagined – elation still accompanied me. As we glided into the Rio della Misericordia, the water flamed beneath the low sun that hung captured at its furthest prospect. The marquis awaited me on the *fondamenta* and I looked across the canal at the palazzo I had often passed, consumed by curiosity and yearning. Now, rightfully, I was to go inside, and nothing seemed more natural. A modest palace by comparison with those along Canal Grande, its high Gothic arches and slender white balconies nonetheless had grandeur.

With exquisite courtesy, the marquis took my arm and we crossed the bridge to enter by the courtyard.

Our voices echoed emptily in the vast *salone*. We sat in velvet armchairs, but the damask curtains had lost their patina and the silvering on the mirrors was worn away. Made morose by this shabbiness, I did not at first notice the count's stiff figure appear, but I raised my head when I heard the tapping of his stick. He held it firmly, its copper and gold top catching the sunlight that fell in through the wide west window. As he came closer, I held his eyes. I saw no recognition.

My heart lurched with disbelief. He was an old man, but not old enough. Oh, I saw Lorenzo in him, in his features, in the faltering, stubborn movements of his lips when he spoke, and in his voice. His father's voice.

I had always asked was he living and well and answers came that he was old and in delicate health. It had never crossed my mind that Count Lorenzo was my Lorenzo's son, a man of 60, further aged by ill health.

This accounted for shabby surroundings at a time of prosperous trade. The count's older brother had died at sea, and he himself was a widower without an heir, the last of the line. The Lendhofs would soon disappear. Trade was no longer their business. Science alone interested this man and distracted him from his woes. He avidly read Poleni's treatises, talked with him about the nature of matter and the stars, shared his passion for astronomy. That triumphant family painting I'd seen must have been sold from necessity.

– May I ask how your father died?

– Nearly 30 years ago, crossing the mountains, on his way to the wedding of a cousin in Vienna. In an avalanche, we believed. He and two others were lost: my mother's brothers. Only their servant survived; they had ordered him to ride out early and seek lodgings for the night.

I sat shocked and silent; the marquis took up the conversation. The ailing count bemoaned his lot. He had his mother's disappointed eyes.

How could I not have sensed Lorenzo's death, living all those years with false trust in his being alive?

It was thanks to Giovanni Poleni that I realised an earlier ambition. Among the many instruments Poleni had acquired for the University's cabinet of physics in Padua were different kinds of telescope. Through the largest of these he showed me Jupiter and Mars, and one winter night I saw the rising of the Pleiades, hundreds of stars packed in a cluster wider than the moon and, Poleni told me, very much further away.

– The brightest are called the Seven Sisters.

He told me their names, borrowed from ancient myth, the most luminous of all named Alcyone.

Through the eye of the telescope's lens, these seven dazzled like great blue diamonds against a silvery breath of light on its way across the sky. Gazing at them, millions of miles above, I felt the universe sweep over me, realigning my significance. What did my years count for in the awesome face of this?

Something else gave me comfort. The knowledge of Lorenzo's death shook me so that breath alone was left in me: no substance, no purpose. I took a step that meant living for another, since I saw no way of living for myself. I made that beggar-child my daughter.

17

Paul put the papers aside. He went to the window and looked into the bay tree.

Absurdly, he was touched by what he'd read; it made him reluctant to continue. Were these emotions to do with Eva? Their night together, her apparent wish to postpone his departure and her offer of hospitality all disquieted and excited him, as did his sense that whatever Eva said, did, and especially what she gave was now to be reinterpreted. In romance, everything is a sign.

Romance. He had uttered the word, albeit mentally. He had let it take shape. The discomfort of this incited a measure of derision. For himself. Wasn't he worldly enough to accept her sensual affection without fearing something deeper? Yet his mistrust had foundations. The papers made him alert to manipulation; how could he believe that they were innocently given, unread. Why did she give them, these stories in which he glimpsed signs, cryptic and equivocal, of something real? And if worldliness raised an obstacle to trust, she was far worldlier for sure.

But remembering her face, her eyes, her body in his arms, he owned that were it not for what disturbed him, he would be moved by her.

To cast out these confusions, he resumed reading.

18

Angela. My beloved daughter, loved by me as I was loved by Donna Merlo, brought by me to begin a new life in the house where Donna Merlo had made me anew. An orphan, without family, since the woman she knew as aunt was a neighbour who gave her lodging in exchange for her earnings as a beggar. I cared for Angela with dutiful desperation, until with growing fondness and delight I discovered what it is to be a mother.

– Have you been baptised, Angela?

– Yes, mother. In the parish of San Salvatore.

I went to the church and found her in the register, so now she could know the date of her birth and the names of her mother and her father, a carrier of coal at the Riva del Carbon. Though she took my name, I wanted her to know these beginnings.

A tutor I employed saw to her schooling, but I would read with her and often listen to her lessons. I wanted her to learn a love of music, so we played and sang together. Everywhere I went with her I taught her to look, not only at palaces or paintings, but the smallest of things. Animals interested her, as they do all children, and whenever we passed one of those round tablets – a *patera* – Byzantine remnants set into the walls or above a portal, we would stop and look at the hares and eagles in relief, the ostriches, lions and galloping horses. Venice is so full of beauty that we often fail to notice it, to marvel at what endures without pretension.

If all these things made her exclaim or laugh with pleasure, she did not entirely trust the truth of them, nor always believe my answers to her questions. Once, I told her the moon's distance from the earth, something I had learned from Poleni when it was measured by a French astronomer. Her look was angry.

– You are mocking me, mother, no one can know how far it is.

– But you asked me, my dear.

Her gaiety was shadowed. She recoiled from her own spontaneous joy. Happiness would have a trouble finding her. I aimed to help it.

When I gave her a kitten she played with it as if she'd found a perfect friend, but asked if she might have another to keep it company; she could not bear to see it so forlorn when left alone without her. I took her to a show of Longhi's paintings, and in pride of place hung the African rhinoceros made a monstrous spectacle for the city's entertainment some years before. She pitied its poor ancient face and dreamless eyes, and on our way home she started weeping.

When she broke a vase of milk glass that I treasured, she gathered all the shattered pieces. For days she tried to put them back together, shedding copious tears, until I finally compelled her to abandon what I told her was a hopeless task.

– No, mother, it cannot be!

Angela grew and I watched her. Time and love worked wonders, or at least a softening alteration. Though her look might quickly darken on seeing another creature's pain – be it animal or beggar – I saw that she herself felt far less need to suffer.

I gave her emerald earrings when she turned 16, and a fan of ivory and Burano lace. I had another miniature painted – the last done when she was twelve. The night of her birthday I had her brought to the opera and for the first time she saw me on stage, costumed, befeathered, gilded, iridescent: a strange artificial being, the mother of no one in the world. I sang Porpora's *Adelaide*, so the rival whom I sang against was not another woman the likes of La Bordoni, but the idolised castrato Farinelli, at that time in Madrid. What woman could match his prodigious voice, sexless but seductive, fabulous in range and breath power? None, yet he spurred me: I was a glittering bird of paradise, my plumage as fantastically embellished as the steep and thrilling crests of sound that issued from my throat. My voice's high agility defied the violins.

Beglamouring my audience meant not half so much as knowing that my daughter was enchanted.

That very night, I had decided, would be my swansong. Finding the right husband for Angela mattered more than prolonging my career. It would consume my energies and require my presence in society. My career, I knew, could not go on indefinitely.

That night earned me new admirers. One of these had a son, and when they called on me in my dressing room, with Angela there, blushing and excited, I could see her heart was lost.

My wish for her happiness made me ruthless. If he were worthy, I would make him love her in return. But I would protect her from any man whose strength and kindness failed. Putting this to the test would take time. Filippo Cavalli proved me wrong. He braved my discouragement and won my approval almost as fast as he had won my daughter's love.

Antonio, his father, was no stranger to me on that evening of my triumph as Adelaide; a bluff handsome man who would greet me as a neighbour, he owned, among other enterprises, the candle factory in Rio dei Pensieri. My charms had escaped his notice until he saw me sing. This, I told myself, was because I did not frequent the grand *saloni*, I shunned the gaming tables and the balls. I was often masked.

But I knew that my powers of attraction grew a hundredfold on stage, when I became another.

I had no palace for a wedding banquet, so we held it in the grandest place that we could borrow. At Ca' Delfin. Under a high frescoed ceiling where deities cavorted, surrounded by vast mirrors, dancing, we revelled in a night of celebration that gave the bride a memory to last her whole life long.

Angela had been fortunate; more than that, hers was the rare luck to be spared the pain of unrequited or forbidden love. Angela so fragile, now made happy. A miracle.

Her marriage plunged me into a new phase of life in Venice. My daughter's father-in-law, Antonio Cavalli, wooed me with sublime and exaggerated gallantry.

He could not offer me marriage, since I already had a 'husband', though I guessed this was what he wanted most of all: a companion's permanence. Yet his wife still ruled him from the grave and he also seemed to fear betraying her. He had mistresses, and I sometimes chanced to see them: occasional beauties, a few well-masked and painted whores I thought might have tricked him into believing them respectable. Or maybe not. It was hard for men to resist the lure of courtesans in a city with so many.

Antonio wanted me by his side, at balls and receptions, or walking in the Piazza. Nobody frowned on us; we belonged to the same family. Everyone gossiped, and I wondered whether any came to know that we did, briefly, become lovers.

For Angela's sake, I never shared my bed with any man at home. I was hers there and no one else's. After the wedding my house felt empty and Antonio gave me sensual comfort.

There was a peculiar formality in our lovemaking, as if to avoid any hint of presumption.

For a month we shared our nights, always beginning with this tentative politeness, gradually approaching voluptuous satisfaction, then releasing our bodies and our thoughts of one another from any lingering grasp.

But when next I saw the moon's fullness I recalled the silvery romance of our first night together, when we deserted the garden's scents and shadows to reach my bed…

– Antonio, you are my friend and almost my brother. Passion needs to grow; ours remains the same, so we should forget it and become good companions.

And we did.

We danced a lot, almost like lovers. Mirrors turning round us. Mirrors within mirrors, candlelight multiplied, so that quivering stalks of flame blinded us and gave our moving forms a dizzying incandescence that obliterated everything beyond it, beyond Canal Grande's many-lustred windows. Once more I entered the palazzo that exhorted God – *Non Nobis* – and danced in that hammer-shaped *salone*.

This was the last grand occasion I allowed myself. Angela had borne two sons and the future by ordinary reckonings was fading from my view, disappearing as the faces around me began to overtake my visible years. I dreaded the exile that seemed my only choice, for I wanted to stay near my daughter, and watch her children grow. But I dared not let her see my agelessness.

Venice helped me; it offered me another kind of exile, an exile without leaving: disguise.

The *bauta*, alabaster-white, the corpse-like *larva*, the *moretta*… Masks.

They gave the old an elixir. Concealing decrepitude, covering decay. And they allowed me to appear as old as I was thought to be. Masked in public, veiled for years at home, my face went into hiding, all to dupe my daughter out of love for her.

I lived on, my unageing face concealed, deceiving everyone. In time my voice too needed disguise; I made it stagger and wheeze. My gait I adapted to the same end, becoming stiff and unsteady. I wore gloves day and night, because hands betray. None of this amused me. The hoax I played on others was at my own expense: my payment for life prolonged, for death postponed.

Death mocked me. Angela was 29 when her first child, Paolo, died, aged 10, from an inflammation of the throat. Until then she had been happy as a blackbird. Crushed by the weight of her grief, I felt trapped in my falseness. I would have shed my vitality, given up my whole profligate life to revive her. I remembered Madonna Merlo's children, taken by the plague, and how I had been the vessel for her thwarted love. Angela was frailer than the grandmother she had heard of in my stories of a distant childhood, the author of my life and hers, a fairy-tale bestower of gifts more fateful than anyone could know. Madonna Merlo's sturdy spirit had been formed by a childhood without shadows, sunlit from birth, unlike mine.

That timorous longing I had seen in Angela the child had reached a final wall of sadness. She tried to smile, but I saw more than she realised from behind my dark veils.

– Your suffering breaks my heart.

– Mother, I am defeated.

Angela plucked at my veils. As gently as I could, I drew her hand away, rigid with panic, lest she expose my face. Words were all I could give her. I took her hand, kissed it and held it to my cheek, but only in my mind's eye. In my caution, I withheld all comforts of touch. Inside me, emotion overflowed; visibly, I contained it.

– Love the child who still lives. Find consolation in him.

Her younger son thrived despite his mother's unabating melancholy. Then, just before he turned fifteen, an infection spread from a dog bite and killed him. Angela was lost to the world. For all her husband's tender efforts, she was lost to him too; when he died, two years later, she entered a convent. Renouncing everything and everyone, she could bury pain by no longer being herself. I wept for her as if she were truly dead, for I would never see her again. She took another name, as nuns do, in self-effacement.

In those years before Angela left me, I lived the half-life of an old woman in a younger woman's skin, cloistered and bereft of family, bereft of song, bereft of any passion of the body. I, more than 90 years behind me, harbouring rebel energies, shed tears of rage for the deaths of children. Until these cruel events, I trusted in my strength to withstand the pain meted out to the one who, time after time, survives. But I had only numb despair.

Grief and unlived life laid their marks on me. Unhappiness marred my face with lines, stained dark hollows round my eyes. I looked in the mirror and believed I was ageing at last. I looked old, withered by constraints, my existence suspended. And the hardest thing to conceal, my monthly flow, had ceased. This provoked dread of decay and infirmity, but thinking of Perulli's words, and feeling cursed by my bodily persistence, I was glad.

These signs were temporary; the bleeding had stopped because my loss of appetite had shrivelled my frame to match my gaunt face. *Col tempo?* Time aged me a little, but did not wreak due destruction. It left me in a wilderness where I had to create new sources of life.

Tedium had become the enemy in the desert I inhabited. I read, and to save myself, I resolved to write, only letters then, but they furnished a use for my threadbare philosophising, a connection to the world. Scavenging for intimacies, I penned my thoughts to strangers whose books had struck some spark in me. I argued or agreed, replies came, and this correspondence nurtured me. And, even though I'm riddled with memories, knowing that these would fade, I began to write about my long life.

When I ventured out, my mask well in place for the year-round carnival that was Venice, I saw them everywhere, the shams of youth, the travestied old and their frivolity. I contradicted them, I the exception, the sole and unknown proof of what they told themselves.

Solo i morti xe veci.

Only the dead are old.

What truer words, spoken everywhere in that declining city as masks hid furious folly. Words that Mozart remembered as if they were the city's motto.

He was a boy of fifteen then, in 1771. These words, a denial of youth, must have sounded sinister to him. In the very year that Hasse predicted he would cause them all to be forgotten.

Mozart. The sun that dimmed those lesser lights forever as a brand-new age was lit.

Part Two

Secrets

Antonia: Tell me the stories you remember, for by them I can
measure what you've forgotten.
Aretino, *Dialogues*

19

The two cats hissed: the sprawling tabby on the wall and, inside the garden, a leaner black-and-white creature that made a show of clawing up towards the intruder. Paul half expected Fatso to execute a sudden lethal drop that would crush or smother Angel, but the game was all feline bravado. Abruptly, Angel abandoned the confrontation and sprang across the grass into the house. Paul cut short Fatso's descent with a warning shout. The cat turned tail over the wall.

From the other side came the pungent, grease-laden smell of fried fish, carried on a hot little morning breeze. The garden had its own, sweeter scents. He couldn't name the blooms that released them. Don't worry about gardening, just feed the cat, Eva had insisted, there's always been one in the house. The tenant before Gail had four; Gail was the American friend said to have much in common with Paul.

He was no tenant but a guest, unconstrained by the presence of a host. So he had made a respectful exploration of the floor at his disposal, and reached some odd conclusions.

The house and the story go hand in hand. Rio dei Pensieri: river of thoughts. That's where he was, though with no canal view from the windows. At first he hadn't noticed the name of the tree-lined street. A good enough name to borrow for sure, but the house too, not just borrowed but commandeered, lock, stock and garden. A garden of delights, weeds notwithstanding: a vine-covered pergola; a profusion of flowers and shrubs around which paths wound into bosky corners, past four tall trees that joined their branches into canopies of shade – persimmon, pomegranate and quince, and one Eva said she didn't know.

On the ground floor a shady corridor ran through the depth of the building. Three locked doors lined one side of it, and at its garden end was a landing from which a flight of steep stairs rose. This arrived at the *piano nobile*, the high-ceilinged first floor. And yes, another long staircase sloped up from there, as Elisa Muto described, a blur behind a locked door of frosted glass.

What to make of it? A fictional abode mirrored in a solid building dating from 1525 – which happened to belong to a friend of Eva's. The questions this provoked had to wait; after installing him the previous afternoon, she'd pleaded sundry obligations and hurried off.

In the gallery at the Querini Stampalia he studied Longhi's painting. It was true: the lady's wrist at the centre, the red fingertips now plain enough. Poor circulation, or a washerwoman's hands? The face: broad-browed, unsmiling, features ill-defined.

He looked up Rosalba Carriera: 1675–1757, Rococo. A long, busy life, her pastels popular with English visitors to Venice and in demand all over Europe, until the blindness. Trying to imagine cataract surgery in the 18th century, he headed for the Accademia to see the work for himself. He liked that self-portrait with the different coloured eyes – too much flattery in the rest. Later he walked to the church of Madonna dell'Orto for a concert of fifteen voices. All the paintings were blazingly illuminated. From a good vantage point to the left of the altar he studied the post-apocalypse frenzies of Tintoretto's *Last Judgment*, letting the music drown him in its pure, rich sounds. He headed back along the moonlit canals of the Cannaregio district and, amply fed on beauty, fell into a deep and dreamful sleep the moment he got into bed. When he woke, rested and becalmed, he wondered at the uncaught truths of dreams, but had no inclination to reach for them.

He would cook a special dinner for Eva. An early-morning shopping trip combined his habit of keeping domestic chores in the margins of the day with bagging the pick of the fish market catch. Packed in the fridge were thick purplish steaks of tuna. He had even found wild strawberries – a one-day wonder, the market trader said.

Who owned this house? Perhaps not the unnamed friend who left it under Eva's supervision. No time for idling; he finished his coffee and took care to lock up precisely as instructed. The city archives were a ten-minute stroll away.

As soon as Eva walked through the door, Angel followed at the red and gold heels of her elegant sandals. Teresa Berganza was singing Mozart arias; an old vinyl recording he had found in the cabinet below the record player. Eva stopped and smiled her approval.

– I prefer this to the CD.

– You can tell the difference?

– I've just listened to her a lot.

He opened a bottle of Prosecco and she stood by the kitchen window, her bracelets chinking as she touched and probed the pots of herbs.

– Don't worry, I've watered them.

She laughed.

– I have to make sure.

Purring, Angel wove back and forth between her bare legs; Eva cooed endearments.

– *Micia, che carina che sei, che simpatica.*

– And she's eaten heartily. So don't be taken in.

– I'm not.

He poured their drinks and set them on a tray with some olives.

– I thought we could have these in the garden. Maybe eat there if it's warm enough.

– I'd like that. But we'll need citronella for protection.

From a cupboard she took three squat yellow candles, fetched matches from a drawer and put everything in her capacious canvas bag.

– This house feels lived in. I can see you're at home.

– Yes, there's always someone here. I make sure... Oh, I meant to tell you about the hot water heater.

She turned away to fuss with a plastic watering can and an unneedy succulent in a green ceramic pot.

– That's all right. I found the switch.

Relief showed in her over-ready smile. She'd been on the brink of a slip about the house. Or was he reading too much into small evasions?

Eva sighed.

– So much to do here. Must get something done about the guttering.

This was almost mumbled.

– The guttering?

– It's leaking. And they fixed it last month. They replaced what was there for 500 years and this is what happens!

– You can't get the quality of work these days, can you? A dying breed, those Renaissance builders.

She gave a breathy little laugh, preceding him out of the kitchen and down the stairs. The cat followed, rushing between them.

In the garden he took her hand.

– Tell me how you are. Did you sleep well last night?

– Yes, and I've been busy on your behalf.

She reached for her bag and a folder full of papers tumbled out, along with the yellow candles.

– More stories?

She gaped at him.

– So you think they're inventions?

Paul's laugh was involuntary, but the wish to convey mockery flared up in it. Unease hovered in the night air. He watched Eva's face, his eyes flicking momentarily towards a large pale moth that skittered back and forth against the curve of the light above the door. The quince tree rustled as the shape of a bird erupted from its branches and vanished into the dusk.

She looked dismayed and suddenly defenceless, a wraith among the shadows, only the sapphire glitter of her eyes asserting vitality. Something made them even more jewel-like than ever. Was it tears? Surely not. They mesmerised him, impelled him to heal that injured look. He resisted. Did that make him unfeeling? No, what he felt was already risky enough.

In observing her, he forgot to ask himself why she should be so offended. A remnant of his dreams the night before pushed to the front of his mind, a faltering intuition. All at once, he remembered he had dreamed of her, and the dream-Eva merged with what he'd been reading. Even as I sleep you follow me with mysteries: the papers, this house, yourself.

To dispel awkwardness, he picked up the candles and placed them strategically around the table, lighting each one with almost ceremonious deliberation.

– There! We're well fortified against mosquitoes.

He gave his voice the warmth he felt it needed to convey, and his next words were gentle, coaxing, making the question they formed penitential rather than an enquiry.

– The other day you told me you hadn't read these papers; is that still true?

– Yes.

He took a deep breath.

– There's a character who doesn't age, the narrator that is, so she has to keep changing her name, but the initials are always E.M.

– Really?

– Yes. I'm wondering whether she's going to turn into Esme Maguire at some point.

His soft laughter was forced.

– And that might be when you give me the real papers – I mean, something less fantastical.

Paul waited. Berganza's voice floated down to fill the silence: *Ch'io mi scordi di te!* Eva tilted her head as if straining towards the music, then the cat absorbed her attention. She continued ignoring his question. He had to prompt.

– What do you think?

– You just have to read on, Paul. I'm giving you what there is in the order I find it, and I haven't got time to read it myself. It might make sense eventually.

Her eyes were disengaged. Touching her shoulder in a passing caress, he got up.

– Time I got on with that fish.

Glad to be alone, he debated with himself. How much did he care about the papers, the real papers that remained undelivered? Did he care more that this house concealed things he might want or prefer not to know about the secretive woman he had taken to bed?

The fish was baking in a fragrance of rosemary and lemon, plates with antipasto sat on the dining-room table. Everything under control. They would eat inside after all, he decided, rejecting the garden's moist romantic gloom. Talk would be less ambiguous without shadows.

It was only in bed, drowsy after sex, that Paul returned to his questions about the river of thoughts and the fictions with which Eva plied him. They were in the dark and he whispered.

– I think you *ought* to read the papers you've been giving me.

– Why?

– This is the house.

– What do you mean?

– The house she writes about.

Silence.

– I'm not sure I understand.

– Don't you?

Silence again. Inside his embrace her body shifted, tensing, stretching as if wanting to be free, then it yielded, her back resting on his chest, her breasts falling into the curl of his arms.

– Whose house is it, Eva? Is it yours?

They were both wide awake now.

– What does it matter whose it is? You're my guest here; it's impolite to ask.

This was jocular, but when she moved to turn and face him, his arms locked her tight. He burrowed into her neck, kissing, murmuring.

– Impolite? It matters. I think you know it does. Are you playing a game with me? I know you own this house.

– How do you know?

Her voice was jagged. She struggled. He wouldn't relax his grip, pinning her closer. He laughed.

– Eva, it's obvious. This is a game and you've made the rules.

– Let me go! You're hurting.

– I can't be. I'm only playing.

Her response to his growing sexual excitement was to wriggle away and use her nails as a defence. With a loud sigh, he let go of her and she jumped out of bed, grabbing his dressing gown.

– I'm going.

She bent to gather up her clothes and left the room.

Naked, he followed. He found her dressing in the dining room;

plates hadn't been cleared from the table and clothing added to the disarray. The cat lay asleep on a cushion, sated with fish scraps.

– Don't be offended. Let's talk. I don't mean to pry, but there's something strange about all this. I feel you don't trust me, or you're making fun of me.

Intent on zipping up her skirt, fastening it at the waist and adjusting it so that the seams were in the right place, she kept him waiting. She reached for the striped silk scarf that matched the blue of her T-shirt. How carefully she dressed. He'd seen her casual, but never without colour coordination; right now, it irritated him.

– What makes you sure I own this house?

– You're at home here. I can tell.

There would be no wisdom in admitting to his morning researches: the proof that Eva Forrest was indeed the present owner of the house, the records predating the Napoleonic survey, showing a Madonna Merlo among its earlier tenants.

– So are you.

Her stern expression had given way to a smile; delicately she pointed a downward finger.

– Well then, would you care to join me back in bed?

– No, I won't, tempting though you are. I'm dressed now and I'm going home. But I'll tell you about the house.

She opened the oak sideboard and took out a bottle of whisky and a pair of tumblers. Trying to deflect his thoughts from desire, he admired the steady hand doing the pouring, the exactness of the measures.

– Listen. The reason I have those papers is that they came with this house. Some of them at least. When Joe – Joe Lensky, whose widow I am – found out about her, he got interested. Later, he bought some more Maguire manuscripts and memorabilia at auction. I've told you he was a collector, and singers fascinated him, not just her.

– So this house belonged to your late husband.

– Yes, he inherited it from a cousin of his mother's. It was how I met him.

Paul nodded, perfunctorily.

– He was looking for a tenant. I turned up, with a notion of spending time in Venice...

She stopped.

– And you rented it?

– No.

Angel appeared, wide awake and nuzzling at her ankles. Eva stroked her. Paul didn't speak.

– I married him and went back to live in London, since that was his home most of the time.

– And the house?

– He kept it on, so that we could come and stay whenever we wanted; he knew I couldn't keep away from Venice for long. Then he bought the flat I'm living in, as an investment.

Paul concentrated on his whisky. After a while she spoke again.

– Money, ownership... it can be awkward, embarrassing to talk about these things. There was no reason why I should tell you about the house, don't you see that?

– Of course, it's your business. But it's in the papers, and I couldn't help but think you knew.

– I understand your curiosity, but if it's a mystery then a mystery it must remain.

She stood.

– I'm off. You don't mind clearing up on your own, do you?

– Wait. I'll fling some clothes on and see you home.

She shook her head.

– Don't be cross with me. It's late and you shouldn't walk back alone.

– I'll be perfectly safe. I have no fears in Venice at night. Cross? I *was*, but...

– I'm sorry. I've been clumsy.

She nodded.

– Tomorrow?

– I almost forgot! I got tickets this morning. Would you like to come with me to the opera?

– Would I! I meant to book tickets myself. Which one?

– Verdi, *A Masked Ball*.

So they kissed and made up. And the kisses, in the doorway above the stairs in this house of many doors, were passionate, and sweeter than before. But Eva didn't change her mind: she went home.

Paul stacked everything in the dishwasher, swallowed another whisky and went to bed.

Sleep didn't come. He fetched the new folder and tried to read but had no inclination. He went to the kitchen and picked at leftovers. He played Teresa Berganza again. *Ch'io mi scordi di te!* It enthralled him; in London he had recordings of it by different singers. How could I forget you! Or was it perhaps 'If only I could forget you'? The aria was full of reproaches towards a cruel lover. For the first time, Eva had shown she was vulnerable; he knew it wasn't an act. Was his insistence cruel? He could hardly be blamed for wanting answers when she presented him with mysteries.

An anteroom led into the bedroom, its narrow space made to appear wider by an old Venetian mirror above a walnut chest. Failing in his attempts to open the chest, he pulled out the single drawer of the writing desk by the bedroom window. Empty. Four light-green wardrobes filled the opposite wall, two of them locked, one for his own clothes, another with its green-tasselled key perhaps forgotten. He turned it.

In zipped-up envelopes of heavy plastic hung a long winter coat of dark grey wool with a fur collar; a black evening gown with sequinned silver trimming down one side; a cream pleated dress of a special type he couldn't put a name to, though he knew it was something made in Venice. Fortuny!

He would have liked to touch them, to finger silk, fur, soft wool, but they were meant to stay untouchable, protected from air, moths, whatever threat precious textiles might face, until either seasonal necessity or grand occasion might release them. Their luxury needed preservation.

Catching sight of himself in the full-length mirror inside the door, he retreated with a guilty start.

20

I stepped into the waves. Nothing had prepared me for the sea.

Water caressed my ankles. Treading on the whitened stones, my feet altered shape.

The tide was out so I waded until water covered my knees. My fingers dipped into its sparkle, disturbing microscopic fish that spread pinprick bubbles in their wake. I trod sand now, at once soft and hard. Discreetly, I kicked, then with a child's unbounded glee I splashed and squealed. Who could hear me this far from shore? I breathed great draughts of salty air that had the tang of ocean's breadth in them. Crouching, to let the water roll over my shoulders, I discovered buoyancy. Lifting my legs, I floated free.

Behind me stood the town with its castle on the heights. Higher still, the seabirds' cries were festive whoops of freedom, so different from the squabbling screams of gulls descending on Rialto to snatch the market's leavings. My memories of Venice were crowded not just with history and my own story, but with the close proximity of others in their thousands. Here, there was space. In the air and in the sea's expanse. There was a wide new century too. It was 1807, a warm June day. Battles were still being fought elsewhere in Europe, but peace reigned on this north-west shore. Trafalgar had ended the sea war.

I had lived many years close to the sea. For the first time, I felt the elemental joy of its embrace.

Fashion had not yet discovered sea-bathing in France, though the English were enjoying it at Brighton. So I learned from my travelling companion, an elderly lady called Mrs Fox. But the likes of Danton and Desmoulins had come to Dieppe in balmier days, before the Terror, when dips in the sea were truly revolutionary.

Mrs Fox thought me shockingly bold. She made allowances, knowing I was Italian and a singer.

– You will catch a chill, Signora Marini.

– The water's cold, *mia cara*, but the sun is not.

Mrs Fox stood on the pebbly shore, parasol in hand, her maid, Liza, fussing around her with a silk shawl to ward off the breeze, while mine, the young Anita, who had set out with me from Trieste, waited to envelope me in a vast bell of linen that billowed about her. She had raised a flapping barrier of sailcloth for modesty's sake as I removed my wet clothes.

– How well I feel, I announced, wanting to hug the whole world with my sea-kindled energy.

The town's air had restored me after the long and dusty journey from Paris, where I had made a week's halt. On the coach I became acquainted with the widowed Mrs Fox and we happily settled on travelling on to London together. She was going home from a visit to French cousins by marriage.

After Angela withdrew from the world, I left Venice for Trieste, as my new self: Eleonora Marini. Yet, for all my pretence and disguise, I had no sense of being someone else. Only when I cast my thoughts back to distant selves in memory did I ask, could that have been me?

Trieste was to be a way station for me to regain my reputation; I hoped then to sing at Milan. Alas, my voice had lost its lustre and needed practice. It took a whole year to win an engagement at the Opera House. Trieste in winter: the bora blowing icy round street corners. A straitened year of fingering coins and looking down the well of hunger. It never came to that, but poverty had stood outside my door and given me a fright.

No invitation ever came from La Scala or from Naples, another goal of my ambition. But when an agent of the King's Theatre in London, a Giuseppe Signorelli, heard my performance as Carolina in Cimarosa's *Secret Marriage*, I was offered a contract for a season there. London promised a new world and I sorely needed to leave behind the old one, the Italy where painful memories held me fast.

Mrs Fox knew a gentleman living in Dieppe, a doctor, who guided us about on the first morning of our stay. Its towers and gateways, its wide brick-arched windows, bore the hand, he told us, of the great master of siege craft, Vauban, for the whole town had been made anew to the design of a pupil of his, following destruction by the English and the Dutch. The old town had been built of wood; what replaced it had an absolute solidity and I liked this style whereby simple curves and arches tempered strength's severity. What rational harmony, I thought, imagining in the course of our tour how it might be to live in this pleasant place. My profession, or the claims of others, had dictated where I made my home and this had always been in cities. It had never entered my head to abandon city life.

We had two days before the packet sailed for Shoreham and I spent them walking with Mrs Fox, or with Anita, through the town's narrow streets and quiet squares, and by the sea in whose silky light I found a calming centre. I felt the better prepared for London by this uneventful interlude. At last I was sloughing off the skin of my former life, my wounds finally mending. Renewed vigour and appetite had wrought a new woman in Eleonora Marini, her face and body scarcely marked by the sufferings of Elise Muto, the gaunt creature in mourning veils who had watched her daughter descend into the hell of self-obliteration.

The human power to recover from wretchedness never ceases to astonish me; time (and some forgetting) does indeed heal, it is only that most of us never have enough of it. I did. The pulse of life had caught me again. It was true I looked a little older than on my visit to Rosalba Carriera, but that was more than half a century before.

When we sailed it was evening. From the deck I looked west at the late sun setting the water on fire. Nature's mysteries continued to prevail over any reason I could ever find.

His Lordship Mount Edgcumbe offered me a dish of tea and began to tell me of his sorrow at Brigida Banti's death.

– A true *voce di petto*. Without a fault. Rich and even…

– I heard her sing in Venice once and much admired that voice's range and powers of embellishment.

He interjected:

– Mind me, wouldn't study. She had the misfortune to come from a class of persons for whom singing is mere pleasure. Her father played the mandolin – in the streets. Many such in Italy, I know.

He paused and fixed assessing eyes on me as if to discover some trace of the street singer, before going on.

– Lazy, but she could afford to be, with a larynx such as hers.

La Banti's larynx, bequeathed by her to the city of Bologna – famed for its anatomists – had startled the world by its size. Its mention, now proverbial, was intended, I sensed, to overawe me.

– Who knows, Milord, what hidden freaks of nature you may be harbouring in London's theatres.

I laughed, aiming to charm him, and he gave a little harrumphing cough, uncharmed but nonetheless reminded that our conversation should move on to other topics.

– We are pleased to welcome you to our great city, Signora Marini.

He enquired about my journey, my lodgings, and whether the language occasioned me any difficulties. Signorelli, I told him, had assisted me, and of course, among the company were other Italians.

I did not mean by this to refer to Angelica Catalani, but the thought arose and set him off on a rhapsody of praise for yet another singer. La Banti was dead. All I knew of her was her talent and I'd had the privilege to enjoy it. La Catalani's monstrous reputation preceded her and followed long in her wake, from Venice, Trieste, Milan and the Napoleonic court. Her greed and overbearing manners were renowned.

What demon possessed her, when nature had endowed her so prodigiously with what should have made her generous and sweet? Countless besotted worshippers spoke only of her searing beauty and a voice universally held to be sublime. I did not relish hearing more of such talk on the eve of my own London debut. Pleading tiredness, I took my leave.

George Lake had deep-set eyes that were narrowed and sleepy most of the time. But when something truly interested him about a person they opened wide and lit up in a warm complicity. He was a Grub Street man, and that was how he introduced himself to me, using Dr Johnson's term and then explaining it with entertaining irony. I fell for those eyes and that wit. He made me smile much more than I had done for years and he could make me laugh, too. He was short of stature and not handsome in the least. Like Voltaire and, from what I had heard, like Mozart, who was said to have been irresistible to women. I fancied George at first a kind of Casanova, for that notorious seducer of women was also a respecter of them, believing that they were made weak only by their defective education, thus impoverished in mind while being equal to men in human dignity and spirit.

He came to my dressing room with hothouse roses the first night I sang the part of Servilia in *La Clemenza di Tito*, and I took this as auspicious since it was my first Mozart role. On the second night he took me straight to bed. He was clever and wild, knowing how to stir my pleasure. I surrendered to his admiration and my need for intimacy. I had been without passion too long to forego it. London, though brimming with music, lacked other delights for the senses. It was a dank, vast container for the insalubrious humours of smoke and fog. George lit up the grey of my first London winter.

Night after night he sat in the pit and never took his eyes off me. He listened hard too and heard things in my voice that no one had discerned.

– You are unusual, my dearest, you have more than one natural shade of expression, a *metallo* that is plangent and sweet, most suited to the great Mozart's mode, and another that is furious and searching, which perhaps has still to find the music that will match it.

How perceptive this was, and I did find that music, although not until much later. And to my cost.

This is how a lover should be, I told myself, and I was right, but I did not keep George as my lover. One evening, when we had finished eating supper, he took my hand, gave me a deep adoring look, and spoke, without preamble.

– Eleonora, I want you to be my wife.

He took some snuff as he waited for my answer, as if this was all the time I would need. The snuff bothered me, reminding my nose of Perulli's dust, but I shook off this tickling memory. I wanted myself wholly in the present.

Marrying George was the worst mistake I ever made.

I married him for reasons good and bad. Husbands had, as a rule (only broken once), been either a necessity or an advantage. With one, much in life was simplified. A married woman had freedoms a spinster could not aspire to, or even an unprotected widow, as I was.

Did I love him?

Love's trueness is often hard to judge when a lover can induce well-being in countless powerful ways, whether they derive from genuine amorous feeling on both sides or on his calculation. What I felt for George bore no resemblance to my love for François or Lorenzo, yet it consumed me. All unseeing, I had fallen for a calculating seducer.

Rivalry played a part too.

My contract paid me five hundred pounds for the season, what each of the company's principal singers received. With one exception. Angelica Catalani earned more than ten times that amount, the value of her talents raised to astronomical heights by a manager-husband who drove a hard bargain. With a husband to puff my own reputation, I might succeed in undermining hers. In all my professional life I had never met a singer who so much deserved comeuppance.

George helped me a little, I admit, for it is always better to have someone of even minor influence on one's side. But it was he who drew most profit from our partnership.

He deployed his irony as a weapon as well as an instrument of charm, and he aimed it where it took his sometimes cruel fancy. I was often amused, sometimes not, for I did not always see the justice in it. He harried one young tenor to drink and ruin with wounding articles that impugned his wife's fidelity as well as ridiculing his talents.

Heartfelt though his affection seemed, his endearments were so wantonly bestowed that in these too I found that irony: my songbird divine, my diadem, my treasure, my little bright-tailed rabbit, my soaring dove, my clever little vixen. Only the last of these suggested a notion that I was in some way out of George's reach, that he suspected me of having secrets – doubtless either to do with money or matrimony. I told him that my family's fortunes had been much reduced by the Serenissima's end with the advent of Napoleon, that I had briefly had a husband, a young poet of slender means, after whose death I had taken myself off to Trieste. But whenever he said my clever little vixen, it sounded like some inner conviction that made him uncomfortable. My husband, I realised, could not bear the thought of any secret I might have. The possibility stung him and bred a simmering watchfulness.

With hindsight, I can see that in this matter of love I deliberately ignored my hard-gained wisdoms of experience, creating the wilful illusion that I lacked them, as do the young. I had wished truly to forget myself.

Those who have not known misfortune know nothing. Alas, those who have can still forget what they know and fall for fresh illusions. Over and over we reconcile ourselves with error, however ill life treats us, however sober it renders our senses.

Being in love was a fount of renewal; it heightened the world's sounds and colours, and showed me the grace of being alive. It lightened me of old burdens, allowed the pain of memory to fade, stripped the years away and left me younger. Illusions are hardy. Lust, excitement and ambition had nurtured mine in George Lake's case. I didn't see the danger.

I could no longer be blind.

– George, you disappoint me greatly.

I had discovered the extent of his gambling debts and the money owed to his tailor. I alone had the means to pay them.

– That displeases me, Eleonora, for I do take pains to make you happy. Do I not amuse you as once I did?

It was a year since our wedding. A year of inexorable revelations. All George's debts and peccadilloes were more tolerable than the now patent truth that the man I had married was an empty vessel with no deep feeling for life. A fatal coldness had been laid between us.

I could endure no more of it. I was accustomed to rule my own life and I resolved to leave him.

Mrs Fox was my only acquaintance outside our circle of music and the theatre, where rumour would at once have led him to me. She was a solicitous woman whose bulky eagerness of manner made her appear ridiculous at times, and these guileless qualities misled me. Taking little luggage, I asked her for shelter while I sought discreet lodgings. With reluctance, she agreed, but was ill at ease. Later, she came to my room.

– I beg you to return to your husband, where a wife belongs, for your own sake, not just mine... you must see how awkward it is that you hide in my house. For where can you go? A deserting wife will find few welcomes; you will be shunned, my dear Mrs Lake.

I nodded, unsmiling, as if to reassure her.

– I'll leave in the morning. You've been kind, Mrs Fox.

I had decided to keep my own counsel; I saw she was fearful of scandal and I could not depend on her. For now I was free of George and would act the following day.

How naive I was. The world I lived in continued to take me by surprise.

The next morning brought a downpour. Its heavy beating against the windows was accompanied around ten o'clock by an insistent knocking at the door. Answer it, Mrs Fox told the servant, consternation on her face, affording me no chance to withdraw.

George burst in, his face angry and wet from the rain, as though tear-stained.

– My dear Mr Lake.

My hostess sounded touched by his appearance.

He dragged me from my chair while she watched, unprotesting.

– I'm taking my wife home, where she belongs. Be so good as to pack her things. I'll send a man for them.

I resisted, but George was strong. He pushed me into the waiting calash and bared his teeth in a frightening animal grimace.

– We'll say no more of this, Eleonora. It is never to happen again.

And with these words, he raised an arm as if to strike me hard. But the blow did not fall. It was meant as a warning, a sign of George's power and my subjugation. He could not afford to hurt me, for his own sake; my singing paid for his pleasures and follies and he meant to continue drawing profit from it. Thereafter he fastened sour and greedy eyes on my every move.

Inwardly, I unleashed furious screams that sent George Lake to hell; I howled at the injustice of my will being trampled on, my freedom stolen. Schooled as I was in dissimulation, I knew better than to let my rage show. I waited, planning for small advantages to make my escape, aware that George could and would do everything to prevent it. All I possessed, he owned and had control of under law. He wished me to know this, and it was the impulse to supremacy rather than any lingering desire that brought him to my bed again. Several times I refused him, then twice he forced me. This provoked the worst of my suffering. I felt caged and tethered, I burned with contempt while knowing that any false step might cost me dear. He paid the servants to spy on me and restricted my ordinary freedoms.

I felt his eyes tight upon me. Mean, all-possessing eyes. Only at the theatre, behind the flats, in the small room where I dressed, could I be free of them. And it was here I laid my plans and decided what I'd need.

My opportunity came one afternoon when I had a rehearsal at the theatre and circumstances granted me some hours of untrammelled movement. George was resting in his room, having drunk too much; his man, Nicholas, had been sent to fetch a horse won the night before at the gaming table of a lord. I, meanwhile, had given leave to my maid Alice – George's replacement for my own Anita, whom he had sent away – to visit her sick mother, although he did not know this. I ordered our driver to take me in the usual direction of the Haymarket. Once at the theatre, I donned a dark wig, made my face look older and my figure stouter, changed into travelling clothes I had kept there, and slipped out unnoticed. I walked a fair distance before I hired a cab. Extreme precautions were called for since I knew that George would question all the local coachmen.

My destination was The Angel Inn at Islington, departure point for northbound coaches. All of George's calculations would have me aim for the south coast, with Paris in mind, or Italy, for he knew how much I missed it. I planned instead to reach Harwich and take ship for Holland. I had my jewellery and some money I'd kept hidden at the theatre.

At Harwich I became ill.

I took a room at the inn and lay down on the narrow bed, my belly torn with agonising spasms. I was bleeding; I stumbled to my trunk to fetch linen. What ailed me was the thing I had suspected but hoped against.

– Help me! Help me!

No one heard my faint calls. I was alone, unaided, without any words of comfort.

After the child I had been carrying was painfully expelled from my body I lay there, weak, helpless, tears and snot smeared on my face, my hands covered in a clotted mess of blood. I felt a surge of pity for that barely formed foetus, and a great amount of self-hatred. I despised myself for what I had made of my freedoms. My first pregnancy of a long, long life to end like this in loss and sordid loneliness! Had there been heartfelt love for the father, had the father truly loved the mother – who was a foolish, selfish woman… had neither vanity nor envy ruled her, that is *me*, for in judging myself I stood back from the person I was… Sobbing, I rued the day.

Nearly a week passed before I could travel. I kept to my bed, but could not avoid the intrusions of the landlord's wife. I grieved, I let myself mourn the child, imagining her whole and grown (or him, I did not know, but I preferred to endow this almost-baby with something of me, and make it a strengthening part of myself).

On the cool, grey morning when I set out again, I felt relief that George Lake would be father to no child of mine. The child now was separate in her death before life, and I had more iron in my soul.

Yet sometimes the thoughts would creep upon me: *that barely formed foetus, that almost-baby*. And I would feel my breast about to burst open from the grief of it renewed. And all my other, older griefs would crowd around, clamouring sorely, as if I had disowned them, when they had only been buried, needfully, in the shallow grave of memory.

George's voice pursued me in my head; I pictured his face, the mean curled lip, the bitter scowl of the man I realised had been jealous of those he professed to admire, those who made music and art while he made lazy exercise of his lesser talents. Free to loathe him now without dissembling, I felt disgust for my earlier infatuation, and even greater terror of falling into his hands again. I feared that this delay might help him find my trail. The landlady, a good-hearted woman, did not question my account that I was Dutch and married to an Englishman in the service of the King – every fourth man at the time was in uniform. But would she not later wonder why I had worn disguise? This, and the postponement of my sailing because of rough seas, compelled me to change my route.

I went to Edinburgh. I had Melchior Cesarotti to thank for this decision.

Through my friendship with the Marquis Poleni, I had met Cesarotti once on a visit to Padua and was impressed by his ardour for ideas. During my veiled exile at the Rio dei Pensieri, I felt flattered to be one of his correspondents, among the likes of Madame de Staël and the poet Ugo Foscolo. He wrote with lively simplicity, as if speaking to an intimate. He firmly believed that language, his own Italian language, should be flexible, not stiff, alive to change and not frozen in time like 'some beautiful corpse'.

… Perfection is illusion, he wrote; *imperfection is a part of life, its constant becoming and renewal…*

I could not but agree.

It was in translation that Cesarotti gave synthesis to these strivings to make language new. The ancients moved him to bring their poetry to modern knowledge, and he published translations of Homer. He also read English and an Englishman in Venice, Charles Sackville, lent him a copy of *Fingal,* the first of James Macpherson's translations of Ossian, the ancient Caledonian poet. Cesarotti wrote to me, ecstatic in his praise.

… This strikes me as the truest poetry of nature and feeling. It is alive with an instinctive and primitive sense of being. Here is an epic of old that can teach us something new, a poem quite different from the classics that have formed our minds and words. Read it, Elisa, and you will find the hot lyric breath of Celtic history…

His own translation was a masterpiece. Its musicality and compelling rhythms would give Italian poetry its modern stamp, while all over Europe *Fingal* and *Temora* inspired Romantic fervour for Scotland's surging rivers and mist-clad mountains, its shining lakes and purple valleys.

I too was inspired. When a pleasant young couple on the coach leaving Harwich that warm May afternoon said they were going to Edinburgh, I pictured a world of invigorating possibility.

I found lodgings in the Canongate, in one of those great stone buildings that followed the continental style of living, with classes adjacent and only vertically divided, a grand bourgeois family spread out on the first and second floors, with the poor above and below them, crammed into small low-ceilinged rooms. Even I could afford to rent the better sort, since those with the means were decamping to the New Town, to its spacious crescents and squares, its houses with porticoed doorways and elegant winding stairs, well away from their poorer erstwhile neighbours.

Gracious and open though the New Town was, for me other skies were needed to give it a true sense of lightness. The grey weather dampened beauty. I craved sunlight; with it I struggled less to sustain faith in my powers or keep sadness at bay.

The Old Town was black and infernal, steps and steep alleys slicing through the lopsided rearing tenements into dizzying drops: a geometry of slopes and mad angles the devil might have designed. Stone merged elementally with rock, spires plunged fiercely into ever-clouded sky. These surroundings only troubled me at night, when I was safe in bed and raised voices or running footsteps in the street woke me and roused my fear of George's pursuit. My dreams would be a torment then.

Daily I moved between the two parts of the city – the Old Town's skewed prospects and thick promiscuity, the New Town's well-proportioned curves and rectangles, its pristine masonry – two different souls within the same body, the one murky and full of hidden things, the other seeming, albeit not being, transparent.

It was in the New Town that my pupils lived: the daughters of the bourgeoisie. I would spend my mornings and afternoons there, only to cross Princes Street at teatime in sight of the Castle on its great basalt cliff and make my way slowly up the Canongate.

Thus was my time strictly marked out in those early months. Edinburgh offered few public opportunities for singers and I had preferred to keep my voice in the background lest word of it should reach George's ears. I gave voice lessons, taught a little fortepiano, and otherwise kept to myself, as folk did in Edinburgh.

Gradually, I received invitations to sing at society gatherings. These improved my financial situation and altered the life I led, prising me from the dream-plagued nocturnal solitude of the Old Town's gothic and bringing the welcome air of cultivated talk and civilised ways.

My name was Elene Mittner, though I called myself Lene. I told everyone I had set out travelling from Innsbruck with a cousin two years earlier, never planning to stay away so long, yet always intending to reach this fine and beautiful country. At the start, when they asked how I had conceived my great desire to visit Scotland, I gave a prompt reply.

– From reading Goethe. In *The Sorrows of Young Werther*, your great Ossian is quoted.

The response might be a pitying or embarrassed look. Or amazement.

– Ossian, Madam, is with us no more.

This answer came one evening at a reception where literary men predominated. I had discovered that Edinburgh was a very literary city, more so than London at that time.

The words puzzled me, and the titters they provoked.

– No longer…? What do you mean, sir? Ossian has not been with us, as you put it, for some fifteen or sixteen centuries, surely?

The titters grew louder.

– No, Madam, only since 1805.

Fortunately, this torture ceased. I heard an account of how an eminent committee had investigated the conflicting claims about Macpherson's translations. To my dismay, 'doubts had been expressed early on, by such eminent men as Johnson and Hume'. Macpherson went to his grave adamant about the epic's authenticity, but the committee sternly deemed that *Fingal* was a fraud, as were his other Ossianic publications. A few genuine fragments in the Gaelic had moved him to invent the rest.

– But Ossian is still admired, sir, across the English Channel. In Scotland you have decreed the truth, but the rest of the world is no wiser. Or else it will not believe in your verdict; it prefers the deception.

– The more fool it.

It was five years since Macpherson's 18th-century translations had been found wanting in third-century originals, and Europe continued to prefer the deception for many more to come. I have puzzled over this and I conclude that the world of letters and music owes Macpherson a debt. Without *Fingal* there would be no Fingal's Cave, and Mendelssohn visited Scotland nearly 20 years after I myself left it. Without Cesarotti's masterly translation, would Leopardi's *Canti* have been written as we know them? Ossian lent Scotland greatness in the eyes of Goethe and Stendhal, and without its Ossianic fervour would Europe have pardoned Walter Scott his bad poems or been eager to read his novels, turning both one and the other into operas destined to endure?

Were the Romantics fools?

Had I asked such a question, my interlocutor might not have demurred. For, besides being the editor of a literary magazine as well known in London as in Edinburgh, he was also a judge, and his looks were correspondingly severe. Judge Jeffrey and I were not suited to close acquaintance.

Legal men were everywhere in this city, and I sang one evening at a gathering of eminent lawyers and advocates; it was leavened with doctors, for they too abounded. I began with a series of Haydn songs, the music set to English words, then Scottish folk tunes to poems by Robert Burns. I liked to end with Mozart, and had chosen a *lied*, 'Das Traumbild'.

Intent upon conjuring this dream picture, I was gratified by the attentive silence that accompanied my singing. A warm late-summer breeze entered through the floor-length windows. The large drawing room was brightly lit and I had a clear sense of the many eyes upon me. Only the shadowy area beyond its wide-open double doors, where gentlemen stood smoking, contained any movement, as guests made their way into the room; murmured conversation could be observed in the gestures of these figures, although no sound of it disturbed my concentration or that of my listeners.

Suddenly, I noticed a commotion there: a man rudely attempting to push into the main part of the room. Someone held him back. I sang on, concerned that nothing should impinge on my absorption in the music. I faltered, though missing only a single beat, when I was jolted by the knowledge that the man was George Lake.

I dared not look at him, and my determination not to have my performance ruined by his arrival impelled me to even greater bravura than I would otherwise have achieved. I was doing battle, music being my great weapon, my singing self my strongest one. As my voice grew in richness and expression, as I found more tenderness and meaning in the sounds that I shaped, so my own strength increased, and while my all was surrendered to the song, so that I and it were now inseparable, I could feel another part of me, deep and distinct, at work in making a decision that might save me.

George Lake was not to have me back. I was untouchable, my own mistress and no man's slave. I sang on, conquering my terror and knowing that my salvation lay in denial. I sang on, fierce with music, curbing my gaze, rehearsing for a part.

The applause was broken by a shout.

– Eleonora!

I ignored it, nodding gracious acknowledgement to my audience, before turning to my accompanist.

But George was upon me, seizing my hands in his.

– Eleonora! I have found you at last. Forgive me. I know not what I did to make you leave me, but it has been my torment. Now, I promise you, I shall make you very happy. Let us leave at once, I have a carriage outside.

Astonishment almost made me succumb to recognition, but I shook myself free.

– How dare you, sir. You mistake me for someone else.

I looked around. I intended to turn this public scene to my own advantage, to rally sympathy and protection. My face displayed outrage. I appealed to my hostess.

– Please! Mrs Ross, I do not know this man.

George turned nasty on the instant.

– You shameless vixen! You're my wife and well you know it!

Shaking my head in a show of utter incomprehension, I did not waver.

He caught my arm, but Mrs Ross outfaced him and he let go.

– She's my wife, I tell you, Eleonora Lake, Eleonora Marini as she was.

– Sir, I ask you to leave my house, Frau Mittner says you are mistaken.

– I know my own wife.

I walked along a precipice whose edge would crumble were my willpower to weaken for one moment. I cast Eleonora into oblivion and infused Lene Mittner with all the conviction I could muster. My eyes flashed indignation.

– I, sir, know my own self. Better than any man might know his wife, therefore my claim is a superior one.

There was a hush. I wondered had I overstated my case. Fear made me doubt whether I could stand my ground, and whether George might have evidence or witnesses. I was in a room full of advocates, in a city where the plain truth had a kind of unvarnished holiness. Everyone was watching. Although I could count on sympathy, for I had kind acquaintances in this company, I would still have to prove that I was in the right. In a French or Venetian salon, things would have been different. Indeed, it struck me that I was not in a salon, where wit and poise are what matter most, but rather in a courtroom or dissecting chamber.

This second comparison occurred to me when I caught the eye of Professor Monro tertius. He was giving me the keenest of looks. I did not flinch.

George clearly felt something of this atmosphere, for he addressed himself to the room.

– She left me a year ago, deserted me with a quantity of debts she'd run up. But I forgave that. I wanted her back, to take care of her. She was my whole life, only wanted to help her career. At the King's, you know, I got her an engagement there.

I bit my lip. This was sheer provocation; I resisted.

He paused for effect, placing his hands on his head.

– I was desperate, travelled everywhere searching for her. I placed advertisements in the press. Look, gentlemen, this came in answer. Here is proof that she is lying.

He fumbled in his pocket and produced a letter.

… a lady resembling your wife goes by the name of Elene Mittner and sings in Edinburgh's best houses…

I let a gasp of indignation leave my lips. I was not the only one. A man I knew by sight as a practising advocate rose from his seat and approached George.

– May I see that, Mr Lake. My name is Hector Bailey. I am a legal man.

– Then you'll know that the law is on my side.

George smirked as he held out the letter. Advocate Bailey read it at a glance.

– Mr Lake, this by no means constitutes proof of your claim. The best it can say for you is merely that Frau Mittner may indeed resemble your wife. What evidence do you have that she *is* your wife?

George had put himself inadvertently at a disadvantage by assuming that his certain knowledge would suffice as proof, and failing to anticipate my lack of corroboration.

– No! She is Eleonora. Look!

His next piece of evidence was a portrait, a miniature he had done of me at the time of our wedding. The artist was a fashionable mediocrity.

At this, Professor Monro tertius stepped forward.

– Allow me, please, to compare the likeness.

He studied it closely, and he studied me, his eyes shifting rapidly between us, me and my painted image. I quailed under this scrutiny, my hands clutching at the skirts of my dress for steadiness. I managed to keep my face composed. The strain I was under must have been apparent to Mrs Ross, for she found me a chair and helped me to sit down. Hardly a breath could be heard in the room. Everyone waited for Professor Monro to speak. His judgement, I knew, would be accepted. Few medical men in Edinburgh had his standing and authority; perhaps only his father, Monro secundus, ranked higher. His grandfather, Monro primus, had been the first physician to hold the chair of anatomy at the University, and it had been in the family since 1720. All three were Alexander, hence their distinguishing appellation by number.

Professor Monro tertius brought his face close to mine and his eyes roved across it in a thorough inspection, then, holding the miniature by its silver frame in his left hand, with his right he gestured, rather theatrically I thought, towards the room in general. Of course, he was used to wielding a lecture baton before a large audience; it was in his blood. That and a scalpel... I shuddered at the thought.

– If this is a likeness of Frau Mittner, it's a poor one.

The words were pronounced with an abruptness that suggested finality. But he proceeded forthwith to present the substance of his conclusion.

– Look at the brow. It's a fair bit higher than Frau Mittner's. Though I'm not saying hers isn't a handsome one.

No one else could see the miniature well enough to judge, so all eyes were turned on me.

– The nose is longer, as if the artist flattered himself he was a painting a member of the royal family.

There was laughter at this.

– And the chin is too prominent, too pointy. Now, look at the lady's.

I began to redden. Professor Monro tertius could have been more delicate. But medical men are blunt, and he was used to showing off corpses.

– Last, but not least, the eyes. Frau Mittner has a fine pair of eyes, as all of you can see, and these eyes are like hers, the same shade of blue, the same sparkle. But they're deep-set, and hers stand out more, and I'm not convinced they're the same.

He paused and leaned towards his audience to encourage them to listen hard for what was coming next.

– Let us suppose that Frau Mittner was indeed the artist's subject. The image is approximate enough for it to be possible. But he failed, for it is not good enough to offer anyone a valid record of this lady's countenance. If Mr Raeburn were here with us tonight, I'm sure he would only bear me out. But, alas...

With this he turned to impress that keen look of his on George.

– He's in London for a wee while, and much in demand by those who can afford him.

George smarted visibly. Did he know Henry Raeburn's work? I had seen enough of the artist's portraits hanging in Edinburgh's grander houses to share the professor's view that he was beyond George's pocket. The professor placed the miniature on the top of the fortepiano.

– If this is your evidence, sir, then I suggest that the law will judge it inadmissible.

With a curt bow to me, he walked away. I felt myself released by his and Advocate Bailey's judgements of the weapons against me, and I wanted to put a distance of several streets between myself and my husband as fast as I could. I stood. George glared at me and as I turned, shunning him, he lunged heavily and almost knocked me off my feet. He caught me in a tight locking of arms and began to drag me towards the door.

– You're coming home, Eleonora. I don't give a damn what your Scotsmen have to say on it.

My struggles were futile. I screamed for help. A shocked inertia surrounded me, though I was aware that something stirred beyond it. Suddenly I was free from George's grip and two hefty constables took charge of him. I learned that Mrs Ross had sent for them at the first as a precaution.

– My dear Frau Mittner, drink this.

Mrs Ross set a whisky glass on a side table next to me, and bustled off. I stared at it, too shaken to move. I sat in a daze, until I looked up and met the shrewd eyes of a woman around my own age. She introduced herself as Susan Ferrier and told me she was a writer, the daughter of the principal clerk of the Court of Session. She raised the glass to my lips. I drank.

– Thank you. I see that the law is determined to come to my aid. I can only be grateful.

– The law may or may not defend you, but from what I have seen your... that man will not respect it. There is too much violence in him...

– Are you offering me advice? If you believe that I am, as he claims, his wife, how best should I protect myself? I mean, it's all one: whatever I say, he still insists it is so, and he won't leave me in peace.

– He'll be locked up tonight; I heard the constables say so. They'll have him down at the Sheriff Court in the morning, and they'll want you there as well. In the meantime, you have a chance to get away. It could be your only chance.

– How? At this time of night?

– I've thought about that and I've spoken to a friend of mine. You'll have to be at Leith docks just hours from now. His ship sails for Gothenburg at first light. With a cargo of malt and coal, and likely some whisky. Maybe it's true what the poet said, that freedom an' whisky gang thegither.

She paused.

– Marriage can be the heart of woman's being and happiness, or a terrible cramped jail.

She said this quietly. I nodded my agreement. I had no need to reflect on my options. It seemed wise to leave the country. Susan Ferrier promised discretion now and in future and, telling me to wait for her return, went off to find her friend the sea captain, Malcolm Stevenson. He was a tall, untidy-haired man; I watched them in conversation. He left almost at once. She wound her way back to me, stopping to chat to other ladies, not making too obvious a connection for others to notice.

– It's fine. You can trust him. I'll go with you now to your lodgings, then we'll find you a carriage to take you to Leith.

All went as planned. As I sped towards Leith harbour, Edinburgh's heights rose and fell behind me against a turbulent night sky. Nothing delayed the *Mary MacGregor* and a fine dawn welcomed us as we made for the open sea.

Alone in my cabin, I let go of my composure. Anger boiled inside me and I called George Lake foul names that for all their power to shock did no justice to his villainy. Had my physical strength been equal to my fury should he come to rob me of myself again, I could have felled him with a casual blow.

I breakfasted with the captain and asked his opinion of the previous evening's events.

– Did they believe him?

– A good many of them would have been inclined to. Either that or they thought him deranged.

– Then why did they take my part?

– You gave them no reason not to. And you were consistent, whereas he... with his snoop's letter and his bad portrait of you. Och, it was a matter of principle. You were who you said you were. Besides, Bailey's a terrible show-off, and Monro's an eccentric with a family reputation to keep up.

I had a long voyage ahead to consider where and who I had been. With the help and kindness of others, I had escaped from my predatory husband. And I was escaping from myself, travelling into another gaping future. I felt chastened. Perhaps this time I had learned a hard lesson, learned so that wisdom would stay in my bones, would direct my feelings and my instinct well. I had learned to fear falling in love. I knew it could destroy me.

21

– A circus tent!

Paul was amused. He knew about the blaze that had destroyed the Fenice. The phoenix would rise as ever from the flames; meanwhile, its replacement lacked glamour.

In the same vein, Eva insisted:

– Surely a proof of devotion.

Day trippers came and went from this hinterland of multi-storey car parks. A German tour bus was pulling out, gusting foul fumes in its wake. A man in overalls raked a mess of litter. They turned through a complex of service buildings and followed a shrub-lined path to the giant marquee.

Opera houses proclaim grandeur and permanence; here, the foyer's hangar-like proportions conveyed an air of helplessness. Marooned in the centre, a table displayed copies of the libretto. Paul joined the queue to buy one, Eva beside him. He became aware of passing greetings, heard cordial voices address her as Signora Lensky or plain Signora.

– You know a lot of people.

– This is a small town once you subtract the tourists. Anyway, they want a closer look at you.

– Eva, Eva!

A young couple rushed out of the crowd. Cheeks were kissed, compliments exchanged and smiles dispensed all round.

– Paul, these are my friends Girolamo and Annie.

Girolamo was lanky, intense with an energy that invaded tousled hair and bushy eyebrows. Annie too was tall, but voluptuous, her gestures calm, her red-blonde curls bundled back with a tortoiseshell comb.

– Paul's from London; it's his first time at the opera in Venice. There may be things he needs to know.

Girolamo laughed as he issued his warnings.

– Canvas isn't soundproof. You might hear planes overhead. The worst is a storm.

Annie turned out to be Canadian.

– I'd never seen an opera before we got married, so here's fine by me; I love the singing.

She turned to Eva.

– Have you heard from Mom? She's coming in July.

– I know. Good news.

– She asked about the kitten.

– Paul's the man to tell you. He's looking after Angel.

So Annie's 'Mom' was Gail, the friend from California.

The final bell interrupted. They headed for their seats.

– I'd have taken them for teenagers.

– They're older than they look. The wedding was six months ago, after they'd graduated. I've known Annie since she was six. She met Girolamo here on an Erasmus from London, where her father lives.

As the lights went down, shadows scurried from the sides towards empty seats in the centre.

Everything dissolved into silence the instant the conductor's arm was raised, his baton poised. Paul always loved the hush of this gesture, its fraction of suspense, the signalling of magic in the darkened auditorium.

Yet the music failed to hold him. Nor was he the only one distracted. Only in rare moments did the mass of listeners surrender to Verdi's melodies and become a single well of concentration.

Act One ended to discreet applause.

Eva frowned.

– You see what a small stage it is, so the director thought he'd extend it outside the arch. The acoustic isn't up to that.

– Let's get a drink.

In the foyer they drank to Girolamo's toast:

– The Fenice's rebirth!

She introduced him to a middle-aged couple, their fleshy, sun-tanned looks at one with a conspicuous air of prosperity. An unseasonal fox fur wreathed the woman's arms, and under it hung heavy gold bracelets.

Pleasantries were aired. They moved on.

– Piero's my accountant. I have to be nice, or he'd overcharge me.

His bills are 'between friends' he tells me. See? Going to the opera isn't just for fun.

She gulped down her wine.

– You're not relaxed. Is the opera so disappointing?

– I'm at the mercy of comparisons; that's the trouble with haunting Europe's great opera houses. I've been lucky; Joe was determined to see everyone that mattered: Callas, of course, and Sutherland, Schwarzkopf, Alfredo Kraus, Tito Gobbi, Marilyn Horne, all the greats. You might say I'm spoiled.

– Perhaps a little.

They took their seats and the curtain rose on the graveyard scene. As Amelia sang, he felt Eva's quick touch on his arm. For him too the music became potent, the singer in control, the colours of her voice enriched by technique. This was the force of opera, its very uniqueness, the blending of drama and music into exquisite spasms of feeling, of joy and suffering at their extremes, the singing voice a prodigious breath of life.

When the aria ended he no longer had the shoulder pain that had bothered him since a stint in the library before lunch, an old injury irritated by computer use. Music acts on the body; everyone knows this. He loved rock, blues, swing – they released physicality, drew out ease and energy. Opera too could cure ills, and not just the soul's.

In the second interval they took a walk under a darkening sky scored by the silhouettes of the port cranes, an atmosphere more broodily fitting than the one inside the tent. Eva was at home among the chatter, but tonight it put her on edge. What did she really feel? He listened, smiled, responded to her words, while driven by a contrary flow of thought and emotion. In his urge to grasp what she wasn't saying, he was alert to every unstifled nuance.

Coolly, they discussed Verdi's themes of friendship, love and betrayal, and all the while Eva's account of her opera-going heyday nagged at him. It didn't add up: Tito Gobbi and Callas had died before Eva met Joe, Schwarzkopf had stopped singing. With shame, he realised he'd been wanting to catch her out.

In the mêlée of exit from the tent, they saw Girolamo and Annie at waving distance. Paul watched some of the city's best-dressed and well-heeled denizens elbowing their way onto a bus already crammed with standing passengers.

Eva led him in the opposite direction.

– Let's take our chances with the vaporetto.

On the crowded deck, he found himself whispering.

– Will you come back with me?

– I can't. I've got an early start, off to Mestre. You could come home with *me* – and not stay though.

– Mestre?

– A yoga class.

A bright moon lit the face of the waiting lion when they opened the street door. The building slumbered, its only sound the canal rippling at the water gate. On the cool stone of the stairs he became intensely aware of Eva's physical presence; her perfume blending with the night scents of Venice, she carried in the burgeoning of summer. It made him ache for her to be knowable, for the riddle of her to be solved, a need as fierce as any sensual craving.

Drinking midnight Prosecco, Eva talked about the opera: the singers, the costumes, the conductor's reputation. Her absorption left no space for Georgian Edinburgh or the poetry of Ossian. His suspicions receded; she'd returned him to the music. He basked in its afterglow.

Finally, they made love.

– I should go. You've to get up early.

– I don't mind if you stay.

– Sleep well then.

– Goodnight.

Questions returned in the darkness. Why did she make things up, like her opera-going with Joe, to hear singers who stopped performing years before? Did this city breed deceit, people packed too close to avoid falsehood, obscuring their secret selves with a heap of social lies?

– Eva?

– What?

– You're a mystery.

– Good. That's how it should be. Now go to sleep.

– I will... When did Joe die?

– Nearly three years ago.

– And how long were you together?

– Nine years. We've had this conversation before. Paul, I'm too sleepy.

In affectionate dismissal, she reached back and her hand touched his wrist.

– All right.

He kissed the hand then rolled away from her.

When he woke he had the flat to himself. Eva's clothes lay muddled with his, but the silence told him she'd gone. He made coffee, showered and dressed. By then the gingerbread clock in the sitting room showed it was nearly nine. What might he find if he took the chance to search those tea chests through the doorway opposite the blue sofa?

Books crowded the wall behind him. He leaned back to scan a shelf packed with octavo-sized antiquarian volumes and extracted a copy of Beccaria's influential treatise against capital punishment. Was this a first edition? The date appeared in Roman numerals: 1764.

He was eyeing the tea chests, reckoning with his conscience, when the sound of a key in the lock made him jump.

Expecting Eva, he turned and faced a plump young woman, rosy-cheeked, with auburn hair in a ponytail. She stepped back, speaking in a language he didn't recognise at first, glaring at him like an adversary poised for any sudden move.

– *Chi è lei?*

The question came from a sturdy youth in the doorway. Paul answered that he was a friend of the 'Signora' and was cut short by an exchange between the two in what he now realised was Russian. He surprised them by interjecting in that language.

– Signora Eva has gone to Mestre. Now please tell me who you are.

He heard Maria whisper it was true, the Signora always went to Mestre on Thursdays.

– I'm Maria. I clean the house. This is my brother, Sergei.

– And you are Russian?

Maria shook her head.

– *Ukraina.*

She explained that Sergei worked in one of the city's big hotels. He had come to help her move some furniture for the Signora.

– Move it where?

He thought it improbable that they belonged to a gang of furniture thieves.

Maria indicated a large mahogany desk.

– Out there.

'There' was where the corridor broadened into a hallway.

His offer of help was refused. He returned to the bookshelves. Picking out a slip-cased volume of Hans Andersen's *Fairy Tales*, he leafed through its pages, pausing at each title familiar from childhood: The Snow Queen, The Ugly Duckling, The Little Mermaid. Maybe Eva also read these as a child. Another first edition came to hand: Diderot's early novel, *Indiscreet Jewels*. Taking care not to leave finger marks, he opened it at random: an imaginary island where marital unions took place on the rational basis of matching genital geometry and temperature, to ensure compatible coupledom.

Halfway through the ceremony establishing these physical criteria, he remembered the bedroom and the evidence of his and Eva's night together.

Maria was shaking out the pillows.

– I'm sorry. I should have tidied up before…

– No problem, Signore. I used to be a chambermaid. I clean rooms but I have other things on my mind: my own life. You understand?

– Of course. Listen, would you like some tea?

She was divorced and had two little girls, back in Kiev with her mother. She answered his questions between hurried sips of the hot black brew.

– How long is it since you've seen your children?

– Two years.

– That must be hard for you.

– It is. Excuse me, I have to get back to work. Thank you.

Reflecting on the tug and flow of money and migration, and his awkwardness with the intimacy of 'servants', he was startled by the buzz of the entryphone. After Maria's footsteps he heard the click of the street door directly below the window, then it thudded shut.

The postman perhaps. Minutes later, from inside, came the indistinct boom of a male voice with Italian inflections. The door closed on Maria's goodbye. He waited by the window until he glimpsed a man in a cream linen suit walking off down the alley, back turned, just a fade of grey hair and the swing of a briefcase.

This small act of spying on Eva's unknown visitor persuaded him he should leave. He'd rather not be hanging around when she got back. He left a note on the kitchen table.

> *Thank you for a wonderful evening: the opera and you. The cleaner came with her brother and they moved your desk. Please call me when you get back. P.*

Restless, as if confined, and with no urge to wander or rifle through archives, he holed up at the Rio dei Pensieri. He read in the garden, turned the handles of locked doors, scrutinised the stones. Eva didn't ring.

22

My feet were wet, my skirts sodden, and my petticoats clung to my legs. The umbrella blown out of my hand drifted along the canal, upturned, gathering water, doomed to sink before the current could push it into the lagoon. Like some half-drowned creature, my beaver hat clung to my head. I sneezed and shivered. Would I succeed in traversing all the water underfoot and reaching the shelter of home? Would the rain ever stop? The soiled and sunless sky had been my welcome.

I could wait for the light-filled Venice I had missed. I was back, after circling Europe and settling in Trieste, a city thriving under Austrian rule, while Venice, its rival, struggled against the tariffs and taxes the Austrians imposed. Prosperity suited me. I had regained my self-possession and resolved to live well. To passion I conceded nothing. Adhering to this course caused something in me to wither, but freedom required that I be constant to myself. *Come scoglio.* Like a rock. Though I might have lovers, no man would rule me again.

They said I sang with a voice that was diamond-bright, unflawed by too much feeling. It was not the kind of voice Italians liked to hear, but many admired it in Warsaw and Vienna, in Prague and St Petersburg, though I suffered too much from the cold to stay long.

Music accompanied me everywhere, and the music that accompanied me best was Mozart's; I knew I had been lonelier without it. A creature like me knows a loneliness few can imagine. Cast adrift from love and kin and friendship, in far-flung banishment, I had walked the alien earth gasping for the oxygen of a world where I belonged. It sometimes felt like living on the moon.

Mozart melted the sliver of ice that threatened to lodge in my heart.

I was Edita Molini now. I could go home, to the Rio dei Pensieri. The house stood empty, up for sale, its garden never greener, its once high branches bowed beneath the torrent.

That year the rain was a plague. It would bring bad harvests. And bad harvests lead to high prices and starvation. It had poured for weeks before I arrived. This was early summer but the stones were puddled dark. Water fell in sheets; wind slapped it in our faces. Yet less of it coursed through the city. Canals had disappeared, filled in by French and Austrians alike. Venice, despoiled and moribund, now had fewer veins.

In August, my swift-streaming river of thoughts, my Rio dei Pensieri, was condemned to this same fate. Concrete dammed the lagoon tides that for centuries had come travelling past my windows. I complained, I lamented, all to no avail. Years of questions cast into that water were petrified. Cities change, alas, faster than the hearts of mortal beings.

1845. Another mid-century. A quickening. Things getting bigger, or cleverly shrinking. Locomotion. Change steaming across the lagoon. Unmeasurable. What would it bring?

There was gaslight in St Mark's when I bought my piano from Fanna's shop. Its glow gave the square an evening beauty I had never seen before.

Mr Fanna knew me; he never missed the opera. He composed music himself.

– Good evening, Signora Molini. I think I may have something to interest you, newly arrived from England. Have you ever seen such a small, neat piano?

It was narrow and high, and just what I wanted, but I was sceptical. Could the size do justice to the sound? Mr Fanna saw my hesitation. He sat at the keyboard.

– Listen, Signora. You'll be amazed.

He played a piece of his own. Though inferior to that of a square piano, the tone was surprisingly resonant and full.

– Mr Meyerbeer was very taken with this sonatina of mine. He thought it rather Germanic.

He looked around the shop with a mischievous smile, his eyes pausing briefly to note the presence of two Austrian lieutenants.

– Unlike this.

He played an air from Rossini's *William Tell*.

I left very pleased at having settled on the space-saving Wornum upright. The Piazza beckoned. I stalked the arcades, watching and listening. The cafés overflowed, argument resounded in my ears, whispers drifted towards me. I listened to the new things they said.

It was 1846.

The years were in a hurry, the speed of change pushing them, rushing minutes into hours, weeks into months. I remembered the slowness of my youth, when the days sprawled and a moment might contain a small eternity. Now, as distances reduced, time's horizons came closer and speech had unwonted urgency.

Curiosity drew me to the Piazza and I would walk alone, the better to hear. Always the city's grand salon, it was now its lung, its throat, its lips. The whispers grew louder. I became alive to the stifled screaming of dissent. I heard those who believed in a Republic, those whose goal was a kingdom, an Italy united and rid of Austria's grip, those who thought they had a whole new world of freedom to gain. I passed the Caffè Florian and caught the splintered talk of Masons, Carbonari and Mazzinians. I only passed, for I could not cross the threshold of that male domain. Across the square, I heard Austrians and Croats, the Caffè Quadri's mirrors reflecting polished sabres, bright gold braid and epaulettes. When the door swung open, the boasts and rumours of vigilance off duty spilled into the air.

Shadow sounds, history's rumblings. I heard everything and nothing.

At home, my housekeeper wept.

– Signora Edita, what am I to do? Help me if you can, he is my only child.

Dorotea was a widow and her son had fared badly in the lottery of conscription. Soldiering for the Austrians' emperor would steal eight years of his life. Her only recourse was the reckoning of prayers on her rosary.

Her younger sister, one of the women who brought the milk every day from Campalto on the mainland, came with news that her husband was in prison for having sung a patriotic air as von Haynau's men marched by. I tried to console her, promising to speak to those who might have influence, while knowing there was little I could do.

It was 1847. Nearly fifty years since Habsburg rule began.

Words grew bolder, echoing in the Piazza. Hunger fuelled them.

Ambition too. I sang on the night when protest resounded at the Fenice as never before, one day away from New Year's Eve. Scores, then hundreds called for Verdi's *Patria Oppressa* to be repeated over and over: the choir of Scottish exiles from *Macbeth*, a soft grey wailing that builds into fervour. Borne along on the rising wave of voices, I wondered. Are tyrants the same the world over? Can history teach us? Had it taught me or was I only learning from the present, only adapting, never catching up?

How would Venice fight against such odds, the might of Austria's empire? Like the Scots, shifting Birnam Wood to Dunsinane?

Lay on, Macduff.

It was 1848. Red, white and green fluttered wildly. Around necks. On the stage. The whole length of Italy was joined by those colours.

From Paris, word arrived of insurrection. I remembered earlier times. *Citizens! Will you continue to tolerate this class who owe their privilege to tyranny alone…?*

Lay on, Manin, president of our newly proclaimed Republic.

It began with bloodshed in the Piazza, bayonets hacking at the crowd, wielded by Croats. Small touch of human mothers in them! Or were there a thousand Doroteas telling beads across the Adriatic?

Shots were fired. At last I entered Florian's, for the wounded were brought there and women's hands could help the surgeons. This violence ended only after eighteen months of siege, Venice the last of Europe's rebel cities to surrender. In the glory of resistance to cholera, famine, shot and shrapnel, the world outside drew comparisons with Thermopylae, with Salamis. I saw a woman's foot blown off. As others ran to help her I fled into a corner where I vomited and wept; I am reckless but not always brave. Whatever blood was shed, day after day the band still played in the Piazza, and people strolled there as before. The poor queued up to hand in spent enemy shells in exchange for a lira; they waited hours in hope of bread. The very rich deserted Venice, taking their wealth to Trieste. The proletarians of Paris sent us their hard-earned *sous*. No more milk came from Campalto.

July 1849. The enemy launched a bombardment from hot-air balloons. The wind blew them back towards enemy lines. This cheered the city. The next night the barrage started in earnest, from heavy guns on land and at sea. For 24 hours Venice trembled, its stones rocked on their millennial mud foundations. Masonry littered *campi* and choked the canals.

Many sought safety in areas to the south and east. I stayed at home. I could hear Dorotea in the kitchen reciting her rosary, praying for her family, for her son, somewhere in Hungary, she believed, helping to put down the Hungarians' own rebellion.

– Oh Blessed Virgin, I beg your intercession. Protect and strengthen Venice's saviour, Daniele Manin. Help him to preserve our freedom, to keep our Republic safe. Oh Blessed Virgin, succour us now, in the hour of our need.

Even above the relentless din, her supplications reached me. I tried to distract my thoughts by singing a few bars of a Verdi cavatina that contained an echo of Dorotea's pleas. *Tu al cui sguardo onnipossente.* Lucrezia Contarini, begging God to save her husband, exiled from Venice unjustly.

Since the theatres had closed I had not sung in public, and despite the music's pathos, my voice refused to obey the feelings that commanded it. I persevered.

I was vying with the deafening blast of Austrian artillery, I was scouring the well of my powers for every drop of vigour and expression. Over and over I sang the same phrases, pounding the piano keys in a rage for the sounds I made to rise above the punishing persistence of the guns. Defiance spurred me and took possession of my voice. I did not know whether what I sang was beautiful or ugly, a mastery of notes or their horrible distortion; all that mattered was that I and the music lived and breathed together, bound by transcendent will and a passionate resistance to defeat.

Exhaustion claimed me in the end, yet I had new energy from a sense of something conquered. My voice, I realised, had deepened, while I still could reach the higher register.

In the kitchen I found Dorotea asleep in a chair. Her rosary had dropped to the floor. I picked it up and joined it to the hand in her lap. It weighed almost nothing, the fibrous beads worn flat by the constant friction of her fingers. I wondered how many thousand decades, how many mysteries she had told on it, and how many of these prayers had been answered. Perhaps none, perhaps faith alone saved her from despair at a life unrewarded. But she did have a son who gave her joy, for all that her fears for him brought anguish.

Dorotea was barely 40 and for three years she had been like a mother to me. Since the time when Donna Merlo claimed me, I had always had someone to look after me. My standing and my income let me take servants for granted. They were there for food to be cooked, things to be cleaned, mended or put in the right place, presences invisible behind the passive voice. I did not think of them much; they were necessary and I tried to treat them kindly, though sometimes Dorotea would cast me angry glances, turning away when I noticed, or relenting into a smile. As I looked at her asleep, oblivious to the thundering guns, I felt an unaccustomed kinship.

All the next day the guns hammered on. Plates fell off the table and shattered. It began to feel normal that everything should shake. My nerves were raw from humid heat and sleeplessness. Nothing could assuage the anxious restlessness I felt. As evening approached I wanted life around me, I needed crowds and talk. If death came, solitude would make it crueller.

To reach the Piazza I could walk as far as the Carità and be ferried to San Vitale. But I dreaded those parts of the city where cholera might have taken hold. Instead I chose to travel by gondola as far as the Rialto and go on foot from there. Luck would have to travel with me; I risked drowning as much as artillery. Although I loved the sea, I had never learned to swim.

It was a cataclysmic journey down the Grand Canal. Projectiles whistled overhead and explosions lit up the palazzi like festive fireworks being prodigally spent to rival the first blaze of sunset. All the while the gondolier rowed with fast and rhythmic strokes. Silence seemed agreed between us, even in rare moments of quiet.

After the Ca' d'Oro we passed the palazzo where Joseph Smith had for so long played host, and I saw that one of its balconies had collapsed. When we cleared the bend within sight of Rialto, even greater ruin met our eyes.

– The bridge was damaged last night.

These were the gondolier's first words since we had settled on the price, a high one. Perhaps he had preferred not to frighten me lest I have second thoughts.

My hands clenched a fear I could not give voice to. The gondolier faced away from me and I needed him to be calm.

It was as if the city were rending itself into so many fragments of my past. As if it possessed some visionary power to unloose the memories held in its shattering stones.

We drew in beside the Fondaco dei Tedeschi, where the Northern merchants traded centuries before. I thought of Lorenzo's once prosperous family. I reached San Bartolomeo in a fever, aghast at the journey I had made, half-convinced I was challenging death to take me. At San Salvatore I turned into the Mercerie, which would lead me straight to the Piazza. I quickened my pace. Sometimes a figure would appear in front of me from a doorway or *calle*, running ahead. Buildings shuddered around me. I smelled decay, recent and cloacal.

I came to the bridge where I had first seen Angela. A crowd of beggars was huddled there, sitting against the balustrades or the facing wall. I threw down a few coins and sped on. Behind me someone shouted, but I dared not turn and look.

The shop where I had spied on Lorenzo's ageing son now sold umbrellas. I stared at them in the window, light-headed with a sudden disbelief that the years had so easily fallen away.

In returning to Venice, each time to live anew, I entered its skin of stone and water; I knew it through my ears, my eyes, through touch and taste and smell. Now my fear of its, and my, destruction made the city a palimpsest, overlaid by sensations and events that had shaped my several selves. This skin, flayed, bled with memory.

My past brushed so close that I could almost touch it, its breath hot in my face. The arc of my life wound itself around me.

I stood and wept. After a while, shaking, I dried my tears. Assailed by thoughts of loss, endured and imminent, hope gone, I made myself walk with a sure and steady step, ready to defy the inevitable.

Nearing the Piazza, I heard more voices, encountered others on my path. The guns sounded fainter and all of a sudden the present rushed into me. Near open water now, I found heart. As I crossed under the arch of the clock tower, two men jostled me, one either side, perhaps by accident, but I could smell the wine in their mouths and see their eyes leer. In my recoil, I collided with a passer-by; he was singing. I stumbled, pulled between where I had been and where I was going. That small collision was fateful.

– Signora, forgive me. I did not see you. Are you hurt?

– No, no, not at all. I'm to blame. I wasn't looking.

I was now. I saw an officer in uniform. He removed his hat and gave a little bow. He was about to go on his way and I stopped him.

– What were you singing?

The words I had heard sounded foreign, though they resembled Italian.

– A song from Naples, my city.

– Neapolitan! Would you let me hear the song again? Please.

With a bemused smile, he complied. He had a very pleasant voice, a light baritone, and seeing my pleasure he sang all the better, the voice, now employed not merely for himself, growing larger, the timbre finding more space.

– Thank you, sir. I like that very much. Can you tell me what the song's words mean?

– They speak of the sea's beauty and the longing of separated lovers.

– How charming.

His name was Francesco Silva. I thought at once of François, my soldier husband, likewise long-limbed and slender. And of Lorenzo too, for his voice was captivating, a voice that took me in its arms.

His tunic had a crackly, not unpleasant smell of gunfire that made me guiltily nostalgic. I could see it had been brushed, just as I noted that his dark hair was pomaded though not sleek, his moustache curled if uneven, his boots polished but discernibly scuffed. These were not the preenings of a dandy but a man's attempt to restore himself in the respite from warding off catastrophe. Though it bore the features of the Mediterranean type, the olive colouring, the full and sensual lineaments, his face was not a common one. It had an irregularity of structure that added to its fascination, and the eyes were a surprising green. As they began to study me I felt their seriousness. His demeanour, and the singing, suggested a will to override what was perhaps a natural melancholy by a seizing of life's immediate joys.

– Signora, this may strike you as impertinent; we are unacquainted, but in a war the claims of propriety lose precedence. Will you dine with me? There is fish and polenta still to be had at the Danieli.

Because of its comforts in one of Venice's safer areas, furthest from the range of enemy artillery, the Hotel Danieli was a refuge for the rich. Major Francesco Silva had sampled the menu on other occasions, but never, he said, in such delightful company.

In a city seething with death, fear and the pride of the unconquered, what happened between myself and Major Silva was the most natural of events: a sweet spasm of desire to live and feel to the utmost. Charmed by the sheer luck of having met, wanting our distraction from hell to be heaven, each of us invented this carnal passion as love and locked ourselves into a spell. Our separation next morning was intense with the ache of suffering and pleasure.

The following night we met again, and the one after, each time in the same room at the Danieli overlooking the starlit *bacino*.

– Sing for me, Francesco.

Each time the guns grew quieter, as we lay in our wide, white-canopied bed, I would ask for one of his sad Neapolitan songs. I never told him I was a singer.

On the fourth night he failed to keep our rendezvous. I waited and, towards midnight, there came a knock on the door. A young *facchino* stood there, a sprig of jasmine in his hand.

– Major Silva is detained by his duties. I am to give you this.

He handed me the jasmine with a note.

My dearest,

We are all needed here tonight and, with a heavy heart, I must forego our meeting. I shall send word as soon as I am free to be with you. Until then, may God protect you...

Sleeping only for an hour or two, I stayed in that bed we had shared. I left the jasmine behind, wanting to recall its perfume in that room rather than take it with me.

I never heard from Francesco again, never knew what became of him. He might have been killed. He might, for all I knew, have had a wife. I preferred to believe the latter, for, sad though I was, my heart was not broken. It had experienced a happiness unalloyed by any sequel.

August 1849. All hope of help was gone.

Two gondolas with white flags left the Riva. All the way along the Giudecca Canal, great crowds on the Zattere shouted as they watched them pass.

– Viva Venezia! Viva Venezia!

These roars resounded all the more gloriously for the sudden silence our surrender imposed on the Austrian cannons.

Days later, forty leaders of the crushed Republic sailed into exile. I stayed. Exile would claim me soon enough, as always. In the Piazza, by Austrian edict, the patriotic currency of Manin's provisional government went up in smoke. Crowds watched these bonfires of millions of lire. The city's resources had dwindled and even more beggars filled the streets. The very rich returned and Europe's outcast royalty washed up in the palazzi along the Grand Canal, clutching at their hopes of resurrection. I despised them. They seemed old beyond my own living. They inhabited the sarcophagi of deadened regimes.

But one more time I entered the palazzo with *Non Nobis* inscribed on its facade. The Duchesse de Berry owned it now and gave lavish parties. I danced again in that candle-starred ballroom, where the mirrors were dimmer than before, doing waltzes and polkas all night long, losing myself in the ecstasy of movement. As the sun rose I was suddenly overcome with nausea.

I had to leave Venice.

My son was born in March 1850, in the countryside not far from Padua, at a small house I had rented and gone to live in five months earlier. I called him Francesco, since that name was the only thing of his father's that I had to give to him. Dorotea was with me at the birth and her joy was like that of a grandmother. No news of her own son ever came.

23

Languor set the pace of walkers, their meetings and partings prolonged by lazy talk, sound clinging to the warmer air. A seasonal
adjustment was underway.

He had a dutiful impulse to buy *La Repubblica*, but a newspaper was
a test of how much you were at home in a foreign culture, how well
acquainted with its shorthands, its trivia. So he bought a day-old copy
of the *Guardian* from the news stand near the church of San Giovanni
Crisostomo, where he'd been to look at the Bellini.

With the gnarled trunk of a fig tree as his desk, St Jerome sat on
a rock translating the Scriptures; behind him a sky of smoky pink
clouds blotted up the sunset, tingeing the green of the fig leaves and
rendering the saint's beard fluffy with its light. In the foreground,
occupying quite a different space, two other saints daydreamed with
sober dignity, framing Jerome like a shared think bubble, Paul fancied, enchanted by the painting's balancing of incongruities. It put
him in good humour.

Eyes on the London headlines, he walked away from the church, in
the opposite direction from Rialto.

After two days without contact, Eva had dropped in unannounced
as he was reading under the pergola. On the table she placed a green
plastic folder labelled 'Maguire'. He thanked her, offered coffee, which
she declined, and asked if he might walk back with her. She suggested
a quick tour of her neighbourhood, starting with Tintoretto's house.

He liked the chipped bricks and worn shutters, the dimmed stone
of the finely pointed arches, preferred these marks of age to the fakery
of restoration, but questioned whether it shouldn't have been better
maintained.

– It's not a monument. People still live there; it predates Tintoretto's
birth but, as you can see, 15th-century houses are no rarity here, and
some are neglected.

She pointed out reliefs and engravings on the buildings they passed,

until they found themselves on Strada Nuova, a plain wide thorough-
fare lined with shops.

– I don't care for Strada Nuova. But I'm meeting a friend and I
should do some errands first. Why not come with me as far as Rialto?
There's a church you should see on the way, with a wonderful Bellini
altarpiece.

The church was closed; their ways parted.

She had come to him and he felt oddly resistant. Later, he rang
and invited her to dinner the next night. Now he retraced their route
along the ugly Strada Nuova, then winding back and forth across the
three long canals to the north of it.

Two bridges beyond the 15th-century palazzo where Eva had half
of the *piano nobile* – in better condition than Tintoretto's more modest
former home – he settled down at a canalside café to read the *Guardian*
with a cappuccino. How remote the world had become. This city
resembled a womb. Or maybe he was lotus-eating, spellbound?

He turned to the Steve Bell cartoon.

Yet, he concluded, reverting at once to his own train of thought,
indolence was no mere Venetian malaise; didn't middle age have
much to do with it?

Reading about 1848 in Venice, he had half expected the infant
Esme Maguire to make her appearance. She was born in Paris, the city
aligned with his own image of that year. There was little use in mentioning these things to Eva.

All that is solid melts into air, all that is sacred is profane... He
thought of those words from 1848, their reverberations in his youth,
in 1968, another year for rocking hierarchies, repudiating tyrants. He
still wanted the world to change, but often had a sense of no longer
belonging in the present.

He returned to the *Guardian*. A cheerful hello interrupted his
perusal of the letters page. He looked up to see the young woman they
had met at the opera.

– Hello there. It's...

Her name escaped him.

– Annie. And you're Paul, aren't you? How are you enjoying
Venice?

She carried bulging shopping bags and looked flustered from the heat.

– Very much. Do you live in this area?

– Yes, in the Ghetto. Our flat is tiny, but we have a terrace and that's bliss.

– Would you like to join me for coffee?

– I'd love to but I must get back. Do come and visit us. How long will you be here?

– Two more days.

– That's a shame… but Eva could bring you for a drink, tonight maybe.

– I'll be seeing her for dinner.

Something had been on his mind. Annie might be of help.

– I'd like to ask your advice about choosing a present for Eva, as a thank you. You must know her tastes better than me.

Annie looked unsure; he waited. It had to be less personal than a gift between lovers. At least, not that in any obvious way.

– I didn't mean right now. We could maybe talk on the phone.

– Okay. I'll have a think. Ring me, I'm in until four, then I'm teaching an English lesson.

She jotted down the number and hurried off, turning to give a friendly wave when she reached the bridge that led into the Ghetto.

Soon he followed. It didn't take him long to grasp how small the Ghetto was; by necessity, growth had been upward, producing the city's highest inhabited buildings. He came across the synagogues and a snaking line of Americans on a guided tour. There were commemorative plaques, listing names and deportations. He felt unprepared for the weight of these surroundings.

He retraced his steps across the *campo*, relieved by its openness.

They were in the dark and he caught her hand. She led him along the narrow alley and he fought a desire to pull her back, keep her body imprisoned in this tight, over-arched corridor while he embraced it.

Sexual impulse did not get the better of his self-possession. Out in the lamplight, along the canalside where the restaurant sign glimmered ahead of them, doubts caught up with him. He reran a script in his head that insisted on his foolishness for being here, entangled in an affair with no future, which subsumed the purpose of his trip. He was glad of the restaurant's bright-lit interior. He'd had a surfeit of Venice's dark romance.

– You said you went back to the church with the Bellini. What did you think of the painting?

– Terrific.

– Isn't it! The colour, the way he used space – all those different planes he creates. I love Bellini's altarpieces. You ought to see the rest… then there's a Tiepolo…

– I've only two days left. And I didn't come to sightsee… though of course I'm glad I've seen all these things. Thanks to you.

– Two days? But you'll come back, won't you?

He smiled.

– By the way, I ran into Annie. She invited us for a drink before I leave. Nice of her.

She swallowed some wine, looking preoccupied.

– Yes, you'd like their flat; there's a great view.

From her forced tone, he surmised that she preferred to keep her friends separate from what happened with him.

Their talk returned to painters, and the conversation didn't flag, but it stayed cool.

He told her about his earlier thoughts, his sense of being alien to the present.

– Yes, I've felt that. The young take over, the agenda gets set afresh, so it matters to value your own experience. You have insights and memories to guide you. I'm sure you encourage your students to think for themselves.

– I try. For the young it's hard to understand what shaped the world we have now; that this wasn't inevitable.

Her rapt gaze made him aware of the intensity in his voice. She had lost sight of herself. It was rare, this slipping of her guard. Then her eyes lowered and she toyed with the ring on her right middle finger; gold, with a gem inset, a sapphire, he thought. When she spoke, he heard a familiar briskness.

– But *you* must always have seen that. Why else would you have become a historian?

– I'm not saying the young are ignorant of history, or incurious. Change is the flow of life. Anyway, ignorance is a gift when you're young. Your hopes are still unshaken… and you're fearless.

He paused.

– I went to the Ghetto today. It disturbed me and I didn't want to linger. Maybe because I ran into a tour group and it felt like a museum. Yet I realise that people live in it, the place has a present.

– When I walk through the Ghetto I always remember that people were confined there, shut in every night, until Napoleon arrived.

– And now you have young friends there.

– On the sixth floor, without a lift. Do you still want to visit them?

They laughed.

Later, at her flat, she held out her wrist for him to unfasten a bracelet. He placed it beside the rest: the thin gold necklace he had seen for the first time that evening, the coral earrings she often wore, her watch, her rings. Perhaps she had done this before, more discreetly. No, he recalled now, as he stroked her arms, felt how slender her wrists were, freed from their clasps, she was different. He touched her throat, kissed it. Her unadorned body made her younger, a less worldly lover.

She asked him not to stay. She needed sleep.

Watching as he dressed, she let out a sigh.

– I'm feeling guilty.

– About what?

– There's something I haven't told you. It doesn't mean much but you might attach importance to it. I know you're mistrustful of me.

He gasped in mock astonishment.

– In my early teens I had singing lessons. My teacher was an old lady who had been taught by Esme Maguire. That's all. Well, perhaps not all, since it was one of the things that set off Joe's interest in her.

He went on buttoning his shirt, while a thrill of anger passed through him, and excitement. Yet again, he was being tantalised.

There they were: he with his back to her, she naked in bed, reclining against a blue pillow. He contained his agitation, reasoned with himself, concentrated on the laces of his tan canvas shoes, tugging, looping, knotting, tightening, struggling to think. Perhaps it didn't mean much, but withheld until now it meant more. He turned, affecting coolness.

– That's interesting. Perhaps you'll tell me about it. Lunch tomorrow? No, why don't I cook you dinner?

Although she had never voiced it, he knew her reluctance to share his bed at the house. And what did it matter? He was leaving anyway.

– Come here instead. I'll cook for you.

– Fine.

His kiss was meant to bruise her lips. What passion, she said, and he thought he heard derision in her voice. As he closed the bedroom door behind him, a thunderclap sounded and rain crashed down. A metal funnel in the hall held assorted umbrellas. He picked out the largest of these, black with a brown leather handle, pulled the flat door to and ran down the stone steps in an adrenalin burst fuelled by fury. Outside, the heavens had opened.

The storm suited his mood. He opened the umbrella and a scrap of paper flew out. Snatching it from the wet, he paused to read its brief scrawled message, put it in his pocket and walked on.

Amore,

Sono passato stamattina, ma non ti ho trovata. Ti telefono dopo.

24

Verdi wore a rumpled frock coat. The hair above his left ear was unsmoothed and his thick beard needed trimming. I had a notion that underneath it he smiled, but something in his look confused this impression.

– Can a photograph be trusted?

Nadar pursed his lips, his eyes twinkling at my question's naïveté.

– It all depends, Esme, on what you expect from it. How much do you trust a face you do not know?

I looked around his studio. For the first time I inspected the other portraits crowding the walls with their fame, the faces quite distinct. The elderly George Sand, a mask of equanimity, all the turbulence of love with Chopin and de Musset locked inside that head with its tight tiers of crimping; Berlioz hieratic; Papa Corot genial and reserved; Courbet a pyramid-shaped rock, every line of his figure and broad countenance expressing mass and weight. These illustrious men and women were arrestingly singular. Had they not intimidated me I would surely have faced them sooner. A few were known to me in the flesh, but only on passing acquaintance. Sometimes here, in this very room. Not Verdi, of whom I had only distant memories, from another life.

– It's some instinctive sense of the person I go by: through looks, movement, speech. The voice always matters.

– It's your instrument, Esme.

– Yes, though the ear can be deceived. What I mean is how personality and physiognomy combine to convey impressions. A fixed image can't do that. Your portraits are images, yet they appear truer to my eyes than any other photographs I've seen, indeed they strike me as so startlingly true as to compel some degree of mistrust. We are all various, in our character and moods, our virtues and our failings, yet your camera takes one mere moment of being and brings it alive as the person.

His laugh was full-throated and generous, like the man. It put me more at ease with the rest of the company I was in. Placing a light hand on my arm, he guided me back to Verdi.

– You're right; there's limitation. But the photograph can add to our perception. You have told me you met Verdi on two different occasions. Look your fill now and see if you detect any feature you missed. See if my portrait has caught something new. I've a matter to attend to.

Alone, freed from inhibition by Nadar's invitation to scrutinise his work, I began to enjoy this gallery of the great.

I was long used to portraits done in oils or pastels, which were slowly given form by the artist's hand and brain, destined to be seen as his (or hers), as well as a picturing of their subject. These instead, so wholly transcribed from reality, proclaimed their own being. They spoke too directly, disconcerting me, as would the characters in a novel were they to step off the pages and live. Something else was disturbing: the knowledge of recognition thus sealed in a face forever. They made the past present.

Verdi's expression was sardonic, I decided, rather than good-humoured. I recalled that the great maestro easily took offence, that he nursed old grievances even through his years of success. He had a look of neatness thwarted, of unruly energies ill-contained. His hands were at odds with one another, the right forefinger pointing down from a set of curled knuckles, the left thumb elongated and straining wide to shape a dark cleft. His face, I saw, was divided in two, with the eye in the light sombre, the other, shadowed, on the verge of being amused. Was this what Nadar had meant: these small insights vouchsafed by the camera?

I ventured the question when he returned. He shrugged.

– Perhaps. The camera captures everything it sees; the naked eye cannot. Movement conceals the nuance of gesture, hiding what stillness might disclose. It might interest you to know that Verdi preferred this portrait above all others.

– Why? Did he think he saw himself in it? His truest self?

– Or else the self he liked best.

My preoccupation with the portrait drew me into a reverie.

Verdi had suffered many griefs: a young wife and children dead, the early public failure of his music before at last it gave breath to Italy's struggle for freedom and independence. And after all those years of turbulence he entered its Chamber of Deputies.

Remembering his operas, I saw a procession of women rich in life, filled with passion, but punished by cruel deaths: poor Gilda, I felt, poor Leonora, poor Desdemona, poor Violetta… Yet, in the song of their pain and their dramas these heroines exert the power to carry us inside ourselves, letting us feel the tortures of loss and injustice to which we even may be blind. Is it our own undoing we see, our never-ending sacrifice, our ill-formed trust in a world of men's making? Verdi shows us this, so do Bellini and Donizetti: poor Lucia, driven mad, poor Norma on the pyre, poor Scottish Queen who had her head cut off. The music that tears at our hearts so truthfully and unbearably, the truth of what men are allowed to do to us. Do men perceive it?

These thoughts saddened me. I turned away.

How might I judge the man beside me by his portrait? One hung near us, of him in middle age, his eyes the salient feature, confronting the camera so that he appeared to reverse his function as the subject on view. I asked him what he was looking at so hard.

– I think… at those in the future who will one day look at me.

I liked this answer. It matched the speaker and his eagerness for progress. He was around 60 and, though portly, retained a boyish vigour of movement and expression. He had lived a multiplicity of lives, and doubtless he anticipated more. Nadar's far-sightedness was comforting. A modern magus, energetically wise. The coming world and many of its changes were set within his sights. His extravagant projects made some regard him as a madman. But he reminded me of others I had known, and time had proved them to be cautious in their visions of the future.

Nadar was extravagant in everything. I realised this when seeing for the first time the building that housed his famous studio on the Boulevard des Capucines. I looked up and saw a large N, then an A, his whole signature across the centre of its red-framed glass frontage. Everyone knew about his ballooning adventures, and the readers of

From the Earth to the Moon had met his incarnation as Michel Ardan in this novel by Jules Verne.

– Nadar, they will indeed look at you, and they will marvel at your genius. They will thank you for allowing them to know all these glorious faces, for giving immortality to La Bernhardt's lovely clever eyes, to Offenbach's smile and Bakunin's beard and Monsieur Baudelaire's...

I was laughing now, aware of how absurd my flattery sounded, ashamed because Nadar had so little need of it. And because I could find nothing at all to say about Baudelaire's appearance. For me it contained the words he had written and no more, though that was saying a great deal.

– Rubbish, ma chère. They will have too much else to marvel at. They'll forget what this means. As we – well, you are too young – have already forgotten. People were stunned then, overwhelmed by this miraculous invention. At first they couldn't believe it: two inventors had perfected a process that could capture an image of reality on a silver plate. We've become so accustomed to the fact of photography that it's impossible now to imagine the enormity of the change it wrought, or the universal bewilderment that greeted its beginning.

– It still bewilders me. When I think of photography I look at the world and have the dizzying perception that all of it can now be copied. There are no more secrets; at least, it's harder to hide what time used to obscure.

Nadar frowned.

– Yes, the camera has already been used to hunt down men and women wanted by the police: the men and women of the Commune. Alas, with photographs they believed taken in innocence. Photographs make fleeting appearances endure, they are proof that something was there. They allow a face in all its exactness to be known the world over. They compel us to see differently, even to remember differently. Never before were these things so, and they make photography the most peculiar and disturbing of all this century's great inventions.

– And flying machines?

Nadar was convinced that machines heavier than air would soon cross oceans. He campaigned for science to direct its efforts towards this.

– Ah! They are still to come, but they will, and who knows where they'll lead.

He was an optimist. What disturbed him also enthused him, in a fearless welcoming of the new. I was ambivalent. Photography frightened me; I believed it could bring about my downfall. Yet I wished with such regret that I could have photographs of those I had loved. Not so much because images would have eased my loss, but because they would be tokens. Proofs, as Nadar had said. I needed those. Whenever remembering caused me to doubt my sanity. Whenever memory failed. I had more than two centuries of memories to cherish and the farthest ones were hazy, slipping out of reach. I had begun to write them down; I needed to tell my lengthening story to myself. As it spread into the future my agelessness would abate, my faculties be blunted, for although I was a marvel I could suffer from the frailties of the body. I saw change in the mirror, the smallest of signs but gradual. And this has sharpened my appetite for life. A day might come when I, as ageing people do, would want a portrait of myself in my prime.

There was one portrait I wished Nadar to make. Not my own, not yet, though he had tried to persuade me, saying I had a strange and interesting face, young but not modern. These very words deterred me. It was my son's photograph I longed for.

Before I left, perhaps sensing my thoughts of photographs and absence, Nadar showed me two portraits hanging side by side.

– These men have been exiles.

Both were exiled for their part in the Commune. One was Jules Vallès, the writer. Nadar had set a great emptiness around him, and he stared at the camera with a tortured, burning look, hands thrust in the pockets of his narrow coat, his clenched jaw jutting out. The other had a name I did not know.

– Élisée Reclus. We went up in the balloon together during the siege of Paris. He's a geographer, and has seen much of the world for himself. After prison, his sentence was perpetual banishment from France. With the amnesty he could have come back, but he chose to stay in Switzerland.

The Commune: what Jules Vallès called the great federation of sadness, the tens of thousands now dead who had taken up arms against 'a poorly made world' to defend a government that opposed the privileges of the bourgeoisie. Their defeat brought massacres, imprisonment and exile.

I looked into the eyes of Élisée Reclus. They were intense and filled with the spaces he must have dreamed of. I thought of our planet's eternal distances, of what was unknown and unknowable. I thought of the eyelashes of the world.

That high-browed open face, so near to mine, made me long to know the man. Histories and fairy tales abound in stories of princes and kings who become enamoured of a woman's painted portrait. What faith in an image that might not be faithful. Now, painting's authority had been found wanting, its substance opaque where the camera was a mirror, reflecting what was past or far away. Here, an absent man was present as if he not only looked at me but spoke, his ardent eyes transmitting a passion that engaged me. And I fell in love with him a little.

Or at least with what he seemed to promise. Even his name was a utopia. While I knew better than to risk my emotions on a fantasy inspired by a photograph, that photograph would stay in my mind.

I hailed a cab on the boulevard and enjoyed the ride to the Opéra-Comique. Omnibuses rattled past, sundry carriages in the English and French styles. All this haste was well accommodated. The Paris of the century's start had been replaced by a wider, more harmonious one, with the long broad vistas of the boulevards opening through its centre. More bridges spanned the Seine. After six months Paris still felt new to me. Baudelaire had been right, cities do indeed change faster than the hearts of mortal beings.

The excitement I found in feeling part of it – I a Parisian – was locked in a tension of doubt and expectation.

My son was 32 and the knowledge that he would soon overtake me in visible years had acted as a spur. For me to see him again, his mother would have to die. In my heart I knew this, despite my plans for her to go on living. Death, the truth, or an out-and-out deception; these were my choices.

With reluctance I had left my son the day after his 16th birthday, fading from his life with the alibi of remote singing engagements, and later giving fragile health as a reason for not travelling to see him. Knowing I had a son alive and well had sustained me in those years of separation and I had written to him often. I had put off two proposed visits with my perennial excuse: a doctor's ban on visitors, a strict regime of treatments. Seawater was one of these, so I had taken a house in Dieppe. It was from there that Esme Maguire posted a letter to Francesco asking him to visit his mother on a matter of family business. Whether Esme or Edita Molini would receive him, I had yet to decide.

– My father was Irish.

To stop it from trembling, he pressed his right hand on the walnut table, but the fingers sprang up again. The hands were broad, though those fingers tapered delicately. Whose hands were they, so capable-seeming and so ready to betray him? Perhaps he felt my gaze an impertinence, for his lowered eyes snapped open in a puzzled glare.

– Drink some of this, you'll feel better.

He jerked the glass aside with his knuckles, then, after drumming them on the small pile of volumes stacked on the table, he raised the cognac to his mouth and drank it in one swallow. I lifted the bottle and he held out the glass. The smell alone was enough to intoxicate me. I gasped. He cast me a quick, indifferent look. I felt sick with guilt and regret, fearful that his anger would lead to rejection. I yearned to apologise, to fold him in my arms and console him, to tell him everything and plead for his understanding. I was drowning in my deception.

– It's best if I leave you alone. I'll be in the drawing room.

– Yes, do go.

The tone was impatient. I closed the study door behind me.

I looked past the white slopes of the dust sheets covering the heavy sofas and armchairs, over the grand piano and spread across the floor, and sought relief in the landscape framed by the windows. Past the beech trees at the end of the garden, past the tangle of blackberry bushes and the undergrowth where I had picked juniper and wild strawberries, on the far side of a pasture in descent, a band of slate-coloured sea was visible. I tried to take my thoughts there, striving for distance from my muddled emotions. Yet nothing could ease the sense that I had made a terrible mistake for which there was no remedy.

Now I heard him howling. The sound was not loud, it remained a private suffering, reaching my ears only because in extremis my waning gift of the senses would return. And in extremis such as this, the gift became a punishment. One well deserved. In his eyes I was a phantom of his dead mother, an irreconcilable creature whose existence could only hurt him.

I sat down at the piano and threw back the dust cover. But there are times when music has to be refused. Better to listen to him.

I turned. He hesitated in the doorway, his face streaked with tears.

– Francesco…

– Do you sing?

– Yes. I have inherited her voice. I sing at the Opéra-Comique.

– Of course, everything about you is as she was. Why did she never tell me I had a sister? Did you know of me?

– I knew only a few years ago, and it was as if we could not see you, as if there were some impediment. It was hard to imagine you as real. Had I known sooner, had I even seen a photograph, my curiosity would have been stronger.

– Why did she hide so much from me?

– Perhaps fearing you would judge her. Other people did.

– Why did you not send for me before she died?

– Please try to understand. I didn't know what to do.

His demeanour became milder. He slumped into one of the white-sheeted armchairs, a long black figure like a dark bird fallen on snow. The Hotel Danieli came to mind, a white-canopied bed two floors above the Riva. I looked and saw his father in everything but the eyes, which were mine. I had left a boy of 16, and for the first time in over three decades, I saw an image of the man with whom I had conceived him. I began weeping and had to run from the room.

The next morning we took the path down to the sea and walked along the beach.

Because of my distraction, the tide almost caught us and we hurried to reach the cliff steps. I was ill shod for the pebbled shore and I stumbled. He took my arm. Our feet were wet to the ankles and we were out of breath when we began the climb, but we both felt the better for this small adventure. The sea air, the exercise and the faint threat of danger had rallied our spirits, while the emptiness and imminent closure of the house inclined us to intimacy. We took coffee and I showed him a daguerreotype of a smiling man in a travelling coat.

– He had red hair. His name was Michael Maguire.

This innocent imposter had appeared to me among a jumble of bric-a-brac at Monsieur Solomon's curio shop in the Marais. He had an appealingly humorous face and made a convincing Irishman, so I adopted him for judicious use as a parent.

– They separated when I was two and I stayed with him and an aunt in Trieste, my aunt Constance. Con, he called her. She was always good to me but she never forgave my mother for leaving. I was 19 when my mother sought me out again, on her way to Prague where she had a singing engagement. By then I understood something of what moved her to abandon me, thanks to my father, who wished me to think well of her. He blamed himself for everything; the disaster of their marriage, his failed attempt to keep her by refusing to surrender me.

I stopped abruptly, disturbed by the fluency of my lies. Accustomed as I was to deceiving strangers from necessity, I could invent a past life with a certain conviction – and sometimes envied the self I claimed to be. However, this elaborate pretence had my son as its object and victim. Moreover, this story of mine would belong inside his. My fabrications courted trouble.

Francesco was bound to ask questions: the time and manner of her death, her place of burial, the life she led and those who knew her. For these I had made some provision, but I risked becoming embroiled in a complicated yarn that might entail contradictory answers or reveal too much. My tongue was running away from the slender fiction I had devised.

I watched him. I saw his hands shaking as he held the fictive daguerreotype, and his mouth began to tremble. I marvelled at the volatile transparency of his emotions.

– My dear Francesco, we must leave soon. A carriage is on its way.

For the first time, I dared to embrace him, kissing his brow. He accepted this affection gladly, and the embrace he gave me in return was so prolonged that I feared he might forget that I was not his mother and that I in turn would remember too well that I was.

Once again, I was grateful for the tonic sea air. Dieppe was famous for it.

Before our appointment with the notary we walked down the rue de la Barre, the town's backbone, running most of its length from the well at the Tribunaux café as far as the harbour. In a small square nearby, adorned with five trim lime trees, I showed him the church of Saint Remy where I would go to hear Saint-Saëns playing the organ.

– Can you believe that I have been his Delilah?

– Will you sing it again before I leave for Italy?

– No. That was in Germany. The Bible is too sacred for the Paris stage. But you will, I hope, hear me sing, though in a different kind of role.

We had lunch in a restaurant under the arcades of the Quai Duquesne. Oysters, turbot, rack of lamb, a creamy bavaroise and some petits fours with our coffee. I was pleased that he had his father's relish for good food and stopped myself in time from remarking that he had kept his sweet tooth. As he talked about his life, his work as a chemist, his love of music and his forthcoming marriage, I confined myself to listening. I was sorely tempted to prompt his reminiscences of childhood with me, but foresaw the pitfalls. All through this meal I found myself smiling: my son here, across the table; for years I had dreamed of him, ached for just a day in his company, and never known how to bring it about.

On the matter of inheritance, our visit to the notary was a charade. Everything had been done, and most of it by proxy, prior to the 'death' of Edita Molini: the deed assigning the house in the Rio dei Pensieri to Francesco, with the proviso that it never be sold, that on his death it revert to the Trieste side of the family; the money, not a vast sum, but a respectable wedding present.

– And you, Esme, what do you inherit?

We were passing the harbour on our way to the station. The sun had come out and gulls wheeled through the high afternoon light as if bent on measuring the sky. I had a fierce pang of sorrow at leaving, my fondness for this seafaring town now blighted by the knowledge that the hours here with Francesco would never be repeated. I spoke without thinking.

– You.

He frowned.

– And I inherit you. But surely our mother left you some legacy. Your house in Paris? The one here?

– Both rented. She arranged a small income for me before she died. And I have the voice.

On the train I used great efforts of persuasion to keep Francesco with me longer. It was his first visit to Paris. By the time we reached the Gare Saint-Lazare he had agreed to stay as my guest for a week.

– There is someone I want you to meet. I want him to help me in making you a gift, which will also be a gift to myself. He is the greatest portraitist ever to wield a camera.

Nadar raised the spectacles attached to a dove-grey ribbon and assessed the resemblance between us. I had told him nothing, merely made introductions, wanting to witness his powers of observation. First he looked into my eyes, then Francesco's.

– What do you see, Nadar?

– I see two people with the same eyes. Are they related?

– Only the eyes? Is nothing else the same?

– Perhaps the answer can be found in a photograph. Is that what you've come for, Esme?

– I thought it might be too late. I know you rarely take on commissions now.

It was true, but he made an exception for us. His supposition that we wished to be photographed together made me nervous. Nadar turned to Francesco and spoke in halting Italian.

– She refuses to let me make her portrait. Can you change her mind?

– I doubt it, sir. My sister has me under her thumb.

He laughed, while I protested, secretly delighted.

– One thing I ask is for his hands to be seen. He has fine and interesting hands. So many of the gentlemen in your portraits have their hands tucked inside their waistcoats and pockets. Even Maestro Rossini.

My tone was unintentionally accusing.

– If you have him stand like Verdi instead, I'll see more of him. I should like nothing to be left out, not even his feet.

In my agitation I avoided Nadar's glance. Too late, I faced a rebuke.

– Don't fuss, Esme. If you wish to stay, sit over there. There is a tray with some cordial, or I can ring for something stronger. As you might observe, feet play no part in my portraits.

I became meek and watched the proceedings from a distance. In my wish to own a total image of my son, presumption had got the better of me. My manner was sometimes at odds with the age I displayed.

Francesco was being charmed and reconnoitred. I couldn't hear the low-voiced conversation, although my extra-sharp ears strained hard. Was it, I wondered, a matter of being deafened by Nadar's will? I had never clashed with him before. I noticed that his feet were large.

He made adjustments to the tripod and ducked several times under the thick black cloth behind his heavy contraption. He slid the square plate inside it then returned to where Francesco sat on a chair with faded damask upholstery, next to a pedestal table on which lay what I knew were volumes by the poet friends of his youth. He took one of Francesco's hands, setting it on the arm of the chair and bending to speak. He smiled, then fetched another piece of his paraphernalia. He came back and ducked under the cloth again. I was startled by a burst of artificial light. So was Francesco. After that the whole process began again. My eyes wandered across the famous faces on the walls.

Rossini filled up the frame of his portrait with his capacious form and strong features, a sensual man even in old age – I remembered those shrewdly veiled eyes. His very own Rosina, Adelina Patti, was there too. I had never met her, nor was I likely to; she sang at Covent Garden. In keeping with the small, pure voice I had heard much talk of, her face was girlish and her figure, cloaked in fur-trimmed velvet, slight and unassuming. This modestly shrinking appearance belied much else I had heard, including the size of her income. Perhaps she has always stayed a child prodigy, one more highly paid than any adult soprano. When I let my gaze linger on Élisée Reclus I felt kinder, less envious.

I needed to sing, but the more time went by the less I wished to be noticed, and this had become a world in which faces were everywhere.

The day after Francesco's portrait session, he came to hear me at the Opéra-Comique. I sang the title role in Offenbach's *La Périchole*, an operetta of masquerades in which La Périchole, a street singer, has a husband foisted on her so that she can take a place at court as a Spanish viceroy's mistress. Poverty has compelled her to accept. By the time she meets her bridegroom she is the worse for drink and in no condition to recognise him as her lover, whom she has reluctantly abandoned.

Ah! quel dîner je viens de faire!
Et quel vin extraordinaire…

As I sang this aria, laughing tipsily and deliberately slurring the words, the image of Francesco, my son, merged with the memory of Francesco, his father, a fuzzy picture in which a swaying chandelier shed its brilliance on a table laden with food and wine.

In the interval, Francesco congratulated me on my performance. He smiled so much that I could see his admiration was genuine. But on our way to supper, I could tell he did not like the music. Both its light satirical style and its subject were alien to him.

– It is not the kind of opera my… our mother would have sung.

I agreed with him.

– This is a different world from hers.

– Alas, it is.

The moment I heard the sadness in his voice, my son seemed older than me. He was an Italian from Venice and I a Parisian, perhaps what explained this impression. Sensibility prevailed, and mine was newer.

Some years later, I sang in a revived production of Offenbach's *Tales of Hoffmann*. I asked myself whether he would have liked it better and what he would have thought of me in the roles of Olympia, Antonia, Giulietta and Stella, different characters in the mouth of the same singer. In this opera, with its melancholy Venetian barcarole, I found echoes of myself.

As the train taking Francesco away from me steamed out of the Gare d'Austerlitz, I wished him happiness and a long life, though the latter might keep me from Venice for a while. In his luggage he carried a copy of Nadar's portrait. I had another, silver-framed, in my drawing room.

He leaned forward slightly from the chair back, elbows resting on the padded arms. His hands lay in front of him, not quite joined, the thumb and forefinger of the right one merely holding the left forefinger, a characteristic gesture. His head was inclined and in his eyes the hint of a question sought expression. What I had taken for hesitancy, here became arrested in a deep and serious thoughtfulness. My son was a man for whom movement was never sweeping and broad, rarely fast or careless; it was well-judged, of infinite delicacy. Had the camera been able to register a tremor, it would have been true to his sensitivity. His hands could be steady too, needed to be, for precise scientific procedures.

His lips were slightly parted, not forming speech, but in the act of listening. His lower lip drooped in its fullness, a reminder of his father's sensuality. His whole face was gentle, yet taut with that dawning question in his eyes. I had seen the passion in him, it was there all the time, giving him a feminine, uncontrolled edge accentuated by his grace. His height and slender figure emerged from the portrait's proportions and scale, while the blue of his eyes and the black of his hair might never be guessed at.

I could hold this image to my cheek as a talisman. It was not enough but it gave me solace.

25

He needed to clear his head. Walking to the far end of the *rio,* he encountered a high brick enclosure with a watchtower at its corner and a uniformed man standing guard. The unexpected sight of a prison made him shudder; it jarred with his sense of this city.

A turning led him away from it, to a wooden bridge, which he crossed. He measured what he could rely on: Maguire was no fiction, but a once living person with published evidence to prove it. If Eva really hadn't read the papers, she was blameless. The scripts might well have put her off: the fading and sometimes illegible handwriting he could decipher only through a magnifying glass.

Alongside her little revelation, he considered the unsettling note that had fallen out of the umbrella. He rehearsed its words in his head: *My love, I dropped by this morning but didn't find you at home. I'll telephone later.* Should this mean an affair between Eva and another man, jealousy wasn't an issue, he told himself, but it made her actions underhand and shabby. It inflated his other suspicions.

The writer had to be the man he'd glimpsed from Eva's window.

He cut along the next *rio.* The Venice of 1848 had taken him back to the libraries. One revolutionary hotbed, the tobacco factory, was here, just around the corner from the Rio dei Pensieri. The building still stood, long-fronted, with a high red-brick chimney stack, little altered from its 19th-century appearance in the illustrations. In 1848 it had a workforce of 700, mostly female. Picturing young Carmen-like firebrands raising the red flag, he checked himself against confecting melodrama from a human struggle with truly high stakes. Life surpasses opera in its extremes of feeling and experience.

At the house, in his room, the sight of the gift calmed him. It had been a relief to spend so much money, obligations well met. It sat on luxuriant display among his notebooks, a splash of exquisite wrapping paper. A parting gift, and maybe for the best. From London things would look different.

Maybe.

Anxious to discharge some of the turmoil in his mind, he picked up the phone.

– I don't want any awkwardness between us tonight, but I've got some questions about the papers.

Tact was essential.

– I've read everything. Esme Maguire isn't named until the last instalment. Can I ask where this is going?

– That's it. I've nothing more to give you.

He had counted on another wad of papers. Disappointment, a surprising emotion in the circumstances, disarmed him. Could she be referring to their relationship? Surely she'd mentioned more material to come. He phrased his next question carefully.

– You mean there are no more papers for me to read?

– I've searched Joe's opera archive and that's the lot.

He thought quickly.

– You wouldn't let me go through it myself? There might be things you've overlooked.

Silence.

– Eva?

– I've told you, Paul, there's too much that's personal among those papers.

– But you spoke about Joe's opera archive. I wouldn't be looking at anything else.

– No, all the same. Joe made notes, personal stuff about singers he'd met.

– Of course.

– See you later then.

So that was that. The Maguire papers amounted to no more than a wild story about a woman who doesn't age. Concocted by Joe? Or Eva herself? That had become the real Maguire mystery. Maguire was real, he reminded himself; she had lived and had certainly sung at the Opéra-Comique. He surveyed possible scenarios. Joe Lensky had inherited this house; he was descended from Maguire, or maybe Eva was. Another: Eva had already sold the real papers and had been stringing him along. A third: Eva was innocent of deception and

Maguire's tall tales were a figment of madness (the oblivion of insanity would explain her near-erasure from opera history).

By the time he reached Eva's flat, flowers in his hand, the fragile gift in a carrier bag slung from his arm, his face was grimy with tiredness. The previous night he had slept little and he'd consumed his remnant of energy in fretful, feverish activity.

– You didn't have to, but I'm very pleased. And the tulips are lovely. White will go well with it.

Tracing a finger across the rippling cobalt of the glass, she glowed with pleasure.

– Blue's your colour, isn't it? It's those eyes of yours. I've never seen a blue so striking.

She accepted this with shyness, clearly touched by the Venini vase.

– How did you know I like these so much?

– I had some help. Venini was a discovery to me, thanks to your young friend Annie.

He watched her face for a reaction. It was serene.

– When I ran into her the other day, I asked for advice.

– She knows my tastes. I'll put the flowers in it then I'll get us a drink.

With his first glass of Prosecco, Paul wilted. Exhaustion robbed him of questions. He listened, let Eva play hostess, pamper him, leave him to admire the simple luxury of white tulips in a blue vase.

– You look shattered. Put your feet up, have another cushion. We'll eat soon, that'll perk you up. It's guinea fowl. I remembered you liked it.

– When did I say that?

– Last night, in the restaurant. They had none left when you tried to order it.

– How good of you to remember.

He complimented her on the guinea fowl and ate heartily. Once revived, he tackled his first puzzle.

– Tell me about your singing teacher. I'm amazed to be in the company of one of Maguire's descendants. That's how I think of you now.

He felt fraudulent.

– I wouldn't say that. Madame Ramirez was very old, 80 at least, a Frenchwoman, the widow of a Mexican. She had lessons from Maguire in her early twenties, so there was a long gap between me and your heroine.

– But your teacher must have talked about her.

Eva shook her head.

– Maguire wasn't famous. My teacher was an old lady prattling on about someone entirely forgotten. I'm sorry it isn't more meaningful. That's why I never mentioned it.

– Eva, tell me the truth, have you read the papers? Any of them?

After a long pause she gave him a reproachful look.

– I've glanced at some of them, yes.

At last.

– Could Esme Maguire really have believed she'd lived for 200 years?

– Is it so impossible? Scientists are working on it now, with serious research money. I read an article the other day; they've calculated that some of the oldest people living now have reached the point where they've stopped ageing. But by then the body's too worn out to cope with illnesses or broken bones. If there's a way of halting the ageing process much earlier, everything can change. It's not a fantasy; it's progress. Suppose somebody stumbled on an answer years ago? I mean, the Romans got there first with central heating and Leonardo designed almost workable flying machines. There were plenty of alchemists looking for elixirs.

The argument was rational in its contrariness. It startled him, even as he detected a hint of irony.

– What do you think of the gaps in this strange story? So many years unaccounted for.

– Aren't there gaps in all our lives? Things always stand out from the past. Don't we best remember the turning points... the peaks of happiness or the things that break our hearts?

He assessed the passionate tone of voice and the steady eyes of the speaker. It attracted him, but he didn't want to engage with it. Instead, he returned to the singing teacher.

– Did your Madame Ramirez ever talk about other figures from that period – say political or literary notables? Reclus, for instance!

– You're asking about conversations decades ago, when I was very young.

Her manner had altered, become a touch exasperated. He smiled appeasement and it worked.

– The night is young, Paul. Let's have another drink.

Drinking was always easy. But his days in Venice had got drier: less whisky, at any rate. Sometimes the cocktail hour slid past without him noticing. The cocktail hour, what Chris always called it. Relieved to be back on the easy ground of flirtation, he let Eva fill his glass. His last night with her.

A night of food, wine, candlelight, a beaming moon outside. Nothing unrequited, no troubling emotions to cloud their pleasures.

In this spirit he picked up his jacket, discarded on the blue sofa, and fished out the note. He would make light of it.

– By the way, this fell out of the umbrella I borrowed last night. It must have been meant for you.

She glanced at it, recognition provoking a mischievous smile.

– And you read it?

– Of course.

She waited.

– And I surmised it was from a lover.

He made the statement unequivocally benign. Eva burst out laughing.

– What made you think that?

– The way it begins. *Amore*. Love, or My love.

– It can mean that, though in Venice people use it as a general term of affection. Even between men, without anything sexual or romantic. Listen to the boatmen, those great macho brutes, and you'll hear them…

He raised an eyebrow.

– Eva, you must think I'm gullible.

– Not at all. You insist on knowing everything, but I think *you* have secrets.

He laughed.

– Not me.

– Well, be more trusting.

– All right. It's not from a lover.

– No, it's not! It's from Nanni, an old friend who is happily married. You've met his son, Girolamo. Nanni said he'd left a note the other morning, but I couldn't find it. He wanted to recommend a builder for the repairs at Rio dei Pensieri. Maybe I mentioned the guttering to you. You weren't jealous, I hope.

– It's none of my business if you have other lovers.

– Good. I'd like to make the most of the one I have tonight.

For hours the conversations of intimacy, mind and body, kept them awake. Physical passion relaxed into talk.

She spoke about being a nomad, following husbands.

– Living in one language makes me forget things I knew in another. The obvious things, the titles of books and films and people's names, but also perceptions that run deeper. My memory's like an overfull suitcase: layers and layers of stuff. Nomads delight in variety, but we also suffer from it. We have no natural environment, unlike people who stay in the same place. The shape of my life resembles an archipelago rather than a unified landscape, though that can help with remembering; I connect different phases with quite distinct places, memory's islands.

– My past has its compartments too: Glasgow, spells in Paris and Rome, a few months in Moscow. London.

He spoke about his father, that difficult man from whom he'd always been estranged, well before the second marriage and departure for New Zealand. The lost child he described, rescued by his aunt, seemed not to be him at all: a boy at the bottom of a long flight of stairs, looking up at the adult Paul without recognition, a boy of seven in a raincoat, with a shivery white face. He's remembering a snapshot, taken, probably by Clem, on a damp summer outing.

– I'll visit Clem soon.

– Your second mother.

– I've been lucky to have her.

He asked about her friends. When he mentioned Annie's mother, Gail, Eva promised they would meet when he came back.

– You have a lot in common. You're bound to get on.

Quickly, she revised the promise.

– If you come back, I mean. I'm assuming you'll go on with your researches.

– What researches would those be? I've drawn a blank with Esme Maguire. Don't you think?

Her answer was barely audible.

– Perhaps.

No promises were made by him. All he said, half asleep, was I'll miss you.

He woke in the night. Eva didn't stir. A solitary truth hit him. It was love he wanted, intensity of feeling. Without it he would live forever in a chill and lasting darkness. It was not just being loved that he missed, but having someone to care for. Eva lied to him. He guessed this was about control, a fear of losing independence after all those husbands. Did he himself have anything to hide? He thought about Chris; secrets aren't always clear. But Eva lied, and love had to be unblighted by mistrust. The love he longed for brightened all of life, its purposes as well as its pleasures.

In the morning she went with him to the house. He assembled his luggage and they walked the short distance to where he'd catch the airport bus. He kissed her, stroked her hair when he saw the worry in her eyes and read in it that this really meant goodbye. Might some emotional weight persist, or vanish when the bus drove off? Would she feel lightened and free, relieved that he had gone at last?

Would he?

Part Three

Keys

But if you take my voice what will I have left?
Hans Andersen, *The Little Mermaid*

26

Art

In placid hours well-pleased we dream

Of many a brave unbodied scheme.

But form to lend, pulsed life create,

What unlike things must meet and mate:

A flame to melt – a wind to freeze;

Sad patience – joyous energies;

Humility – yet pride and scorn;

Instinct and study; love and hate;

Audacity – reverence. These must mate,

And fuse with Jacob's mystic heart,

To wrestle with the angel – Art.

September 1880
    Memories are not for this journal, they belong in other pages, and some day, perhaps when death finally approaches, or when someone arrives who can believe my impossible truths and trust me, I shall offer them for reading. The writing of memory takes me inside my younger self; she lives again.

October 1881
    Francesco is to be married. All is well: my son has a profession and soon he'll have a wife. How I should like to see him. It will be hard to arrange, but I am resolved…

January 1898

A letter has come from Francesco, addressed – as ever now – to his sister, Esme. Reading it, I felt I had robbed him of so much: myself, a knowledge of his father, but he wrote only of what his mother had given him. This forgiveness is undeserved, a matter of pride and shame.

I understood then that by having a child, watching him grow, I myself became another. For you are his creation as he is yours.

I have observed the most pathetic and vainglorious, the most ignorant and foolish be shaped and redeemed by this experience. I have received the gift that the chain of generation can bestow.

June 1905

Francesco has written with news of my granddaughter's wedding, planned as a grand occasion. I wanted to see her for myself, so I set out for Italy. I wore a veil and dressed in black like a widow, an accidental observer. Carla is a dark beauty, but blue-eyed like me. By her side was my son, heavy-bodied in middle age, contented and grey, his wife a plump and gracious mother of the bride. So I spied on my child, now older than I am. How many generations of my blood might I see born and die?

January 1920

Only one of my line left, Camilla, my great-granddaughter, living with an aunt in Trieste. I contrived to meet the girl last week and found a sad orphan, her father killed by shellfire, her mother and brother by the influenza plague. Not knowing who I am, she has no need of me, but I long to claim her; there may be a way.

December 1925

Perhaps George was a man born out of his true time, and this was what afflicted him, perverting his talents, freezing his heart and his conscience. He was right: there was a music still to come for me that would match the fury and the searching passion in my voice. And how prescient he was to call me vixen. I have been that cunning little vixen, at home amid Janáček's troubling chords…

September 1928

A disaster! Two days ago I discovered that my secret has been stolen. Eager to know more about Janáček's new opera, his last now that he is dead, I laid hands on a translation of the play by Karel Čapek on which it is based. Čapek once visited me in Prague after we'd met at a theatre party. It was careless of me, but while attending to an unforeseen household problem I left him alone in the room where I wrote. Now I see he read my papers, for he has used my story! He must have found my reference to Perulli's letter, he may even have pried into this journal, for he invented Elina Makropulos, making me Greek, keeping my initials. And it disturbs me, fills me with terror, because I know the power of art, and Janáček's music draws me deep into its world…

February 1929

I have seen the opera. Alas, the music matches me too well, reaches something in my soul, speaks to me as if it were my fate. My double, Elina Makropulos, has lived for more than 300 years. She knows her days are numbered unless she can find her father's formula and take the elixir again. She dreads death, yet is weary of life, unable to love. I do not tire of life, but sometimes I tire of being endlessly remade. As for love, long ago I learned that it is dangerous to surrender oneself to a man's mercy.

Elina Makropulos. If I become her on stage, will I be tempting destiny?

October 1943

I hide inside the narrow beauty of my life while all around the world is crushed and tortured… Again I fled to London and from there, escaping bombs, though not their carriers in the sky, to Deal and almost sight of France. France denied me, Italy too. Instantly I am shocked by these words that I write from safety, while millions are denied their lives and freedoms.

I live in the creases of history. Shame on me.

November 1970

My voice shows alarming signs of weakening. Small things: the richness of its timbre suddenly stifled, a note I cannot reach. This brings more than

the pain of failure felt by any artist. Each time, and they come at closer inter-
vals, a fear shoots through me. The fear of ending, of despair. If I cannot sing,
will I die? If I cannot sing, can I go on living?

January 1983
I have sung her, I have become Makropulos. It is too much to bear.

April 1990
Yesterday I looked out of my window and saw men chisel and hammer
at bricks from a ruin they had pulled down. A ruin I had cherished, roofless
and open to the elements, each season settling into its gaping structure where
the branches of an overhanging elder burgeoned with tiny dark fruits or grew
the rust of autumn and shook against the wind, where blackbirds hopped
between the rafters, and the powdery blue of jay's wings flashed among
spring leaves.

Reclaimed bricks fetch a good price. Here, in place of my ruin, another
house will rise, a new roof will crown it, its bare blond timbers a sign of
hope.

The present gives me no home, yet I can prize each of its separate
moments, make them keen and fluent to my senses. My pain is for memories,
the ones I have and those I lose with every year, with every week that passes,
things seen and felt in brightness or fury that now are as hard to catch as
thistledown adrift. In my youth I was someone else. I must have been, for I
remember her dimly, as if in another skin.

Yet the skin was mine and her eyes the same I have now.

January 2000
I know I can still find joy in first times. But these become fewer, the shores
and faces of the world either too familiar or remote, threatening new intoxi-
cations and perilous nostalgias.

The new millennium disturbs me, as if the calendar were no mere human
invention, but the markings of my doom. It places me in the world that is
past. Today has been cold and grey and I stepped out only as night fell. I
have no wish to meet my neighbours in the street and feign nonchalance. I

yearn for a new connection to the world, a look, a touch that will give me intensity.

There is a man who wants to know about Esme. His name is Paul Geddes. He is persistent. He intrigues me.

May 2000
I've met him now. He's lonely and he doesn't know it, like many men who prefer to shun their need for intimacy.

All long lives have passed through crowds that would clamour in our thoughts were it not for the rub of time that blurs them to a murmur. I am agog with memory, and forgetting.

Life consists of always stepping forward. We learn from Lot's wife, and our image of happiness belongs to the time our own existence has assigned us. But I am going to do what I've never done, and hand my memories to another: the stories of Elena and Elisa, Eleonora, Edita and Esme. To him. This diary will stay my secret.

27

– Nice cup of tea.

  – Fancy another? I'll put the kettle on in a minute.

  – No hurry.

Paul didn't stir from his wing-backed chair. Children played in the grassy square below, their faint cries lacking urgency. Sun lulled the streets.

The long-limbed man sprawled across the sofa was Alex Clay. Alex was elusive, apt to disappear to France or somewhere mountainous for months on end. He changed addresses. This time it was Paul who had vanished; in his habits of loneliness after Christine left, he'd often ignored the phone.

When Alex rang Paul had been pleased to hear his voice, that self-ironic public school drawl.

  – Can I interest you in a pint at the Magpie and Monkey?

Paul said he'd be delighted, except that he'd never heard of the pub in question.

  – It's probably a sushi bar now. I'm out of touch.

They met instead at the Lorelei, and later adjourned to Paul's flat.

While Paul made tea and put on some music, Alex rolled another joint.

Lazy afternoons were an unaccustomed luxury. Today took him back to the time when hours and weeks stretched further, when he was younger, or spent weekends with Christine, and those were as detached from him as someone else's life. When you live alone, doing nothing is slothful and lonely. He said this to Alex.

  – You should get out more, Paul.

  – You're not listening. It's staying in I find hard. There's a compulsion to keep busy. Going to things. Plays, films, concerts, dinner parties.

  – I wouldn't know. I avoid leading a full life.

He was clever. Uselessly clever, he would say, whenever people tried to chivvy him into making more of his talents. They had been best applied, he insisted, in the world he had left and to which he would never return. Paul knew the whole story.

They sat absorbed in John Coltrane.

Alex had been married to Gemma. They had earned a lot of money in the City and saw no need to save, regarding their hefty mortgage repayments on a tall house in Notting Hill as sufficient sacrifice. They had a small place in the country, near Bath. The cottage. They had a daughter, Kate, now twenty. They took expensive holidays. They gave dinner parties and drinks parties, always lavish; they footed the bill for family gatherings at restaurants, and invited friends to the cottage for weekends. Eventually they both had affairs. It was implicit in the lifestyle, said Alex. Where they had been showy and generous with the world, they became mean with one another. The marriage turned brittle. He frequently used that word to describe it.

– When the glassy edifice of my marriage crumbled away to sand…

He was prone to recalling that period, but warded off questions. He had constructed another kind of edifice.

– …I often went in for staying up all night.

Paul's thoughts lagged back with the glass.

– Yes, sand makes glass.

He knew this only because Eva had told him, explaining the chemistry of early glass-making techniques. How the sand needed to be fine and very pure, was brought from Sicily or the beaches of Istria, sometimes made by crushing pebbles. Sand and ashes, ashes from plants high in sodium content, ashes from Syria, potassium for brilliance. Exotic necessities to feed Venice's old secret. He began relaying this information to Alex, but found himself at a loss for precise terms, furnace temperatures, remembering only undiluted colours: saffron, cadmium, aquamarine, viridian. Dawns, sunsets. Chemistry and sound mingled in his mind, riffing across the inside of his eyelids.

– I can see you're obsessed.

– With glass-making?

– With her.

– Hardly.

Three days back and he still felt dislocated. He recalled the misery of last winter, when friendships had seemed so paltry, inadequate to fill the emptiness left by Chris. He'd been going under with the knowledge that he, not Chris, had been the destroyer, that he'd wrecked his own life. And those friends had brought him to the surface. Once more in the world of well-being, of appetite and energy, he sees friendship for what it can be: a luxury as well as a necessity.

Why does he find transitions hard? Another reason for not going to his father in New Zealand. Did it have to do with his want of a mother, a terror of being between places, having to let go of one to reach somewhere else.

– You were thinking about her, though. Dwelling on all those things she told you about La Serenissima.

He broke up the Italian syllables with aggressive emphasis. Paul had expected some laddish mockery, though Alex only made a pose of it. A warmer attention had filled his eyes when Paul had mentioned Eva in the pub.

– As if I would risk boring a cynic like you, even if I was – thinking about her, I mean. You're too world-weary to waste an obsession on.

Hanging out with Alex always became a regression to youth, though they'd first met long after youth had ended. It was only with Alex that Paul ever smoked grass (of the best quality), and Alex (the grass perhaps helping) always nudged him inwards, to some naive illumination that simplified. Now, in stoned introspection, he examined himself: the rationalist who strove to deny the romantic, the romantic with reasons to resist.

By this tortuous route, his thoughts, flushed yet clear, settled again on Eva Forrest. Where did the affinities of love begin? In the physical, or in some rapturous bond of shared recognition? With Eva, potential lay in the first, but he doubted he would find the second.

He leaned back and closed his eyes until the CD ended.

When it did, he got up, stretched and went into the kitchen, trailing a question meant decisively to change the subject.

– Tell me how things are with you, Al. Are you still seeing Barbara?

– Ah, Barbara, the archaeologist. It never took off. She disappeared from my radar.

– So *you* haven't found love?

This was provocative. Alex never spoke of love. He spoke only in the vaguest terms about anything he was doing. For the last three summers he had guided groups of walkers across the Cévennes. He wrote the occasional travel article. His work was always short-term, marginal, or a very finite labour of love, like the photographs he had taken for an overlooked section of a book on wild orchids, which involved tramping around the foothills of the Dolomites at his own expense. He was learning Hungarian ('another string to the bow'). He was 49. Nothing he did could be called a career. Never again would he be 'sucked in'. This vow seemed to Paul to refer equally to women, from whom he always disengaged himself without apparent chagrin. Paul liked Alex, he even liked his opacity; a solid reality lay behind it.

– Love has not found *me*.

Paul had not imagined that love would ever be allowed into a conversation with Alex. Even a stoned conversation. His question had been lightly meant. The answer made it weigh a little more. As a consequence, he dithered in the kitchen.

When he returned bearing a fresh pot of tea and some biscuits, Alex had dug out an old Van Morrison tape.

– Takes you back, eh?

Paul's smile spread, slow and benign. A bee loitered behind the curtains, its drone occupying the spaces of the music's silent beats. In the slanting light the dust on his books, the flame-orange paint on an art deco vase that had been his mother's, the glowing wool pile of the rug he stood on, had all gained a perfect natural clarity. He knew what Alex meant, a little piece of time, of youth, regained in melody, in the euphoria of a sunlit afternoon. He felt no pull back. He felt nothing missing. He even allowed that what was meant to be would always come about.

Alex seized the tea tray.

– I'll take this, before you drop it. That smile's too dreamy to be trusted with breakables. She's done you the power of good; I've never seen you looking so well.

– I wasn't actually in love's dream, Alex. I was enjoying the music.

– Okay.

They idled for another hour.

– Are you happier, Paul?

Paul hesitated.

– You know, with Christine I had no idea of what I risked with that first little affair. Little, I thought: insignificant. A woman who had a husband as I, more or less, had a wife. I thought I could avoid any hurt so long as I kept it hidden from Chris. And I got away with it.

He let out the bitter rasp of a laugh.

– The trouble was the second affair, and her finding out. You know all this, but the thing I've never really understood is why I did it at all. Maybe, after all the years in a kind of marriage, I needed to know I still could draw women. Yet Chris was all I wanted – I couldn't imagine another woman who would make me happier. So I blew it. And it turned out she wanted a baby, though she'd always said it was fine if I didn't.

– Surely you realise that was because staying with you mattered more.

– Yes, I realised. I saw my own selfishness, I deserved all I got.

He paused.

– I've moved on.

– Because of Eva? Does she know your past sins?

– No reason to tell her. She's helped me leave the bad stuff behind, that's probably all there is to it: her and Venice together, a temporary rapture.

Alex pursed his mouth.

– Rapture. Can't be gainsaid.

After that, Haydn prevailed over speech, until hunger prompted Paul's mouth open.

– Al, what do you say to some spaghetti, then we could always take a stroll, maybe the flicks at Camden Town.

– Terrific.

Leaving the sauce to simmer, he excavated in the larder for a bottle of Barbera he'd been saving. He splashed a taster into a glass and sipped. Right now he loved the present, he felt the perfect hold and swing of sensation, of the instant and the prospect immediately beyond. The smell of dinner cooking, the complex liquid flavours in his mouth, the eating of food and the darkening city's rumour of summer evening. He felt in the right place. Nostalgia was an illness, diagnosed in the 18th century, a melancholy longing for the sound of cowbells suffered by the Pope's Swiss Guard. Regret for the past acquired a sour taste if gnawed on too long. His miseries had fallen away from him.

Eva too felt remote. This gave an illusion of emotional omnipotence. He could choose to forget her. He need not be a slave to desire or recent memory. She, after all, could easily do without him.

At once he wanted to negate this thought.

It was Alex who rescued him from descent into self-puzzlement. With a shout demanding company and the promised glass of wine. Alex, suddenly voluble and curious about Paul's own plans.

– So life has triumphed over biography. Living it, and a good thing too. If you stay with this Eva, one of these days I'll come and take a look. In fact there's a chance I'll get to Venice soon, at least the Dolomites. My orchids went down well and I suggested a modest little guidebook. I'm waiting for the go-ahead, and a contract.

– Great. Let me know if it works out. Even if it doesn't, I'd still recommend Venice. Who knows what it would do for you, Al.

In the morning he hurried to check the post. Only bills.

Two weeks and nothing from Eva. He'd sent a card soon after getting back: a greeting and a thank you, a reproduction of Lorenzo Lotto's *Young Man in His Study*, in the Accademia. What he wrote was casual, not meant to be conclusive.

July was cooler than June. The academic year was over, leaving weeks of empty freedom. Returning from a Sunday lunch with neighbours, he knew he wanted to hear her voice.

The phone rang several times before an answering service clicked on.

– It's Paul. I just called to say hello and find out how you are. I hope you're well.

He expected nothing from her, nor was there anything he craved, but he didn't want to be forgotten.

198

They hit the motorway and crossed the city fast. Rain drizzled at their backs until the Campsie Fells came into view.

– Didn't I tell you we'd get better weather over this way?

Clem assented with a grudging laugh.

At Balmaha they took a short walk to stretch their legs. Boats idled on the surface of the loch. On their right the forest rustled damply.

Rowardennan was where the road ended and the serious walking started. Clem strode ahead up the gentle slope towards a stand of beeches while Paul retied the laces of his boots and peered into the undergrowth in the hope of seeing a red squirrel. Something moved in the cave of thick branches that trailed among the bracken. Clem shouted to hurry him. It was gone.

– Come on, slowcoach.

When he reached her she was sitting on a tree stump with the thermos flask out, waving a packet of biscuits at him.

– This'll speed you up.

– Nothing like it, eh? Fresh air and birdsong.

– Aye. And knowing there's nothing but wildness ahead.

– You're right, Clem. The forest belongs to us.

The forest wasn't entirely wild. It was managed, protected, designed for enjoyment. But this preserving of its beauty, so spend-thrift and varied, moved him as if he were a prodigal son being feted on return. They walked for an hour, encountering solitary hikers, a young couple then an older one, a family with a dog, the laughing, skeltering children and it taking over the quiet path in a commotion of shrieks and barks, exuberance streaming out of them like good medicine they'd been sent to spread about.

– I've never walked the West Highland Way before, Clem. You know it, don't you?

– I come sometimes, with my walking club.

– Did you ever come when you were young?

– Only the once. With your mother and two other girls. I would have been about 19, just after the war.

His mother walking here, a teenager, with no knowledge of his future existence.

Around noon they turned back, taking the lower path along the loch side.

Tour buses had filled up the Rowardennan car park and all the pubs were crowded. At one of these they took their chicken salad outside.

At this point the loch was narrow, the water a dense stinging blue that Paul found almost unbearable. It forced an inexplicable yearning for something he couldn't name. Maybe it was being in an ancient place where ancestral ghosts roamed impervious to the coach parties. Or else he was disquieted by too much beauty in the land he'd left behind.

– Will we have another wee walk?

– Paul, I feel a bit woozy after that glass of wine.

– I've an idea, Auntie Clem. What do you say to heading for the seaside?

It was blowy on the seafront at Helensburgh, but warm enough for ice creams.

– The sea's the best tonic I know. It makes me feel light as air.

– Well, you always wanted to be somewhere else. You should have come here, closer to home.

They drank tea in a café and argued gently about Paul's youthful decision to escape from Glasgow and the friction it had caused.

– You were certainly thrawn.

He'd wanted to go where unknown histories lay. So he'd got a research grant for a year in Paris, another for a term in Rome, a summer in Moscow. London. It was embarrassing to think how little he knew Scotland. He'd have to turn into a tourist some day and visit the Highlands and Islands. Clem said it was high time and they launched plans for a trip the following year.

At the beach, Clem sank into a deckchair and took out her knitting. Paul walked to the shoreline.

That was the thing about leaving the place you came from; it turned into memories, it got stuck there. Pictures in your head from so far away you wondered at yourself having been there at all.

He looked far across the Clyde estuary and remembered his granny's single end in Duke Street: one room, one door, a pulley for clothes to dry on squashed against the ceiling, always emptied when visitors were due. The corner by the window with the cooker and the sink, where the body was washed as well as the dishes; the bed recess: everything doll's-house neat and clean, like a fairy-tale abode. On his last visit he was 15, his mother was dead and Clem was younger than his own age now. He didn't remember it as poverty, or wretchedness.

He stayed another day, returned the hire car, took Clem shopping for some sandals and treated her to lunch. The city centre had that buzz he'd got to like in the years of coming back. While Clem returned a too-big skirt in Marks & Spencer's he walked up to Garnethill, enjoyed the pitch of the streets down to the misty nothingness of the river, thought of a girlfriend he'd had at 18 who'd lived nearby. In the evening he met Clem's new friend, Harry, a humorous man who fidgeted with his glasses according to the tenor of the conversation. The friend who would stay a friend, for Clem had pronounced she would always stay a widow. Free, she said.

The journey south was changeless, always the same thoughts, the same sights that struck him through the train window. An aftermath of quiet turmoil, for every return made his mind overactive with emotions unresolved. Three days in Scotland had engrossed him in a past that seemed boundless. The crossing of the border hills, smooth-humped like an animal's hide, faithfully marked this movement's reversal. Scotland and England; the hills made it easy: two places, two separate phases of his life.

Among his post were a letter from New Zealand and a card with an Italian stamp. Still in the loop of family, he read the letter first. The writing faltered, he wondered about Parkinson's: *I'm not too well. It would be good to see you, I'll help you out if the fare's a problem, and it should be cheaper at this time of year.*

He felt the impact of an unexpected blow. This pleading wasn't like his father; something was up. Consumed at the kitchen table, a small Grouse stiffened him. He lifted the postcard.

Dear Paul,

I've been away – Berlin, then an island in Croatia (sea wonderful but very cold) before the Italian invasion hits. Nice to hear from you. I'll be in

Venice for the next few weeks. If you're not busy, perhaps you'd like to come and be my guest (if you can brave the heat) – here at the flat.

Fondly, Eva.

He reread it, considered Eva's elegant scrawl and peered at the small print under her signature: the Gemäldegalerie in Berlin. A Longhi, *The Singing Lesson*. He read it again.

New Zealand was still too far for him.

28

– No need to look doubtful. You're here.

– I haven't got used to it yet.

– Tell me about London... No... We'll talk later. Look at all this.

She wanted him to notice everything: the lagoon's traffic of small and large craft, its seabirds and shallows. She wanted him to be amazed, as if at first sight, to restore the awe Venice inspires in those new to it.

At Marco Polo they'd boarded a boat instead of a bus. He felt thrown between worlds, some part of him left behind. Fixing on the middle distance, on the unrippled path through the markers ahead, he tried to be fully present.

Venice came closer, its architecture suddenly defined. At San Marco the opulence of light and water made its stones appear weightless, the entire *bacino* a vision conjured by some genie's puff of magic in an oriental tale. The launch rocked. The Doge's Palace swayed.

By the time they reached Eva's flat, he felt drunk with the unlikeliness of being where he was.

An American voice called out; loud, disconcerting.

– I'm running late, Evie.

A tall woman appeared at the end of the hallway, hurrying towards them, her smile apologetic.

– Paul, this is Gail Terry. I think I've told you we're very old friends. Gail's staying at the Rio dei Pensieri.

– Glad to meet you, Paul. I've heard a lot about you. Must dash. Have a nice evening. Hope to see you soon.

They waited, their faces worked by eloquent smiles, as Gail hurried to the door. They even allowed her time to reach the street before they moved closer.

– She couldn't resist waiting to see you.

On their first night together they wandered hand in hand. Venice's shadows were intrinsic to its romance, the darkness rendered voluptuous by the sounds and reflections of water, by the lustre of marble and the paleness of stucco against a sky whose depth and colour was revealed only with the open view of the Grand Canal. He still marvelled at the theatricality of it all.

When they reached the spotlit splendour of St Mark's, they walked the length of the Piazza. The café orchestras had gone home, leaving Florian and Quadri in the dark. A young tourist with a backpack sat propped against an arcade column, plucking at a guitar. It was 2am and the day's heat clung to the humid air. On the Riva the breath of the sea refreshed them.

They were too tired for lovemaking. Curled together, Eva's body and his own became a single sensual surface. He drowsed. In his half-dreaming state he knew something was different; her invitation, his return, had altered the over-careful balance of feeling.

He woke early. Light flowed in through the bedroom door. He cast a tender look at Eva as she slept, her face relaxed and tanned.

Coffee cup in hand, he stepped onto the balcony. Seeing people pass on their way to work, he had an urge to share in the day's newness. Perhaps he'd find a baker's open. He scribbled a note and took the spare keys from the hallway table.

He thought of Eva's cheek on the pillow. Her face stirred him so much that he needed to be away from it, to savour his joy, the immense, euphoric helplessness of it.

The nearest bakery was closed, but the smell of fresh bread led him to another. He chose *tartarughe* and a *ciabatta*, as well as croissants filled with yellow cream. Tired and unshaven, the baker didn't look at him as he made these choices, then he gave Paul a thin smile.

– You're my first customer.

Paul left the change on the glass-topped counter. From the greengrocer's on the corner he bought a bag of fragrant peaches. What else could he spend money on? Flowers. He found the florist's locked and shuttered.

Eva hadn't woken.

He studied her face for a while, then went to the kitchen to prepare her breakfast tray.

London slipped from his consciousness. He was free of teaching until September. Esme Maguire had become remote; not quite abandoned, more a spellbound statue, petrified by time, waiting for him to bring her back to life. She might wait forever.

He liked the beach in the morning, before it got too hot. Or they would set out when everyone else was heading back from the Lido, since Eva liked to swim in the early evening. In the sun, Paul's Celtic complexion required a permanent coating of cream; Eva soon retreated to the shade.

– Wrinkles will gather fast enough without being invited.
Paul shook his head.
– Age cannot wither her, nor custom stale her infinite variety…
Eva squinted at him.
– Who are you quoting?
– It's Shakespeare.
– Age cannot wither who?
– Cleopatra.
– Ah, like Sarah Bernhardt. I saw her once as Cleopatra, she was 72 and had only one leg. But on stage the years fell away. It must have been a trick, some special radiance that made her appear young. It was all in the voice, she said. That was her power as an actress; Victor Hugo described it as golden. You could say those lines were written for her, a woman unwithered by age.

– How could you have seen her? She must have died long before you were born.
Eva burst out laughing.
– I meant I saw her in a film… or else it was a television programme, you know with someone playing the part of Sarah Bernhardt.
– It's true, some women never really age. I'm sure you'll still be a beauty when you're 72. I hope I'm around to see it.
This got a sharp look.
– Isn't that unlikely, you and I both wrinkled and old?
– Maybe. Maybe not.
She answered his smile in kind.

Nothing had come of Eva's talk about Paul and Gail getting acquainted. Until a chance meeting on the boat to the Lido.

Gail had a man in tow: Jack Newhouse, also a biochemist, dark enough to pass for an Italian, though it turned out he was a Mancunian lured to the US by a research job. Conversation was lively on the crossing, and when they disembarked Gail invited them for dinner that evening. Eva wavered, then seeing Paul's enthusiasm, went along with the idea. He had taken to Gail, liked her fast talk and generous, inclusive manner. When they spoke about Italy or London she saw with eyes that had learned to be European, while her friend Jack displayed a presence and an accent more American than hers, though he said very little. Paul had an impression of effortless patience, a man not displeased by the company he was in but with his mind elsewhere.

They ate in the garden at the Rio dei Pensieri. Citronella candles glimmered under the pergola to keep mosquitoes at bay. Gail cursed them loudly.

– Damned mosquitoes! There's a population explosion this year.

She was a New Yorker. With a husband in flight from the draft and the Vietnam War, she'd moved to Toronto, then to California after the divorce. They'd stayed friends, because they shared a daughter and, Gail said, a political network from the old days.

– It's shrunk, but it's never disappeared. There's comfort in it, in having the same vocabulary for that past. We argue though – about how things are now.

Paul was disinclined to talk politics.

– How long have you known Eva?

– Seventeen years. But I started coming to Venice when Annie was small, which makes her practically a Venetian. After I got pensioned off early I wanted to spend more time here.

The next remark astonished Paul.

– It was in New York that we became friends, when she had a singing engagement. Which husband was it then, I can't remember, Evie?

Eva gave an embarrassed laugh.

– It was Victor.

Paul interrupted.

206

– I'd no idea Eva sang professionally.

– Well, Evie's a great one for secrets. It's her prerogative, so maybe I shouldn't have said. That voice of hers, you should have heard it. Evie honey, can nothing persuade you to sing for us?

Eva made a face.

– My singing voice is in the past.

She continued, even more forcefully, Paul felt, for his ears in particular.

– And I don't like talking about it.

Jack Newhouse leaned towards Paul, adopting a stage whisper.

– But now you know who to ask.

Eva frowned. Gail looked repentant.

– Time for dessert.

She gathered up plates and fled inside.

The revelation baffled Paul, showing Eva in yet another light. Later, he raised the question.

– What happened?

– I was ill. My voice gave up on me.

– That must have been tough. I can understand that it's hard to talk about. You know, you have a beautiful voice. I've always thought so.

– What do you hear in it? Sadness?

– Hardly ever. Anyway, we all have some reason to be sad.

Gail would tell more, given opportunity, he suspected, and he remembered this when she called with an invitation to the house she'd rented in the mountains with Jack. Eva seized on the prospect of mosquito-free air and respite from Venice's humidity. One clear morning on his previous visit she had taken Paul to the Fondamente Nuove to see how close the mountains were, jagged and glistening an icy white against the sky to the north. He pictured this vision as their destination.

The Dolomites appealed to him. Venice could be claustrophobic, too womb-like.

An early train got them to Trento by ten. On the local run to Bolzano, the station names slid past in twos: Italian, German. Eva fell silent and looked out of the window. Since his arrival he'd felt a kinship grow between them, a sense of the world's nearness or distance shared. Now, again, he caught sight of her otherness.

As if impelled to inspect the landscape, she stood, her face to the glass. He could see her reflection, blurred and inscrutable. She spoke in a monotone.

– We'll soon be there.

She still had her back to him. He caught her by the waist.

– Come and sit down.

She did as he asked, her face composed. Then, her mood shifting, she began telling him about a journey she'd made the year before with a friend, from Graz to Vienna, the train climbing and dipping between mountains as they sat in the restaurant car and drank Turkish coffee with freshly made apple cake.

– We were travelling old-style. The train had started out from Istanbul.

It made him nostalgic for the journeys of his youth.

– You know, this is our first time outside Venice together, in the real world.

And on neutral territory, he added mentally.

At Bolzano, Gail and Jack met them with a hired car.

– We thought we'd see the sights and have lunch before heading up to our Tyrolean chalet. It's outside the village where Freud spent his vacations. You'll love it.

Despite the heat in the valley, Gail had a busy programme in mind.

– There are two castles, the Mareccio and the Roncolo, or the Maretsch and the Runkelstein if you prefer. There's the cathedral, and the cloister at the Dominican monastery; it has frescoes. And something else... A few years ago they found a prehistoric man frozen in the mountains – like a mammoth. Well, he's here, in the museum. And that's not all. There's another find from the mountains, not that ancient, though maybe stranger.

She paused for effect.

– They found three bodies buried since the 1700s. The glaciers are retreating, which is why they keep finding deep-frozen people. Yesterday, for the *very* first time, they put them on show. We *have* to go and see them. This I don't want to miss.

The first shock of the day was Paul's. Entering the cool foyer of the museum, he fixed on a tall figure browsing by the bookstall, struck by its familiarity: the stance more than anything, a graceful angular droop that reminded him of Alex Clay. Something in the man's gesture of reaching for a book made Paul look again.

– Alex!

Alex turned, eyes narrowed behind reading glasses.

– Paul Geddes? I don't believe it! I sent you an email; did you get it? The idea was to drop in on you when I'm done with the mountains.

– So your publisher gave the green light?

– Yup, the non-skier's guide to the Tyrol.

– And you're visiting the Icemen?

– I've seen them. They're going in the book. The press office gave me pictures.

Alex was scanning the faces surrounding Paul. When introduced to Eva, he gave a charming bow of the head.

– Delighted to make your acquaintance, Eva.

But it was Gail his attention stayed on, and Paul noticed Gail's eager eyes. He whispered to Eva.

– Alex is a fast worker. What about Jack, though?

– Don't worry. They're just friends. They had a brief affair two years ago, but now he's in the throes of coming out as gay.

– Well, well. Good luck to all three of them.

Only two of the bodies were on public view. Their clothes, weapons and money placed them in the Venetian merchant class. All three had been on horseback and speculative scenarios accounted for the absence of their mounts: a quarrel, a chase, a blizzard.

Reading this, next to Eva, Paul heard her mutter some kind of calculation.

He followed her through the dimly lit corridor to the viewing room. She stood, blank-faced, her fists cupping air, then clenching, in small, slow movements that appeared both involuntary and effortful. He realised the whole thing must be upsetting her. They were about to see human remains, preserved perhaps like the fully dressed 18th-century figures he had seen once in a Naples church, skin still attached to their skulls and skeletal hands, but shrivelled and blackened.

Visitors processed in single file. He caught her elbow.

– Are you all right? Would you rather leave it to another day?

– I'm fine.

The queue moved slowly. Eva's breathing contradicted her assurance. He turned to Gail; she failed to read his anxious look and sent a bright smile. He stopped Eva in her tracks.

– Let me go first.

He edged past, giving her hand an affectionate squeeze. It was limp.

Steps led to a plate-glass window with room for only one viewer. Beyond this chilly surface lay the first body. It was not what Paul had expected, not so alien and dark, more like a stale waxwork, the face yellowish. Exposure must have altered it at once; it might even have resembled a living body when found. Now it looked like someone newly dead after a wasting illness. The man must have been handsome, his features regular, the mouth still with a hint of fullness. He felt a lump in his throat. The finery made this worse: the fur-lined black cloak, a deep-cuffed coat under that, of a once rich crimson, and, in the same material, a buttoned tunic over black breeches and silk stockings. The panel next to the window gave the Venetian names for these: the *tabarro*, the *velada*... There were silver buckles on the shoes, and this detail took Paul back to the illustrated nursery rhymes of his childhood: antiquated images that, to his child's eyes, depicted a past just before his own short span of years. Our clothes outlive us. Like the dresses his father had kept in the big bedroom wardrobe, unable to part with the cotton and wool that had clasped his dead wife's body, relying on their ghostly shapes for a paltry lasting comfort.

Grace had made her own clothes; he remembered the paper patterns from Lewis's bundled into a lidless shoebox on the wardrobe shelf.

Two rings lay beside the body: a cornelian set in gold, a narrow band with an emerald, displayed together with a silver dagger and a pouch whose contents of coins and threadbare bills of exchange spilled out. Long gloves, fur-lined to match the cloak, seemed to reach for these objects. He tried to picture the scene all those centuries before.

Becoming aware of holding up the queue, he moved to the next window. Eva took his place.

He glanced back and saw her shocked eyes. Immobile, mute, she dully conveyed distress. He went to her side. When he touched her she began to sob.

– What is it, Eva?

She shook her head. Her sobs grew louder. This convulsive weeping astonished him, as if Eva herself had melted, lost the contours of her self-containment.

– Eva, let's go outside and you can tell me what's wrong.

Gail rushed to join them. She put an arm around Eva's shoulder.

– Try to calm down, honey. Maybe you could do with a drink.

In a nearby café, Eva became even more distraught. A large whisky made no difference. They all soothed and pleaded; Paul kept hold of her hand. He watched the tears bathe her cheeks, smudging her make-up, crumpling her face. Unforeseen emotions had burst out of her, leaving a cool, clever woman with her self-control undone, wailing like a naked infant. He was paralysed by confusion: he felt pity for her, and tenderness, and something akin to fear.

– Tell us, tell us, Eva.

Finally, still sobbing, she managed to speak.

– How can I? You'll think I'm mad.

29

July 2000

There are always new griefs, and this one has torn my heart out.

Lorenzo in the ice, forever cold, the arms that held my enraptured young body now lifeless, yet their flesh intact. Lorenzo, the love that has haunted me for centuries, given me the joy of its memory, Lorenzo a frozen ghost, chilling the new love that had almost abolished my fear.

It's a warning.

August 2000

When I sing, I am freed from the pangs of remembering and forgetting. The present rewards me. It releases me from envy, from grief and disappointment. This is my only answer now. How can I risk everything for Paul, for something as fragile as a love affair?

Love alters its pitch and urgency at life's different stages. In youth it's absolute, it devours; I've come to know its transience, and this passion instils the dread of repeating earlier follies. Yet each love is unlike any other, and whatever moves us can give us energy, an incandescence that renews our waning selves. With Paul I've found happiness, but I mistrust love.

I must leave him, and the thought is unbearable. Not yet.

30

– It's not the first time.

Gail's gesture, teaspoon in hand, was peremptory.

– Though it's a while…

Hesitation clouded her eyes, but Paul's curiosity had been replaced by a wish to know nothing.

She dipped the spoon into brown paper bags scattered on the kitchen table, the spoils of long mountain walks, names scrawled in pencil: juniper berries, camomile flowers, wood betony and valerian, motherwort and lady's slipper. Gail was simmering a herbal brew to help him sleep. He'd drink whatever she put in front of him. Shock had left him helpless.

Down in the garden, plates and glasses lay uncleared. Gail mumbled an apology and lit a candle. Emerging from the bushes, the cat crept beside him. He touched its head, stroked its fur with a hand that felt disconnected.

– You'll stay here tonight. I'll make up the bed in the study.

He nodded. Irrelevance surrounded him. Gail's guilty conscience, the cluttered table, encroaching mosquitoes, the fragrant night air. It was Eva's garden, the air she used to breathe. But Eva was gone.

Nothing had prepared him for this. He'd seen her through the crisis, so he thought. *Paul, you've been wonderful.* If only they hadn't gone to Bolzano.

– I'm sorry you missed Alex. I nearly went with him to the airport. Just as well I didn't.

He hated this chattiness. On the way to the Rio dei Pensieri he had longed for Gail's kindness, the solace of sharing his terrible news. He had blindly counted on her help. Now he resented her, Gail here in Eva's place; Gail whose fault it was they'd gone to Bolzano; Gail made happy by meeting Alex. These feelings shamed him. She'd gasped when he showed her the letter. 'Oh God, Paul, it's not the first time.' He dreaded hearing more.

– Tell me tomorrow. Not now.

– I'm not sure what I can tell you.

– She's alone, I'm sure of it.

– Yes, I think so too... But she's always been able to take care of herself. Except for the time...

– Stop!

Paul stood up, his cup left on the table, still half-full of Gail's concoction.

– I'm going for a walk.

For 24 hours he had walked until exhaustion.

The day after they saw what the newspapers called *i signori del ghiacciaio* – the lords of the glacier – Paul and Eva returned to Venice. Gail's concern prompted an offer to go with them, but Paul could see she'd rather stay, and he preferred that. She gave him a plastic phial with five or six pills: tranquillisers to calm Eva for the journey.

– They're old, but still effective.

A pattern set in. Eva would cling to Paul, weeping quietly, demanding reassurances. Could he endure this until she was better? Would he stay if she promised to answer all his questions? Then, at some innocent but misplaced word of his, she would flare into fury.

– What do you think I can give you? You understand nothing. You don't know me. I don't know myself any more.

Paul found the strength not to feel insulted. He kept his voice steady. Hers rose hysterically.

– You've tried to find out everything about me, prying, quizzing my friend. I told you things. I gave you the papers. You wanted something romantic, but she isn't like that; maybe once, when she was too young to know any better.

This made no sense. He concentrated on giving comfort.

– I love you, Eva.

The words were spoken without thought, as words are used to soothe a crying baby. In the same instant, he regretted them and knew he meant them.

– Who do you think you love, her or me?

– Her?

Eva sneered.

– Esme of course. *Your* Esme. The one you made up for yourself. How do you think women survived on the stage? Unless they have someone who'll protect them, or they're exceptional. I wasn't.

– Then tell me how it was, tell me the truth. That's what I want to know. About you. Esme doesn't matter.

– She does! They all do!

This teasing madness persisted.

Next morning he retreated, said it might do them good to have a day apart. A boat to Murano with its cooler, breezy air offered relief in solitude and refuge from the familiar. He walked aimlessly, ignoring the glass shops and factories, sat in a café on a floating deck with striped awnings and a pleasant, unglamorous vista across the wide canal. Eva's messy emotions lay beyond his control, and the failures of insight had hardened. In the evening he reached her flat no less weighed down.

Gail and Alex arrived, inebriated with romance and wanting to be alone now that Jack Newhouse was heading for Milan. Paul and Alex went to a bar while Gail talked to Eva, and this conversation seemed to lift her spirits. Later, Gail spoke to Paul and advised a doctor, the one Eva had owned up to seeing in Mestre.

– So that was it! Not yoga: a shrink. Why didn't she tell me?

– Why should she have?

– A question of trust. Why is she so secretive? Is it to do with this… illness?

– Shortly after I first knew her, she collapsed and had to give up singing; her life was falling apart. I've been thinking back. There were things I'd forgotten…

Gail paused. Paul had a sense she was loath to tell him everything, though she went on.

– She was married to Victor Murnau. Did she talk about him?

– Hardly at all, but I've heard the name.

– From what she told me, he was her great love. They met in Vienna when she was 19 – he was married and ended the affair. She was devastated. Marrying somebody else helped her get over it. A mistake, of course, on the rebound. A few years later she ran into Victor in Paris. His wife had died and the outcome was that Eva and

Victor got married. They wanted children but when Eva finally got pregnant the baby was stillborn. The marriage didn't withstand her depression. When he left her, she had to give up singing.

– Had to? What do you mean exactly?

– She no longer had the energy, couldn't handle the stress.

– I knew nothing about this. Poor Eva. What terrible things she's gone through.

– It's life, isn't it? People do go through awful things, but they pull themselves together and sometimes make it work. Eva did that. She met Joe. He was older, but he made her a new woman and he left her well provided for. She's kept her looks – though I'd bet with a little help from the surgeon's knife. Facelifts aren't unusual in the world she used to move in.

Paul ignored these last remarks. He frowned.

– Couldn't she have gone back to singing?

– She told me her voice had deteriorated.

– What happened to Victor?

– He had two sons, with a much younger woman. Sadly, he died in a skiing accident last year, maybe what upset her at Bolzano. Has she talked about it?

– No, though I've asked, as delicately as I could. Surely to do with Victor's death... What did he look like?

– I never met him, never even saw a photograph.

Paul struggled to picture Eva's great love. Jealousy endowed this Victor Murnau with formidable, almost demoniacal, talents and attractions. Later he asked Alex what Gail had told him.

– Not much. She's been very concerned. To tell the truth, I want to take her mind off the situation. Gail's life hasn't been easy either. She's...

– Another time, Alex. Not now.

He saw this was brutal.

– I'm sorry. It's all a strain.

Paul remained in lonely bafflement. Eva shut him out.

In the darkness he lay next to her, accompanying her restless, angry sleep with his own turbulence. Opaque dreams held him prisoner in those stretches of the night when his eyes closed and he let go of listening, loosened the clasp of his hand, the embrace of his arms. He woke wracked by anxieties: the dreamscapes he could never clarify, the fever in Eva's mind to be grappled with. Every part of his consciousness and the layers beneath it had absorbed her pain. He ached for a tiny corner of himself to be inaccessible to her claims, to the blame in her voice as she issued a stream of laments and accusations in mingled German and Italian. Old hurts, he thought, that he couldn't cure. He told himself not to despair. *Love is not love... all tests of it worth enduring.*

He wanted to kiss her and have her respond, and this was urged by something more than the desire that still flickered through their intimacy. His instincts told him that, just as someone saved from drowning needs resuscitation through another's breath, she had need of his. A kiss was life, and he longed to reanimate the vitality now extinguished in her. She refused this sensual remedy.

Then nights came when she turned to him, calm and dry-eyed. Her anger subsided, melancholy replaced it. With this rest, the flame in her revived.

He longed for her to speak of herself.

– Do you want to tell me about it?

– No.

– Don't you think it would help?

– It would be too much; you've been through enough with me already.

– Will you tell me about your marriage to Victor Murnau?

– No. What's past is past.

Slowly, change came. Recovery was helped by her trips to Mestre; after a month of these she reported Doctor Amadeo's satisfaction with her progress. Paul would take the train with her and wait at their agreed café. One day she announced with airy confidence:

– I could go back to singing.

He was astonished.

– Does the doctor agree?

She looked bewildered, then shook her head slowly.

– It's possible now. I know it's right.

– Didn't you say you'd lost your voice? Are you being realistic?

– Are you an expert? Do you think I don't know I'll have to work at it?

She softened.

– Paul, maybe it's hard for you to understand. My voice failed because of problems in my life. But singers can go on past middle age; I have the potential.

He could see she was happy. Some radiance lit her eyes. And happiness deserves encouragement, even if its origins are misaligned with reality.

– I'm glad. What made you decide?

– I suppose I was shocked at myself after Bolzano. That's too complicated to explain, but I saw I should use what talents I have rather than being idle. And you helped me; you put up with me, gave me enormous support. You're loyal.

Her idealised view pierced him with guilt. He hadn't been loyal to Chris, and he'd never owned up to this with Eva.

– Well, this is great news. Thanks to Doctor Amadeo.

– Most of all, thanks to you. You've been wonderful, Paul.

This praise provoked mixed feelings. He listened to it again in his head and heard its warmth tinged with dismissal. Eva's decision struck him as wild, not a little unbalanced... but perhaps the course she needed to take.

– I'm not perfect either, Eva.

Paul had postponed his departure; a colleague was covering his teaching commitments. They spent three days at a borrowed beach flat. The weather had cooled, warning of autumn, but the light cast a blue-gold brilliance over everything. They swam lazily, slept well and ate with relish. On their last evening they loitered in the setting sun, Eva at the water's edge, iridescent in an emerald-green costume. Glimmering through the dusk, she appeared a fabulous creature, a dragonfly, fragile in its splendour. He reached her quickly and draped a towel around her shoulders.

– You'll catch a chill.

Her hand touched his cheek and the life in her eyes cancelled the shadow that had brought him running. He could shed his fears and accept the summer's fading perfection. Eva was a new woman and Paul had no qualms about the future.

Return to the city was dictated by the prospect of an evening with Alex and Gail, due back from the mountains. Paul was impatient for them to see his regained happiness with Eva. In Venice, they found a disappointing message: the new lovers would spend one more night in the Dolomites.

Next morning threatened rain and the leaden sky supplied a reason for the sombre alteration in Eva's mood.

They'd planned to see an exhibition after lunch.

– Go without me. I'm tired. It's the change in the weather perhaps.

– I'll stay with you.

– No. It closes tomorrow. Go.

Sunlight sheared away the clouds as he crossed Rialto Bridge and it helped him cast off a fresh unease. He stopped for the famous view, sharing it with camera-wielding tourists three-deep by the parapet.

The Correr was crowded. Its survey of 18th-century views of Venice had been assembled with loans from London and the Hermitage. After the first two Canalettos he lost interest and bypassed the others. Half an hour of cramped progress brought him to the café. He downed an espresso and left, gripped by a compulsion to be with Eva.

When the key turned twice in the lock he knew she'd gone out, though he called her name. By now he was used to her always being there, either with him or waiting; in any case, she'd have expected him back later than this. He headed for the kitchen and took a bottle of mineral water through to the sitting room. The blue sofa was long enough to accommodate his full length and he stretched out.

Loud bells roused him. Still drowsy, he turned to look at the gingerbread clock, the one Eva claimed had been Wagner's. Propped against it sat a white envelope with his name on it.

My dearest Paul,

This way lacks courage, I know. But had I faced you I would have stayed. I cannot. Not only am I burdensome to you, but also to myself. My life lacks purpose. I need to sing again – I've told you this. Try to imagine the effort; seventeen years since I stopped. I might not succeed. Being alone is my only chance, without emotional ties.

Stay on for a week or two if you like. I won't be back before the winter, and perhaps much later. It's probably best not to meet again.

I am grateful for all you have done. And I do love you, though that can scarcely mean much to you now that it is over. From the second time we met (I scarcely trust first encounters) I felt happy with you. That sense of being utterly in the right place with a man, choosing and feeling free, is something for which I am also grateful.

It's hard to live without love, but love can stop us from living. When I was young I couldn't imagine life without it, that mad, scalding love I'm sure you know about, and later, married to Joe, I found the kind of quiet love that brings serenity, and in between there were other kinds. But I've feared for a while that love would cause trouble, robbing me of something precious: the will to resume an artistic life, with all it demands.

Despite my rash promises, I didn't answer your questions, though you may discover answers of your own. As for what we saw in Bolzano, I was reminded of someone I had lost.

There's an attic room at Rio de Pensieri that you will find unlocked. This key fits a trunk I've left in it. The trunk is to stay there, its contents not to be moved from the house. They should be put back and locked up again before you leave – please respect this. I'm sure they'll interest you. Make of them what you will, what you can. You know how to piece lives together.

Whatever happens, there will be no loose ends. My notary has instructions. Please don't search for me. It would be useless.

You have taught me much more than I thought I knew about constancy. This is not a fickle choice but it is goodbye.

Eva.

Midnight. Paul's head ached. Looking for Eva, he had lost himself. He walked with a crazy stagger, his surroundings unfamiliar.

A boat went past with music blaring. He followed, losing it to silence, but reached a corner where a promising light was visible. A bar.

Meaning to ask for directions, he ordered a drink instead. He'd already drunk so much that the fog in his brain made it unreceptive to anything as complicated as distinguishing left from right in a foreign language. Eventually the barman guided him, one arm round his shoulder, into a small *campo* with two empty benches. He lay down, collapsing into shallow sleep until dawn. As he made his way back to the flat, shop shutters were being rolled up to start the day. He groped for the letter in his pocket. Had he imagined it, and would Eva be asking where he'd been all night?

Disbelief again, like the shock of his first reaction and the race to the railway station, in case she was waiting for a train to Paris or Vienna or Rome, perhaps delayed. He'd dashed from platform to platform, thought of grabbing a taxi to the airport, but some instinct or false hope convinced him to stay in Venice. He'd found no one at the house in the Rio dei Pensieri, and so began a search of the city that led to one glass after another. A whole night in which Eva moved further away from him.

Aspirin and coffee restored him to the certainty of finding her. If he never gave up the search, kept on walking, even getting lost. Chance might favour him, so long as he didn't stand still.

Opening the trunk filled him with dread. It was Eva he wanted, not heartbreaking answers. He nearly threw the key into a canal, only stopped short by the thought that it might lead him to her. Another thought resurfaced: Gail might know where she'd gone.

It was dark again. His desperation made Venice an unkind labyrinth. He battled through it.

Paul would have lost himself to the night again had Gail not kept some tranquillisers in reserve. She had spiked his hot drink and when he tried to leave she restrained him with a more pacifying line of talk.

– Stay here and sleep, Paul. We'll talk in the morning. There's stuff I should tell you, then maybe we can look for her in earnest. She's done this before.

31

Paul pushed open the unlocked door behind the curtain and climbed the stone stairs with dreamlike strides. At the top he had to stoop before entering a high-ceilinged attic where the early morning sun plunged through a mansard window. The dark-brown trunk greeted him in the centre of the room, a straight-backed Biedermeier armchair facing it. He accepted its severe invitation and examined his surroundings.

E.M. The monogram was tooled in elegant script on the trunk's leather lid.

He wasn't going to rush at this. Finally, he took a deep breath.

Books packed the floor-to-ceiling shelves, beside bound journals and magazines in different languages, all of them to do with music, opera mostly. A specialist collection, with runs of *Dwight's Journal of Music*, *The Musical Times*, the *Gazzetta musicale di Milano*, the *Revue musicale*. A glass-fronted cabinet contained what appeared to be the rarer items; he opened it. A first issue of the *Allgemeine musikalische Zeitung* from 1798, complete sets of *The Musical Antiquary* and an Austrian journal called *Thalia*, published in 1810–11. What impressed him most were the six volumes of *The Scots Musical Museum*, a compendium of songs, predominantly settings of Robert Burns, published between 1787 and 1803.

Copies of recent publications were stacked on assorted surfaces. He spotted a pile of *Discovering Opera* on an oak credenza. Joe Lensky's passion was being kept alive.

Tight in the palm of his hand he held the small brass key that Eva had left in his keeping. He thought of it now as the key to her past. He pressed it to his cheek. When at last he fitted it into the lock, there was a moment's resistance before the click.

His curiosity took him no further. He wasn't ready to face whatever the trunk contained.

– Is that you, Paul?

Gail's shout hurried him downstairs. He smelled fresh coffee.

– I woke up early. I've been to investigate the trunk.

– You opened it?

– Not yet.

– Paul, I think I should put you in the picture about when I first knew Eva. Seventeen years ago.

– You said she had a nervous collapse. What else?

– The thing is… she went crazy, you know, madness, insanity.

– Madness means different things to different people. What do *you* mean by it?

– I mean she lost her hold on reality. She no longer knew who she was. Her perceptions of herself and others became utterly distorted.

– Stop!

– You don't want to hear this? Okay, it's up to you. But I…

– Yes, only stop all this vagueness. It's like some clinical condemnation. I want exact details. I want to try to understand.

– I was getting there.

Gail fumbled in her bag for cigarettes. She offered one to Paul; he shook his head.

– She believed she'd lived for more than 300 years. She believed that when she was 16 she'd been given a potion to make her live forever without ageing. Sound familiar to you at all?

Paul started.

– In what way?

– You're not a great opera lover, are you?

– For Christ's sake, Gail, get on with it. I listen to opera, I go to the opera. It's one of the things that brought me here in the first place. Are you saying she imagined she was a character in an opera?

Gail closed her eyes momentarily.

– No, she imagined the character was *her*. The opera was *The Makropulos Case*. Janáček wrote it in the 1920s, drawing on a play by a Czech writer called Karel Čapek. Eva sang the principal role in a New York production 17 years ago and at the end of the first performance she broke down in her dressing room, convinced she'd known Čapek and that his play was about her, that he'd discovered her secret: that she was Elina Makropulos, that she'd lived for 300 years. This was shortly after Victor left her. She was in a fragile state. The opening night tipped the balance. I guess that fantasy was preferable to coping with being herself. She had a full-blown breakdown.

Paul lost track of Gail's words as he struggled to absorb this revelation. He tried to match it with the Eva he knew, the Eva who had guarded herself from him. And, with a hard effort of detachment, he measured it against the papers. Questions collided in his mind. Was Eva deranged? Had she tricked him, had she used him? Which was worse: madness or cruelty?

– What happened then? Presumably she recovered.

He felt Gail's touch on his wrist. She took his hand.

– Paul, I'm sorry it's so upsetting for you.

He realised his face was wet with tears.

– Go on, Gail.

– She did recover, with the help of pills and rest and doctors. Then she disappeared. Same as this, except she wrote a note vowing she would never sing again. It was at least two years before her New York friends had any news of her. Next time I saw her she was married to Joe. She never spoke about what happened. I've given it a lot of thought. Opera is full of women's deaths and desertion by men. Maybe it got to her too much, all those suicides and stabbings. Maybe moving on was a way of refusing that passivity.

– I see.

Paul stood up.

– I want to be by myself for a bit.

– One more thing, Paul. Since Joe died Eva's had a few affairs, all short-lived, nothing serious, she's told me about them. She seemed to need men in her life; it made her feel younger, more alive to have a lover, but before things got involved she'd disentangle herself. She'd had enough of big emotional relationships. You were different, which must have scared her. It's you she's run away from.

… *It could be said that the resemblance is persuasive, and our father did serve in Venice at that time. Alas, he died eleven years ago, shortly after the death of our mother, to whom he was devoted. But your claim to be his son shocks us both and we must treat it as groundless at best, to say nothing of the slight it casts upon our family. A photograph can be no basis for alleging paternity. Our dear father was an honourable man and a faithful husband. We must, therefore, refuse your request for a meeting, nor can we engage in any further correspondence. My sister thoroughly endorses this refusal.*

Yours,

Avoccato Enrico Silva

The trunk gaped open. Paul had settled to his task, after a frantic half hour of delving willy-nilly into its layers of papers and packets in the hope of some instant discovery. When he saw that his haste was creating muddle where some kind of order seemed to exist, he began placing these in piles on the floor.

A grey-marbled cardboard box was the first thing he opened. In it he found the letter from Enrico Silva – addressed to Francesco Molini at the Rio dei Pensieri – along with what he took to be the photograph referred to, of a dark young man whose style of dress roughly matched the date of the correspondence: 1892. The photograph was signed by Nadar, and there were others. Paul set them aside to be studied later.

Tissue paper enfolded a dress that floated free in his hands like a gossamer cloud. This garment, although miraculously preserved from moths and apparently without holes or tears, had its colours so faded and its silver brocading so frayed that its small size, a child's fit, seemed of a piece with a natural process of time's erosion, as if it must have shrunk across the years. Studying the pattern in the silk, Paul made out trailing tails of plumage.

Under it, among gauze pouches filled with dried lavender that had long since lost its scent, lay another tissue-wrapped gown, this one more ragged, its silk sleeves hanging in streamers to which a few wisps of lace were still attached. He laid the two side by side across the table and the subdued afternoon light tinged what remained of their colours with some life. A pale watered blue, a ghost of green behind the silver.

Inside a black twill cover closed with a zip he discovered a third dress, pristine by comparison with the others, and exquisite; made of the finest ivory cotton lawn, it rippled with scores of tiny pleats that fell from the neckline to the embroidered hem. A more luxurious twin of the Fortuny gown he'd seen in the wardrobe.

A velvet drawstring bag contained two fans and a silver-framed portrait in miniature of a blonde-haired girl holding an unidentifiable fruit. Masks of various designs, some elaborately sequinned and frilled, were bundled into a flower-printed sewing bag. When he opened a small rosewood box, a single handwritten page sprang out. A short letter, illegible at first glance, and undated.

There were many letters, sheaves of them tied with ribbon, or folded vellum sheets with their seal broken. He aligned them on a shelf, aware that he ought to preserve sequences. Some would be beyond his linguistic reach, even if he managed to decipher the script.

Pocket Baedekers offered advice to the German-speaking traveller in the Italy and France of the 1840s. There were Tauchnitz editions in English, and packed into the large Kraft envelopes where he found these small volumes were old maps, of 18th-century Marseille and Vienna, of Haussmann's Paris, of Regency London and Edinburgh, along with many of Venice and its lagoon. But the two military maps among them, one plotting Napoleon's first Italian campaign, the other showing battlefields in the War of the Spanish Succession, were in garish modern colour, from a series titled 'Warfare in Europe', published in the 1970s. A battered copy of Montaigne's essays had tiny marginal notes in French, too faint to be legible.

Three sizeable boxes were stuffed with playbills arranged in series, one devoted to Venice alone. Quickly he perused the names of the theatres: the San Moisè, the San Luca (which became the San Salvatore), the San Cassiano, the San Benedetto, the San Samuele... and, in abundance, the Fenice.

This collector's mania was not what he'd expected.

What did he expect? A family album with baby likenesses and wedding pictures? Eva three years old, a schoolgirl, an unblushing bride? Mementos of her travels and stage life? Revelation? What can explain madness, self-deception?

Disturbed by these thoughts, reluctant to satisfy his greed for clues and explanations with what first appearances delivered, Paul yielded to tiredness. He left everything where it was and closed the door on the room's dusty light.

Drifting off to sleep, he thought of Eva's different names: Eva Murnau, Eva Lensky, Eva Forrest – the name by which he had met her. Two were missing, her maiden name and the one her first husband gave her, the man she married on the rebound from her youthful affair with Victor Murnau. He needed them to complete the picture of the public Eva, though he now saw that for herself she was Eva Murnau. E.M. Had this encouraged the delusion of being Elina Makropulos?

Next morning he asked Gail about Eva's first husband.

– I've forgotten his name, if I ever knew it. He was American, maybe Canadian.

– And her maiden name?

– I've no idea. Eva didn't talk about her early life, and in fact I never heard her say a word about her childhood. She sang as Eva Murnau, though maybe she had a different professional name at the start. She must have.

He spent the morning in the garden, half feeling that he should leave rather than be a burden on Gail, yet loath to forsake the peace of its walled greenery. Work had begun on dredging the canal outside Eva's flat and it promised to be noisy. And he wanted company, not constant, but a comforting background presence: Gail, the cat. At lunch, he broached the subject.

– Eva meant you to be welcome here; her letter says so. I'm her friend and you are Alex's friend, so I'm all the happier to help.

– Thank you.

He set himself two simple tasks.

First to acquaint himself with Janáček's opera. Instead of returning to the attic, where a brief study of the books on the shelves might have supplied all he wanted to know, he headed for the library at the Querini Stampalia. He needed air, and normality.

The *Grove Dictionary of Music* convinced him that the Esme Maguire papers were written by Eva. When the opera begins, Elina Makropulos is known as Emilia Marty. In the course of her prodigiously long life she has been Eugenia Montez, Elsa Müller, Ellian MacGregor and Ekaterina Myskin.

Elena Merlo, Elisa Muto, Eleonora Marini, Edita Molini... had Eva invented them all? Were these the elaborate fantasies of a woman terrified of ageing?

Esme was real. He could be sure of this, despite her absence from every music dictionary on the shelves, along with the rest. Esme was reliably documented elsewhere.

His head was clearer by the time he got back. He set about his second task. To unearth Eva's maiden name.

The letters to Eva proved a disappointing oracle. Most were personal... Dear Eva, Dearest Eva, Dearest E., My dearest, either handwritten or badly typed, and with no envelopes. There were others, addressed to Joe Lensky or sundry names unknown to Paul, collectors' items mostly: correspondence with agents and theatre managements dating from the 18th century and earlier. He found two thick bundles of legal documents in French and German, the ink on them clotted and discoloured.

One envelope bulged with press cuttings, yellowing, crumbling at the edges. An Edinburgh newspaper headlined the Burke and Hare case. The words Doctor Monro caught his eye and he read the faint type quoting a pronouncement of his:

... the brain is very soft, as it is often the case with the criminal classes, showing a very limited intelligence.

Another envelope contained three pamphlets from the 18th century. 'Epistle from a Werewolf' was credited to Giacomo Casanova, published 'in no place, in the year 1000700702', with sections underlined in pencil. 'Man is never pregnant, nor does he have to fear bloody misfortunes with the full moon; woman has both, hence she does not think of becoming an architect or of rounding the Cape of Magellan, nor of military honour, nor of demonstrating cycloids or spending six hours with her eyes glued to a telescope to observe whether a comet may appear in some corner of the sky ...' ... 'Forced by her education to admire man's prowess without being able either to comprehend it or imitate it ...'

It was among the playbills that he came across his answer. Attached to a programme booklet for a performance of Mozart's *Marriage of Figaro* he found a gilt-edged white card with a wedding-bell motif and an elegantly handwritten note on heavy cream paper. From the scrawled signature Paul could make out only the initials M.K.

Wishing you a wonderful wedding day and a happy life together. The Countess deserves it.

He looked at the programme. Vienna, October 1968. Singing the role of the Countess was Eva Sanderman, in the part of Susanna a singer called Margarethe Klee. Susanna wishing the Countess well on the eve of her wedding. A charming reversal.

Under a blurry photograph of the cast, in which Eva was faintly recognisable, a biographical summary announced this as her debut in a principal role.

Sanderman. Something about this name nagged at him, but he couldn't place it. At any rate, he was glad that Eva hadn't started life as E.M. It would have been too unsettling. He began combing through the mass of opera memorabilia. Sanderman was his first quarry, Esme his second.

Chronological sequences went awry. One buff-coloured pamphlet had been misfiled: a monograph on Joseph Smith and Giovanni Poleni published in the 1960s. Joseph Smith, it seemed, was one of the great collectors of the modern era, and the man who sold all those Canalettos to George III. Joe Lensky must have had an interest in him because as well as art works and manuscripts Smith went in for musical instruments and scores, and both his wives were singers: Catherine Tofts, then Elizabeth Murray. Paul decided to ignore this new coincidence of initials.

A clutch of Rossini ephemera made him wonder about Elisabetta Manfredini, who sang in the first staging of *Tancredi*, at the Fenice in February 1813, and Ester Mombelli, who belonged to Rossini's circle and made her name in *La Cenerentola*. He came across an Edith Miller in a London production of *Hansel and Gretel* at Daly's Theatre in 1894.

It took him over two hours to finish the three boxes. By now he thought of E.M.s as red herrings. He had found no further mementos of Eva's operatic career, no other references. Her Viennese debut tantalised him. Nor had Esme Maguire made a single appearance. He was having doubts about her too. Yet he knew she had really existed.

He took stock of what he did know. No more than when he first met Eva. He had already encountered Esme's name, first in two footnotes, relating respectively to Berlioz and Élisée Reclus, there was the Meyerbeer reference, and finally the piece with the two photographs in *Discovering Opera*, whose author had never replied to his letter requesting more information, sent a good six months after the article's publication. It might not even have reached him. The article had been short on biographical detail but rich in context, suggesting the Parisian theatrical world that Esme would have inhabited. It had pointed him towards Venice with its mention of a stay there and some papers held by a Venetian collector.

He looked across the room at the oak credenza and the pile of *Discovering Opera*. He had sudden misgivings.

Even when he lifted out the issue he sought, he feared the article would be missing.

It wasn't.

ESME MAGUIRE – A DIVA IN THE WINGS?

And below the title:

E.M. Sanderman on a Forgotten Fin-de-Siècle Singer

He had a moment's dizziness. He was astonished by his own stupidity, his failure to put two and two together. How naive he had been, what an appalling dupe.

He needed to sit down. He needed a drink so he stood up again and went down to the kitchen.

To his relief, Gail was out, making the most of her last days in Venice. He poured himself a large measure of whisky and drank in quick gulps. It failed to soothe his sense of humiliation but it calmed his nerves. As he sat at the kitchen table, his struggle to unravel the chronology of Eva's deceptions became less labyrinthine. Paranoia subsided when he remembered it was he who had pursued the article's author (and got no answer), it was he who had always assumed that this author was male, it was he who later advertised in *Discovering Opera* for information. Up to that point he was hardly the victim. Eva's motives might be mysterious, but they couldn't be perceived as mischief.

Nothing changed the fact that Esme Maguire had lived; there were proofs. Whatever Eva invented came after that fact. Maybe there was even a son called Francesco, and maybe he wrote to his father's family in Naples in search of acknowledgement.

After a professional singing career, E.M. Sanderman is now engaged on research into fin-de-siècle opera in Paris.

Paul almost blushed when he read this note, his role as historian already usurped before he or Eva knew of the other's existence.

He forced himself to reread the article. The tone was altered from what he had remembered, less lofty and academic, more a heartfelt plea to remedy past unfairness.

... what we know about her so far suggests a poignantly lost talent, a woman too overwhelmed by personal difficulties and professional rivalries to win the recognition that her voice deserved...

Back in the attic room, Paul surveyed the scene he had created: the trunk almost empty, its contents scattered around; papers still to be read, objects whose significance escaped him, while others clamoured for interpretation. All this had the makings of some message, its words scrambled and incoherent; but he could impose a syntax, could treat it like a game, a challenge set by Eva. Or perhaps there was no overriding order, no meaning, and anything more would have to come from Eva herself. If she were truly deluded by madness, these would be her proofs, rather than the stuff of fabrication, the components of a made-up history.

He touched the things she had touched, and found himself moved by them. The broken silver threads running through the child's dress with its once brilliant pattern of plumage; the tattered silk of the gown that might have been worn by some learned lady who brightened 18th-century salons with her wit, and maybe sat to be painted by Pietro Longhi. The combs and miniatures, the fans and masks. Vanity's relics. Venice's downfall.

Returning to the letter rejecting Francesco Molini's claim to Neapolitan paternity, Paul removed the photographs from their box. He looked at them all: the presumed portrait of Francesco: melancholy, fine-featured and with delicate hands; Berlioz; the fur-clad Adelina Patti; then a bearded face he did not recognise, high-browed, the eyes candid and fervent. Only the first two were signed in the distinctive Nadar hand, the N lunging slantwise, the R curling and slashing down into a final flourish. Showy, self-proclaiming, yet inspiring a certain confidence, that flagrant sureness exactly what the time required.

He opened the small rosewood box, and out, once more, flapped the handwritten sheet. This time he read it. The letter's first page was missing.

... when he died Cosima gave the clock back to me. She said he had wanted me to have it, but I suspect that it was not to her taste. Since you were my very best Gretel I wish you to be its owner now...

The signature might be a forgery, but it pleased him to think he had given the gingerbread clock a fitting name since it was, as the letter suggested, originally a present to Wagner from Engelbert Humperdinck, composer of *Hansel and Gretel*.

Paul's smile became a yawn. The sun was setting. He would leave everything as it was and replace it the following morning. After a moment's thought he left Gail a note on the kitchen table. He longed to sit on the blue sofa, to look at the gingerbread clock, and sleep in the bed he had shared with Eva. Whether to tell Gail about his discoveries remained undecided.

Vibrating windows roused him from sleep. He opened the shutters.

The canal had been drained and water lay in thin puddles. Clumps of mud and slime peaked above it. Sluice gates had cut off the tidal flow and a barge dragged for debris with a dangling shovel reminiscent of a penny-in-the-slot machine where a metal claw relaxed into motion over a heap of plastic trinkets. A narrow platform gave workmen access to the newly exposed stonework. One man cleaned with a noisy high-powered jet and, following behind, another filled in cracks.

Paul retreated to the kitchen. He was pouring his first cup of coffee when the phone rang. It was Gail.

– We could have a late lunch together; I'll be back by two at the latest. Do you need to be in the house before then?

– No. I only have to tidy up in the attic.

He breakfasted slowly, scanning neglected newspapers. The morning slid by unused. This blankness eased his cluttered head.

Shortly after two he reached the house. Gail had set the table in the garden with a tempting spread of salads. She shooed away the cat.

– Have you heard from Alex?

– He's rung a couple of times.

Gail was smiling broadly and Paul gave his head a quizzical tilt.

– We miss one another.

– Glad to hear it.

After his first glass of wine, he turned the talk to Eva. He pressed Gail for memories, for clues from the past. She answered, he pressed for more.

– You're a bloodhound Paul, never letting go.

He frowned.

– It's all right. Not always a bad thing. On the contrary, I admire you. Tenacity and loyalty go together.

She poured more wine and they both relaxed.

At four she went out to meet Annie and Girolamo. She was leaving next morning and they said their goodbyes. Paul was saddened. There would be no one to share Eva's absence with.

– I'll make sure I have news of you from Alex. I'll be in touch with him soon.

– I'll want your news too. And I'll let you know if I hear from Eva. Don't despair, Paul. Not that I think you will.

He lingered in the garden before climbing the stairs.

There was so much he hadn't read or made sense of. But it *was* time to let go of what the trunk contained.

Observing the layers in which he'd found things, he would pack the trunk neatly. First he cleared some small objects lying at the bottom: a bunch of dried flowers, a child's rag doll, a handful of tarnished coins. Gathering them, his fingers slipped into a fold of the thin leather lining at the base and found another layer. He encountered a small glass bottle, dark blue, from which he removed the spherical stopper. It was empty and smelled of ancient staleness. Perulli, he thought, and smiled at this absurdity.

Next he felt the edges of a book, and pulled out a thick volume bound in worn burgundy leather. It proved to be a diary. A separate page had been pasted onto the inside cover, a handwritten poem in pale violet ink.

It trembled in his hand. He set it aside, conscious that he would ignore Eva's request, yet convinced that the find was his, a secret delivered from hiding.

Calmly, methodically, he put everything back and locked the trunk. He was meant to leave the key at Eva's flat; he put it in his pocket for now and left the house, the diary under his arm. For the last time ever, he thought, closing the front door behind him.

32

– You're waiting for her.

Paul saw the danger in accepting this. All his efforts at self-improvement were conceived as aids to life without Eva.

Winter resolve had replaced the melancholy of autumn, when his calls were met by an answering machine, then a disconnected line. He would become the best of himself, the man she thought he was.

He stopped drinking. At first completely, as reformed alcoholics do, then maintaining moderation. Three times a week he swam at the pool and felt the better for it. He took a refresher course in Italian.

Work absorbed leftover time and energy. He welcomed extra teaching hours, and a commission to contribute entries to a historical dictionary – a Dictionary of Exiles – meant days spent in the British Library on Euston Road and the Marx Memorial Library at Clerkenwell. He walked from one to the other. He read about Élisée Reclus, an anarchist precursor, it transpired, of today's ecological movements.

Meetings with Alex were more frequent than before. Though they did him good, they unsettled him, sweeping gusts of luxurious memory through the spartan chamber in his mind where he aimed to keep Eva confined.

– I'm not.

Alex shook his head.

– Okay, if you say so.

At Christmas, Gail flew over and Alex asked him for lunch with them on the 25th. He refused, averse to their pity and Gail's well-meaning questions, foreseeing that their reunion would sharpen his sense of loss. When they turned up on the afternoon of Christmas Eve, their good humour persuaded him to change his mind. He recognised that the irritation Gail provoked in him arose from her knowledge of Eva's past: he had to protect the Eva he loved from the one Gail saw as mad.

Madness was the reason he hadn't mentioned the 'diary'. It was Eva's secret. One he half wished he hadn't found. Reading it he told himself he was seeking clues, was no voyeur. He had left it in a sealed envelope with a note at Eva's flat.

I shouldn't have taken this. I wasn't meant to see it, but I thought it might offer some idea of your whereabouts. My apologies and all my love. P.

Could all of this be explained as delusion? The diary entries deepened the mystery that was Eva. Thinking back to their last conversations, he recalled her wish to convince him that living for 300 years was not unthinkable.

Gail cooked a goose with red cabbage. She showed him snapshots of Annie at different ages. One was from 10 years earlier, in Venice, beside the triangle of bridges near the Rio dei Pensieri, and memory pierced him. Gail noticed and put the pictures away.

– Whatever you're feeling, I'm sure it's not too different from what she's feeling.

The words consoled him, because he was certain of their truth.

Paul won at Scrabble, so they let him choose the film they watched on TV: Hitchcock's *Spellbound*. Later, in the darkness, they ventured out to Highgate, where they found a pub open. He got home at midnight. The day had been easy and familial.

New Year. A corner being turned. Paul always felt it that way, but the thought of even greater distance from his time with Eva brought a relapse in his spirits. He missed even his mournful first months back in London. He missed his hope. Yes: he had been waiting.

Alex helped him rally, picking him up when a descent into alcohol laid him low, dragging him to films and organising concert trips. They saw *Der Rosenkavalier* at Covent Garden. Reading about the opera, Paul discovered that the Marschallin, an older woman renouncing love, was only 32 in the work's original conception. Thirty-two and past it. He read the libretto and her words, the music insisting, became a splinter in his head. He brooded over them:

Die Zeit, die ist ein sonderbar Ding…

Time is a strange thing. As our lives go by it means nothing, then all at once, we're aware of nothing else. It is everywhere around us, inside us too. Gently, it falls across our faces and into the mirror; it streaks my temples. On and on it flows between you and me, noiseless as an hourglass…

Later, listening to a recording, above the soprano voice he heard time stretched and stilled in the movement of the music.

Eva, he realised, was close to 60, though he found it hard to believe.

He persevered with self-improvement.

At Easter his father died, a death sudden though not unexpected. Numbness turned into an ache of remorse. Obstacles of his own making had always stopped Paul from going to New Zealand, but this loss without seeing him had never been imagined. His grief took him by surprise. He told Clem that if they'd only acknowledged their estrangement, he or his father might have tried to end it sooner. Christmas and birthday cards had come without fail for over 25 years, the two of them pursuing their lives out of sight.

Life's changes were closing in on him. A week later Alex and Gail announced they were getting married. He had been the occasion of their meeting, and the couple gave him due credit. Gail was to move to London.

He took a lot of walks on Hampstead Heath.

One Sunday early in May he came back from one of these to find an email he almost deleted before noticing the name Sanderman in the address.

Dear Mr Geddes,

My aunt, Eva Forrest, has been ill. She is much better now, I am glad to say, but I'm still dealing with her affairs. There are matters in Venice that I must attend to on her behalf, and you yourself are involved.

Would it be possible for us to meet there soon, perhaps at a weekend? Please let me know. I can arrange for your airline ticket, and the house at Rio dei Pensieri will be free for you to stay in. Or, if you prefer, I shall book a hotel.

I should be most grateful for an early reply.

Yours,

Camilla Sanderman

PS. You should soon receive a small package in the post, a gift my aunt asked me to forward.

It was a warm afternoon. Paul made a cup of tea and took it to a chair by the window. Spring had come early, only to have second thoughts, and the cherry tree across the street was denuded of its premature blossoms. Staring at the wind-torn branches, he tried to hold back a small surge of anger.

He was used to feeling angry with her now. Before leaving Venice he had searched for her doctor in Mestre. There was only one Amadeo in the phone book and he turned out to be a singing teacher. Paul went to see him with a photograph and recognition had been instant.

– *Una bella voce.*

Maestro Amadeo's praise for Eva's voice also made him jealous.

Why did she want him to go back and still not see him?

In his convoluted state of bereavement, the soreness of her desertion became acute. It was how he had felt when his father left for New Zealand all those years ago.

In the morning his mind was clear. He replied that he'd book himself into a hotel.

33

Nothing about the landscape interested him at first. He'd come to get away from what was too interesting, too dense with stones and history.

The road that dwindled into a path was thickly hedged; he envisaged fields with vegetables growing, all the fresh air and greenery he'd missed in Venice. Eva's garden hardly counted; it blended into the artifice. He walked at a brisk pace, so relieved by his unexceptional surroundings that it occurred to him to renege on his appointment with Camilla Sanderman.

Pride and anger urged this thought. Curiosity rejected it. And something nameless. On the flight from London his blood raced with excitement, but from the moment of arrival regret took over, sharpening his loneliness. He felt a fool for agreeing to be there at all, resenting Eva's refusal to face him. In the morning, he shrank from the city. The lagoon offered escape to marshy oblivion, to islands ignored by the guidebooks. To ward off unwelcome echoes, he caught a boat.

The path opened out and he saw a restaurant perched above sloping lawns and pretentious fountains with plaster-cast satyrs. He preferred the solitude of walking; he had chocolate in his pocket.

Camilla Sanderman was due on the train from Trieste at five.

Would she have things to say about her aunt? Would he ask her outright about madness? About singing? He recalled the article in *Discovering Opera*. '… a woman perhaps too overwhelmed by personal difficulties and professional rivalries to win the recognition that her voice deserved…'

Suddenly poplars soared above him, birdsong descended. In hedgerows frantic with colour and wing beats he spotted wild flowers familiar from the English countryside. Bramble bushes crowded into the roadway, fruitless, a season too early, but they reminded him of home, the rural byways of his Scottish childhood. Ahead he could see farm buildings; a red-feathered hen crossed the road at a purposeful diagonal and made him laugh out loud.

A giant bay tree oversaw the farmyard, its great trunk branching into stout and tortuous ramification, its boughs tipped with a new green. Around it a trio of goats munched on corn cobs. Chickens roamed. Cut logs were stacked against the wall of the farmhouse, which was shuttered and quiet. Towering at the centre of this ordered stillness, the tree acquired a magic presence. He thought of *Hansel and Gretel*; thinking of opera brought Eva's package to mind.

It had arrived two days after Camilla Sanderman's email and contained a CD, nothing else, with the label handwritten: Sanderman '*Il gran dono*'.

In the moment before the aria began he heard a quiver of breath. The voice was heartbreaking, crystalline yet full of emotion, and the thought that this was Eva's voice, surely the voice of Eva when younger, filled him with yearning. If he could only be in the same room as the singer again. Just once, for an hour, for a minute, a wish so irrevocably denied to him that it was like Eva being dead.

With this voice of the past he entered her sorrow. The music let him feel what she felt, what she was feeling now. Time collapsed in that voice, for it seemed to embody the singer's pain that her powers to sing like that had gone forever.

Until late that night, he played the CD over and over, unable to hear all the words, not caring, wanting only the voice, the voice being the heart and soul of Eva. Drained by this craving, he fell into a deep and wretched sleep. In the morning he put the CD in a drawer, intending never to hear it again. But return to Venice felt right.

Being here was no mistake; it promised a conclusion. Yet the voice and its heart-rending music would not leave him in peace.

Shade came to an end when the road curved into the open and cut through an expanse of fields. Compact vineyards were set among vegetable plantations: beans, leaf salads, courgettes, aubergines. Near the road's edge a stone marker tilted into the grass, the date inscribed in Roman numerals: 1662. In the last year Paul had read enough about Venice and its lagoon to have forgotten a great deal, until a prompt like this would jog the knowledge back. He remembered that this narrow island marked the lagoon's eastern boundaries, the limits of the city itself. Then, as now, things grew here, produce ferried to the markets at the Rialto.

Old maps are usually approximate, partial, often fantastic projections, but over the centuries Venice really had changed shape. A thousand years ago there were eight river mouths through which lagoon tides could climb or drop. Time and engineering displaced deltas and redirected river flows, land was lost and elsewhere reclaimed. The wash of mud debris made new sandbars rise from the water, and to this day shoals appeared and disappeared in altering configurations shaped by tides and wave erosion. Salt water and fresh water followed different currents.

Out in the lagoon, the soil mixes sand with clay. He began to notice this fertile partnership of earth and sea as the fields gave way to salt marshes.

The path had turned into a causeway lined with low, thin-limbed tamarisks, some still with the fading pink of their blossoms, a short-lived spring fire. In the channels alongside, duckweed coated the water's surface. All around were banks of profuse marsh-rooted vegetation. A network of canals became apparent. Crossing a bridge over dark, brackish water, he passed asparagus beds, then an area that seemed to extend all the way to the sea, covered with tall artichoke plants. These he recognised from the purple globes that poked out through stiff foliage. Swamp food, primeval in its spiky lushness. Was this what dinosaurs ate?

He felt he had been walking back in time.

From here it was a short distance to the vaporetto stop at the island's north-eastern end. Waiting, he looked across the lagoon and identified Torcello by its square-topped bell tower, Burano by the lurch of its own. They stood alone, strange, eminently beautiful relics of a vanquished era, now bound by wilderness and water. He remembered what Eva had said when he'd asked why she had taken him there. That this was where Venice began.

He recalled his awkward conversation with Gail in the pub on Christmas Day while Alex got drinks from the bar. He'd said that Eva always struck him as wise and secretive, that he could not see her as disturbed in her valuations of reality. Gail had nodded in agreement, then demurred.

– Yes, that's true. But the fact is she was convinced...

– That she'd lived for three centuries?

– Yes. I still find it unbelievable. I mean, that she could have so completely lost...

– Well, it's hard for anyone to believe it, but...

Gail frowned.

– Maybe there was some logic in this idea of hers, so it wasn't that she lost her mind.

She shrugged and smiled in a way he read as humouring him. His own smile was retaliatory, pursuing an impulse to provoke.

– And Gail, what if there really were some chemical compound that arrested ageing? There are scientists searching for that very grail right now in high-tech labs across the world. What if someone stumbled on it in the past?

Her look mingled warning with concern, suggesting his own sanity was in question.

– Paul, I know about that stuff. I'm a scientist, remember, albeit retired. This is of a different order.

Alex arrived with the drinks and the conversation shifted.

They didn't know he was back in Venice, nor did they know about Camilla Sanderman's emails or the CD.

Back at the hotel he considered a final option to avoid the meeting. But Camilla could corner him at the airport if she were so minded. In any case, it would be cowardice.

What if she were the one who failed to appear. The thought arrested him.

34

Paul

Still in a rush, he squinted up at the arrivals board. Another five minutes. His breathing relaxed. Leaving the uproar of the concourse, where tourists queued and public announcements gurgled through an underwater megaphone, he emerged into bright light, facing the tracks and the sky. With near certainty, he knew it was Eva he expected.

Since the first email he had strained to picture where she was. In vain, he willed his mind's eye to see through the fog of separation. He thought of a place where she could sing. Logic pointed to Trieste, recurring bolthole of her stories... yet the clues didn't mean she wanted to be found. Some opaque neurosis held her but he knew she couldn't be mad – unhinged from reality, as Gail had hinted.

Eva

One night a month earlier, in a small flat in Trieste, two floors up, close to the Botanical Gardens, she woke with a jump of fear: he would take her voice. She calmed herself, rational knowledge coming to the fore.

Her sleep was fitful. She woke again, shaken by a nightmare of helplessness, of being bereft of her infinite sense of life, of a future unbounded. In it she opened her mouth to speak, to sing, and was mute. She turned on the light and lay open-eyed, examining the dream, drawn back inside it as she probed her way free.

After a while she let old, opposing feelings speak to her, of how lonely and cold the future could be. The faint but continuous rattling of the wind against the bedroom shutters accorded with the bleakness of this prospect. A ship's foghorn sounded far off; perhaps entering harbour, perhaps sailing out. She drowsed. It sounded again, startling her. In the dark she drifted, shed anxieties, as if in the wake of that ship. Trieste always brought her back to the sea's openness and freedom. Trieste, where West became East, where South became North, a windswept boundary as fluid as herself, a place of self-preservation and remaking. This slow city beached on the rim of the Balkans was where she could be safe now.

Off her guard, she succumbed to thoughts of Paul. Desire to be with him fluttered free. She stifled it, with a sickening doubt that without him half her world would be empty. Did he feel this too? She fretted through a list of dismal possibilities: that he despised her, had cast her out of mind. She had treated him badly, repaying loyalty and love with rejection. She thought of him suffering on her account. Weeping, she finally fell asleep.

Early in the morning she put on a linen dress and dark glasses to hide the redness of her eyes. She walked down the short hill and through the Botanical Gardens, where busts of the city's eminences, all of them men, sat on plinths among the pathways. The stone heads of these poets and scientists streamed greenish-yellow with guano; she checked that James Joyce still had the shelter of flowering branches to spare him this indignity. A momentary cloud obscured the sun. A flock of grey crows hovered in the treetops, their calls muted, in keeping with a park whose strollers and solitary readers were shielded by introspection.

At the Caffè San Marco she had the high room to herself. Once the waiter took her order, she set the journal on the table. She laid her pen on a fresh page, but didn't begin writing until he returned with her tray. The coffee revived her; the daily ritual of the table by the window in the sun was always comforting.

You leave someone, in time you get over it. This is what I thought.

Before I met him I had no more appetite for love and its disappointments, its endings, whether by death or desertion. I had no more wish for vows that could be broken, bonds easy to betray. To sing again would restore me, I thought, restore me to myself. Then, alas, I was moved by him, waylaid in my cherished intentions.

If you take my voice, what have I left?

These words from the flotsam of the night echo in my head. How could I bear it if I chose him then we parted, if he loved someone else instead of me? How can I know love will last? I'd have nothing: no love, and no voice to sustain me.

Madame Stuparich, my singing teacher, a Slovene, has told me I must put music above everything and never swerve from my resolve. I've done it before, regained that phoenix voice of mine by dint of will. And what a glory that is, to sing again, my voice touching every note with perfect subtle strength, agile and unforced, colouring it with passion. To sing so well that I'm impervious to hurts, to sing so well that it cancels loneliness, makes my art my best companion, makes me my truest self. In my long years I have surely loved enough.

My emotions are divided. My soul – whatever I call the core of my feeling for life – won't accept this turning away.

She closed the journal and ordered another cup of coffee.

That afternoon she sent the email. She wanted another chance to see him, and if she got cold feet less harm would be done with the subterfuge of the niece, though he might well see through it. Was she being capricious, unfair? No; she weighed up her own seriousness. The CD was a gesture, paltry, she later judged, of recognition: Paul had a right to hear her voice, to know its worth.

In the evening she drank whisky and listened to that voice. A rare thing for her to hear; she preferred the music of old friends and rivals, those she admired. Her own revived too much memory, its qualities out of reach, perhaps forever. How we change with the times we inhabit, transforming ourselves while remaining the same, recreating ourselves in the daily course of our remembering and forgetting, never sure entirely of who we were in the past, now that we've become the great-grandmothers of our younger selves.

Once she had seen Paul the die would be cast. He lived in her dreams after that admission.

When the day came, despite her farewells to the city, she wavered. Renunciation could be reversed at any halt along the line: Portogruaro, San Donà, even Mestre. She foresaw a small future, her own death nearing. Did she have the willpower?

Somewhere past the halfway point the pull of regret weakened. Wasn't it futile to hold back the tide of years? Hasn't she lived too much to hunger for the oceans of experience, the way the young do, or those who see time speed by misspent or short-changed? The sweetness of what lay ahead took the upper hand and that small future gleamed with the promise of happiness.

The train drew into Santa Lucia. Little more than two hours, but she might have been travelling for days. Time at last to wake from her dream of agelessness.

Doors opened and banged shut, voices clamoured. Ignoring the bustle around her, listening to the movement of her breath, she lingered in her seat. The sounds dwindled. Her feet touched solid ground.

The train slowed towards him, fifteen minutes late; enough time to sow doubts. Supposing she'd caught an earlier one or come by road, and was now at his hotel, impatient.

He stood by the buffers watching the first passengers. Was it really Eva he was looking for? Maybe the niece existed after all. He checked every youngish female face and no one glanced back. Fewer and fewer carriage doors banged shut. Eyes straining behind every pillar, he scoured the farther reaches of the platform.

A dark-haired woman appeared, something familiar in her walk.

She saw only a figure in outline; tall, his shoulders broad, a little agitated, straining to see. Her pace quickened. Now she observed the delight in his face. Something happened then, a kind of magic: her skin felt warm and smooth, her breasts alive, her limbs moving with lithe ease. She sensed the beat and flow of blood, the pulsing of her heart. The burden of years had lightened. Quickened in her new knowledge of mortality, she gladly let go of the past. Against all expectation, life's wholeness came back to her.

– Eva.

– Paul.

Eva's dark hair emphasised a pallor she'd never had before. Glowing eyes offset her tiredness. After this long look, Paul took her in his arms.

– You must have found out how old I really am. You can see it in my face if you look for it. Don't you mind being younger than me?

He touched her cheek.

– How could I?

They walked arm in arm. By the steps overlooking the Grand Canal, they stopped.

Beyond the high bridge they turned right. The house was ten minutes away, round the same quiet corner that ignored the tourist hubbub. Paul had thought never to see it again.

In the kitchen she poured wine, but neither of them lifted a glass.

– I haven't always been honest…

She paused. Paul raised a humorous eyebrow. She went on, almost whispering. There were amends to be made.

She felt light-headed.

– My mind should have been clearer before I drew you into my life… It's human to wish to be other than oneself, to escape one's nature, one's history. Singing let me do that in the past. I was afraid you would stop me from singing. That's why I ran away.

Then, her speech hoarse with emotion, sounding older and unlike the voice he knew, she asked:

– Did you listen to my song?

– Many times. But I had no idea what you were singing. It was your voice I wanted.

She spoke clearly now.

– I must have meant it as a message. It was an aria Farinelli sang, about the gift of mortal life. Because we know that we must die, that life is short, we must live well enough to enlarge it.

Could two people be closer? She looked beyond love's illusion of oneness and saw, with maturity's insights, that for all this thrill of human connection, there could be no symmetry of souls. Yet here they were, the two of them in the depths of feeling, fiercely and gently bound to one another. She bowed to the guidance of instinct. Love may be illusion but can be hard-earned reality: a utopia in the making.

– I've left Trieste. I've said goodbye to my singing teacher.

– But you can go on singing. And you'll sing for me one day.

– Yes, very soon.

So little time was left.

They raised their glasses and drank their wine.

DAWN

‒ We're near now, said my mother.

Soon the air changed, clearing as we crossed narrow streams and canals. When at last we stepped outside, the grass by the banks of the inlet was too tall for us to see beyond the short path at whose end the boat sat waiting. Birds called and clucked among the thick shrubs. One of the boatmen shouted. An impatient voice. A hot sun struck at our heads. I could hear the panting breath of the young boy who went back and forth carrying the travellers' baggage on his shoulders. Then, quickly, we were all on board.

After leaving the river mouth we passed two small fortified islands where sentry boxes lurked among the trees. One soldier stared at us, another took no notice, mopping his brow, spitting at the ground. Ahead, the water opened out and across it we saw sandbanks and low-lying islands. Some had stone buildings topped with crosses. Monasteries, my mother told me, where prayers never ceased.

Our view widened again as the boat cut between more marshy islets. A long strip of land seemed to drift beside us, flat and woody dark. Two towers interrupted the sky's emptiness, the one square and straight, the other leaning as if towards a thin white stain on the azure above. I asked my mother if this land had a name and she answered with two, for the towers stood either side a channel that lay out of our sight.

We saw vessels of different kinds, some rowed fast by men standing, others with nets being cast from them. There were places where people stooped down in the water, which only reached their knees, yet they were far from any shore. This perplexed me.

Hardly a breeze stirred. The water was a plate of glass. Everything above it ‒ all the boats and the figures in them ‒ was doubled beneath.

‒ Mother, how beautiful it is.

Her eyes sparkled, glad at my pleasure. Blue eyes, like mine, and a head of blonde hair so close to mine in colour that people always said I was her in miniature, and would be her to the life when I grew. Yet we shared no blood, my mother and I.

– Wait.

At last, in the distance, we saw a sun-blinded outline.

– Look, Elena, there it is.

I kept my eyes on what began to take shape in the south. Towers, cupolas, spires and palaces began to rise from the sea. A gilded city afloat amid the vastness of water and sky. In my amazement I turned to my mother and she answered my look with a smile. Yes, it was real.

She told me how much she had longed to take me there, to watch me see it for the first time.

The first time I sailed down the Cannaregio Canal and under the bridge of spires I was 14 years old. There were eight of us in that boat and it was the thirteenth day of the sixth month in the year sixteen hundred and eighty-four. I have seen Venice change since then, for all cities change, even faster, alas, than the hearts of mortal beings, and I am no ordinary mortal.

Venice, of course, is no ordinary city.

Patrons

Jean Arundale
Michelle Ayling
Pete Ayrton
Marietta Bearman
Anne Beech
Suzanne Biggs
Anna Birch
Jill Boswell
James Brown
Lindy Burleigh
Celia C
Erica Carter
Jane Carter
Norma Clarke
Andrew Coburn
Michael Conniff
Harriet Cunningham
Judith Easter
Elizabeth Ellis
Jennifer Elvins
Sara Flanders
Iain Galbraith
Kerry Hale
Andrea Harman
Lucinda Hawkins
Antony Howard
Margaret Jull Costa
Richard Kuper
Lorry Leader
Lizzie McDonnell
Angela McRobbie
Carla Mitchell

Michael Ann Mullen
Carlo Navato
Angela Neustatter
Jill Nicholls
Donald Nicholson-Smith
Claudia Nocentini
Denise O'Connor
John Peacock
Sarah Perrigo
Andreas Philippopoulos-Mihalopoulos
Deborah Philips
Stef Pixner
Janet Ree
Christine Roche
Beatrix Roudet-Ellis
Marsha Rowe
Ros Schwartz
Richard Soundy
Juliet Steyn
Sarah Stoller
George Szmukler
Paul Trevor
Cara Usher
Pat Wooding